W9-CBT-107

# RULES for VAMPIRES

# Rules for Vampires

Alex Foulkes

ALADDIN
New York London Toronto Sydney New Delhi

This book is a work of fiction. Any references to historical events, real people, or real places are used fictitiously. Other names, characters, places, and events are products of the author's imagination, and any resemblance to actual events or places or persons, living or dead, is entirely coincidental.

ALADDIN
An imprint of Simon & Schuster Children's Publishing Division
1230 Avenue of the Americas, New York, New York 10020
First Aladdin hardcover edition November 2021
Originally published in Great Britain in 2021 by Simon & Schuster UK Ltd

For information about special discounts for bulk purchases, please contact Simon & Schuster Special Sales at 1-866-506-1949 or business@simonandschuster.com.
The Simon & Schuster Speakers Bureau can bring authors to your live event. For more information or to book an event contact the Simon & Schuster Speakers Bureau at 1-866-248-3049 or visit our website at www.simonspeakers.com.
Designed by Heather Palisi
The text of this book was set in PS Fournier Pro.
Manufactured in the United States of America 1021 FFG
2 4 6 8 10 9 7 5 3 1
Library of Congress Control Number 2021940853
ISBN 978-1-5344-9835-8 (hc)
ISBN 978-1-5344-9837-2 (ebook)

# Contents

*Human, come closer, and listen well:*
*This tale may give you a fright.*
*For while you are tucked up safe in your bed,*
*There are creatures who lurk in the night. . . .*

# 1
# One Hundred and Eleven

There are two ways to kill a vampire.

These methods promise CERTAIN DEATH to the bloodsucking beast, according to *The Novice Hunter's Murder Manual*. It is a mysterious and little-known book that is nevertheless found in every library worldwide, if you know who to ask. Choose the crinkliest librarian and give them the secret signal (close one eye, tap the end of your nose, and hoot twice like an owl). They will direct you to the back of the room, perhaps through a suspicious revolving bookcase.

There you will find the *Manual*—in one of its many editions and translations. This book contains all a first-time hunter needs to know about dwellers of the night and how to slay them. There is advice on every monster from banshees to zombies, imps to werewolves, fey folk to flesh-eating mermaids. On hunting vampires it helpfully suggests the following:

> 1. *Sunlight. Unfortunately, in newer editions of the* Manual, *the exact details of what happens to a vampire in the sun were deemed too horrible to include. In older versions the pages have been torn out, lest they give young hunters nightmares.*
> 2. *A stake. That is, a* stake. *S-T-A-K-E. Not S-T-E-A-K.*

A S-T-*E-A-K steak* is a delicious dinner that might clog your arteries if you eat it too often, but it won't leap up and stab you in the back.

An S-T-*A-K-E stake* is a horrifying wooden spike traditionally hung on one's belt and wielded like a dagger. It is a vital piece of equipment for any budding hunter who does not wish to become lunch. Simply plunge deep into the vampire's heart before their snapping teeth can reach your face. Twisting is optional.

The first *Manual* was written in a time that has been swept away by history, before even your oldest teacher was born. But many years before the *Manual* even existed, before it was ink on paper, there was a girl who already knew these vampire-killing methods very well indeed.

After all, her survival depended on them.

Slow as creeping moss, stealthy as a stalking cat, the girl slunk closer to the door. Set in a stony archway, its brass doorknob reflected the light of the girl's candle, sending shadows skittering back down the passage behind her. For a moment, she longed to follow and flee back to safety. . . .

The girl did not blink. Nor did she breathe. A tremor shook her, making her teeth rattle and her bare toes curl. She had come too far to lose her nerve now.

This was the sort of door that was bound to open with a foreboding creak—and, sure enough, its rusty hinges gave a bitten-off squeal when the girl inched it open. She hesitated for a moment, listening intently.

Inside, nothing stirred.

Willing her frantic heart to slow, the girl slipped into the murky space beyond.

The circular room was a welcome change from the suffocatingly tight and twisty passageways that ran deep beneath the castle. Cobwebs stirred about the domed ceiling. The girl held her candle aloft, eyeing the ancient portraits that hung on the walls in gilded frames. All the faces were obscured by dust. The furniture was covered in white sheets and had been pushed to the far corners of the room.

The coffin took up a lot of space.

It was enormous, cut from rough stone that winked with half-hidden geodes. A thick vein of amber ran through its center, dotted with the furry bodies of fossilized moths trapped within. Great iron chains bound the coffin to the ceiling and floor, crisscrossing off in every direction. Old runes had been carved into the heavy lid, concealing the horror that lay beneath.

Bending stiffly, the girl placed the candlestick on the floor. She couldn't draw her gaze from the coffin: the resting place of a creature so foul, so vile, and so unspeakably cruel, even the fiercest warriors would not face it on the battlefield.

The floor was damp underfoot as the girl picked her way carefully through the maze of chains. She placed both hands gently, reverently on the stone box. It was strangely beautiful, she thought; the way it glimmered in the candlelight was mysteriously inviting. A trick, perhaps—a devil's trap. But the girl wouldn't be deterred.

The coffin came all the way up to her chest—she had to lean her whole body forward to budge the heavy lid even an inch. Her thin arms strained beneath her cape—

There was a grinding sound as the stone slid farther aside, revealing the slumbering monster within. A skeletal face was framed by a pillow of lush green velvet, its bulging eyes covered by lids too thin to obscure their dark pupils. The cheekbones and jaw stood out in high relief, as did the tendons in its long neck, leading down to a silk nightgown. The body beneath was wasted away, nothing but skin stretched over frail bones.

A VAMPIRE—more than a millennium old and in possession of a primeval power.

She wanted to look away. She wanted to run. Her body seized in instinctive fear, yet the girl knew what she had to do. Reaching into the pocket of her cape, her fist molded tightly around the object concealed there.

A vampire hunter's weapon of choice had to be the stake. The crucifix and the garlic and the silver were nice—they were useful for weakening a vampiric foe—but the pointed spike, whittled sharp, was essential.

Yet the girl was not holding a stake at all. In her hand was a small bell.

It chimed out, ringing clearly through the silence. The girl stayed very still. Electricity crackled up and down her spine, zapping her toes and the tips of her ears.

Inside the coffin, the vampire's bulbous eyes cracked open. A low hiss escaped from its sunken throat. With a malevolent glare, it looked straight at the intruder.

And rumbled a bleary groan.

"Oh. It's *you*."

The girl hastily pocketed the bell, stumbling backward over a thick link of chain. The vampire began to rise up, levitating, its arms folded over knobbly collarbones. Its gaunt face was set in an irritated scowl.

Before the girl's awed gaze, the frail body was filling out. It became slender where it had been feeble, angular where it had been hollow. A cascade of silver hair sprouted from the vampire's bare scalp, spilling down its shoulders. Dead eyes now glimmered like black ice, flinty and shrewd.

Sieglinde von Motteberg—the Great and Terrible Sieglinde—came down to hover comfortably above her coffin.

"Well, Leo?" she demanded. Her low voice rolled from her like the tide, sucking its unlucky victim out to sea. "Why, pray, would you ever dare to wake me at such an hour?"

The girl (*Leo*, for that was her name) flinched. She realized too late that she had been staring; she looked instead to the ceiling, as if seeing through the complex maze of tunnels and chambers right to the surface. Though not a shred of light could reach them, she knew the sun was up.

"I . . ." Leo's voice cracked. She cleared her throat and tried again. "I just wanted to make sure you didn't forget about tomorrow. That's all."

"Tomorrow?"

"It's—it's my . . . I'm one hundred and eleven. Tomorrow."

Humming, Sieglinde idly inspected her knife-like claws. "Ah. Your birthnight."

"It is," Leo confirmed hopefully. A tiny, horrible thrill shot up her spine when the vampire looked down at her.

"Then you will be undertaking the Hunt."

It wasn't a question. Sieglinde spoke with complete certainty, just as she would say that the night sky was black or that winter followed autumn.

"I will," Leo croaked. "I'm going to Otto's End. Will you—will you be here when I get back? Dad said you're going away?"

Sieglinde flicked a speck of fluff from her clawtip. "I leave at first dark," she purred. "The Council has requested my presence. Lord Ayman has had a most unfortunate accident—torn apart by a wolf ambush during his last diplomatic outing. Simply tragic. We are in need of a new Head . . . since they have yet to find his." Her lip curled in a satisfied sneer. "I will most likely be away for some time; there will be much ceremony, I'm sure. There is a rumor that the leadership will fall to me. The *correct* choice."

Leo couldn't disagree. There was no one stronger or more ruthless and cunning.

Despite her sympathy for Lord Ayman—or what was left of him—Leo couldn't help but feel sorry for herself too. Was Sieglinde really going to miss Leo's special night?

"The Hunt of the Waxing Moon is an important rite of passage for every young vampire entering adulthood," Sieglinde continued. "I will inform the Council of your success, just like your older sister before you."

Sieglinde never failed to mention Emmeline's accomplishments. It was tough for Leo, being the younger sibling. She wondered whether Sieglinde might talk about *her* with such pride one night in the future.

There was, however, one problem.

"But," Leo started to protest, "I haven't yet—"

"You *will*," Sieglinde interjected. A vein began to bulge in her forehead. Her black gaze ensnared Leo's own, trapping her with her stare. "A failed Hunt would be an embarrassment. All the noble families are watching. Generations of aristocratic vampires, ALL OF WHOM completed their Hunt on their first try." Her voice conjured up the image of vampire daughters and sons out for their first kill, growing up to become powerful—and rich, and *influential*—in their own right.

Turning her face away, Leo fixed her gaze on the dancing flame of the candle. Her chest felt tight.

"You *do* want to make me proud, don't you?" Sieglinde intoned, looming above her. Her nostrils flared. There was a staticky *pop* that made Leo's hair stand on end, bringing to mind a memory of a hundred frantically flapping wings. It was a warning.

"I do!" Leo said quickly. "I will!"

"Good. The future of our family name depends on us all. My standing will never recover if you fail to complete your Waxing Moon." Sieglinde's thin ribs heaved. Her eyes rolled in their sockets, envisioning Leo's failure and the resulting shame. "No child of mine will ruin the Hunt! *Every* von Motteberg passes; no second chances! It's practically tradition."

Leo's eyes felt hot. The electric charge in the air dissipated, as did the phantom sound of wings. Left behind was a heavy feeling in the pit of her stomach.

"Yes, Mum," she said.

Regaining her composure, Sieglinde relaxed down into the coffin. Her fangs shrank back past her lips, her expression smoothed, and she laid her head against the velvety lining.

"Then we are done here."

With the wave of a bony hand, the candlelight died, spluttering a faint thread of smoke.

"Do not let me down, Leo," Sieglinde cautioned as the crystal-encrusted lid scraped back over her. "You are to be one hundred and eleven. The Hunt is your birthright—and your duty."

Cloaked in darkness, the girl called Leo didn't dare move. Sieglinde's voice echoed from within the coffin, sounding everywhere and nowhere all at once.

"*I will see you when I return. . . .*"

# 2
# Through the Dreadwald

Yanking aside the heavy curtains and flinging open the shutters, Leo looked out on her one hundred and eleventh birthnight.

At first glance, the unsuspecting world far beneath her bedroom seemed quiet. The distant lights of the town were mostly extinguished, and the piney treetops of the forest swayed gently in the wind. This high up on Mount Moth, the dark sky felt endless and the pale shape of the moon could have been cut from parchment.

Across its white face, a swarm of winged creatures flew

westward away from the castle. A shower of dust fell like fine snow in their wake, carried away on the air.

Disappointment stung, bitter and sharp, before Leo brushed it away. Of *course* Lady Sieglinde hadn't come to see her off on her Hunt. Her time was so important. Leo would see her on her return—however long the Vampiric Council business might take—and they would both have good news for each other.

*Good luck with the Council, Mum*, Leo thought, staring out into the inky night. *I won't let you down.*

Her cape fluttered behind her as she stepped up onto the windowsill. She leaned farther and farther forward, until the forest was tilting dangerously and the wind was ruffling her hair.

*Here we go, then!*

Leo plummeted.

The thrill of the drop made her stomach flip. Her feet worked frantically beneath her, running on thin air, until they connected with the stone wall. Leo sped toward the earth, cold air rushing in a deafening roar as she sprinted down the tower.

The Dreadwald, the vast forest that lay between Leo's castle home on Mount Moth and the sleeping town of Otto's End, was deep and dark and full of mystery.

She swept through the trees as nimbly as a running stream. She sailed through the leaves, she leapt from branch to branch, and she ducked under low-hanging vines that reached to snare her. She whizzed and zipped and slithered on her belly. Leo had spent a long time out in the Dreadwald (a long, *long* time, in fact), and she knew every damp and dreary inch of the place.

For example, Leo knew which berries and flowers to grind to make healing salve. She knew which types of mushroom were lethal when eaten. She also knew of a particular sap that would make its victim dance uncontrollably until they collapsed, their legs still performing a frantic jig.

Vaulting over a fallen tree, she ran alongside a startled hare, keeping pace before it veered off into the shrubbery and out of sight.

Leo could identify every species of forest animal and insect by name, right down to the carnivorous grubs that hitched a ride on the ants feasting on worms in the undergrowth. She knew all the best places to build a den or a base or even a heavily armed stronghold. Whether undercover or underground, concealed in a fallen tree or an old badger den, Leo's secret hideouts were second to none.

But she wasn't here for any of these reasons.

This was her most special of birthnights. Her one hundred and eleventh. And Leo was on a DEADLY HUNT.

The forest was awake and it was displeased. It sensed what she was going to do. It didn't care about the Hunt of the Waxing Moon. It didn't care about the vampire way. It didn't care about Lady Sieglinde and the Vampiric Council, and what she might do if Leo failed. . . .

Taking a life was against the natural order of the Living world.

Thorns ripped at Leo's arms as she crashed through a tangled bush that hadn't been there yesternight. Thin branches whipped her in the face. She grimaced as her bare foot sunk down into a swampy puddle of muck.

"Blurgh!" she blurghed, and took off again in a rocketing bound.

Finally, with her wild hair full of twigs and her mouth full of moss, Leo stumbled free of the forest. Nestled in the bottom of the valley, the town beckoned. The windows of the squat stone houses were all shuttered. Above them, the peaked rooftops and chimney stacks were silvery in the light of the moon.

Leo scraped moss from her tongue. She swallowed the uneasy lump in her throat. It slid all the way into her belly, where it became a squiggling knot instead. She knew, should she turn around, the jagged peaks of Mount Moth—and the castle—would be watching. Behind her, the Dreadwald pines rustled a warning, but Leo knew what she had to do; she had trained too hard and waited too long for this night to stop now.

She zoomed off down the hill, close to the ground, the dry grass swooshing past her ears. She was spiderlike as she crept down the crooked lane that led into town—and to her unfortunate, unsuspecting, soon-to-be rather unhappy victim. Someone in Otto's End would meet their *own* end tonight.

All was quiet and still. Every door was closed and bolted. Leo's feet made no sound as she passed by a stable in which two horses were dozily dreaming. The butcher's yard was empty. The marketplace was silent. It appeared that not a single other soul was awake: a stroke of good fortune.

There was a big difference, Leo knew, between an ordinary death and a Suspicious Death. An ordinary death—by accident, or disease, or old age—was no risk. But a Suspicious Death—*that* invited questions. Noses poked where they didn't belong. TROUBLE, with a capital T.

The Living, and humans in particular, had a nasty habit of using an offensive formation known as the ANGRY MOB. Mum would be EXTREMELY IRKED if they turned up on the castle doorstep, and then there would be no humans left at all. They would all become supper faster than one could say, *Wait—what are you doing? Wha-aaauuugh!*

When it came to who she would choose to eat, Leo would have to be very cautious indeed. All her training, her studies on tactics, her hard work—it all hinged entirely on this first bite. Everything had to go *exactly as planned.*

Though she had no way of knowing at the time, nothing could have prepared Leo for what was to come.

# 3

# St. Frieda's Home for Unfortunate Children

You've probably gathered by now that Leo was not an ordinary eleven-year-old girl. Or, at least, she wasn't anything like the young girls of Otto's End who were tucked up snug in their beds.

It was true that she was resourceful and clever and swift for her age. But these are qualities that all eleven-year-olds can have.

Entirely unlike all eleven-year-olds, however, Leo was rake-thin and six feet tall. Her claw-tipped fingers reached past her knees, and her skin was a luminous gray. Her eyes were dark caverns that turned into catlike slits in lamplight.

Her hair was a black nest that stuck crazily out from her head at all angles. Her smile was full of needles: her *teeth*, sharp as any blade.

Leo—or Lady Eleonore von Motteberg—was a VAMPIRE.

Not only this, but Leo was the youngest daughter of the Great and Terrible Sieglinde von Motteberg, who had famously once wiped out the entire population of a small country in only three nights. Sieglinde's wrath, Leo knew, was legend. The whisper of her name was enough to make even the bravest human tremble and dash for the nearest loo. But Leo just called her "Mum."

There were highs and lows to being a vampire. On one claw you got cool powers like beastly strength and hypnotism and the ability to GRIMWALK (a skill so fantastically, breathtakingly, spectacularly amazing, it required an *Oooooh!* just thinking about it).

On the other claw, however, vampires were bound by the Vampiric Laws: rules to protect the balance between the worlds of the Living and the Undead.

***The Eight Vampiric Laws***

*1. The Vampire will not enter uninvited.*

*2. The Vampire will not stand in the light of day.*

*3. The Vampire will not touch the purest silver.*

*4. The Vampire will not partake in the foul bulb, flower, or stalk of the garlic plant.*

*5. The Vampire will not gaze upon Holy artifacts.*

*6. The Vampire will possess no reflection.*

*7. The Vampire will consume the blood of the Living, thus sustaining their immortal unlife into eternity.*

The seventh Law was troublesome, especially when you were only eleven years old. The Living didn't hand over their blood willingly; it had to be taken from them, so every vampire had to learn to bite. While she was still young, Leo's parents had hunted for her. The castle dungeon was where the magic happened. A Living victim would go in, and a cup of delicious blood would come out. Up until now, Leo had never bitten a human. She hadn't needed to.

But Leo had been an eleven-year-old vampire for exactly one hundred years. That is to say, she was now one century, one decade, and one year old. It was on this hallowed night that young vampires would undertake their most important rite of passage to become a full-fledged grown-up.

The Hunt of the Waxing Moon.

*8. The Vampire will undertake their first Hunt on the dusk of their one hundredth vampiric year.*

To be a grown-up, you had to track and kill your prey—ALONE.

*Happy birthnight, Leo! Time to bag your first human!*

She should have been brimming with excitement, but no. It was the absolute crummiest birthnight present Leo had ever received. Maybe a close second to the time Emmeline had given her a box of spiders. Leo rolled her eyes, remembering how they had exploded all over her bedroom like wriggling creepy-crawly confetti.

Or perhaps this was actually *worse* than the spiders.

She paused beneath the cover of a leaning tree and crouched among its gnarled roots. A wooden wind chime tinkled gently on the breeze, at odds with Leo's racing mind. Danger was all around, in the silent houses of sleeping enemies, ready to awaken and attack at the slightest disturbance. . . .

Leo clung to the trunk of the tree as though it might reach down a branch and give her a motherly pat. Because, truth be told, she wasn't really sold on the whole EATING HUMANS thing. It wasn't so bad when they arrived already juiced, as they had for the past century.

A delicious cup of cherry-red blood was one thing.

An actual *human*, walking and talking, singing and burping and going about their humanly business, was another thing entirely.

There were too many ways a hunt could go wrong. What if her victim was deceptively strong? What if they were wearing silver jewelry or had eaten something (yuck!) garlicky? And, unthinkably—what if she was interrupted?

Leo could be about to tuck into her very first human and then be rushed from behind by someone wielding a stake.

To be fatal, it had to pierce through the heart, but the vampire heart shrivels with age and becomes easy to miss. Her mother's heart had shrunk to the size of a smallish plum. Leo's heart, being young, was still quite large.

She shook herself. If she was going to grow up and become a proper all-powerful vampire—like Mum—then she had no choice. Lady Sieglinde was probably already planning how to brag to the Council about her success.

"Come on, Leo," she urged herself, still clutching the cold bark of the tree. She imagined her sister scowling at her. Emmeline's imaginary voice was already rattling mockingly around her head: *"Come on, grub-for-brains! Cockroach! Mealyworm!"*

A shower of leaves fell and Leo was gone, melting away into the cramped Otto's End streets.

She could have used the GRIMWALK—ideal for speed and stealth, and helpful over long distances. With this technique, a vampire could transform their body into a flock of bats, or crows, or something equally spooky. Sieglinde was somewhat rare in that her GRIMWALK was a hurricane of giant gray furry-bodied moths. Secretly, the sight always made Leo itch.

The general idea was that the flock of bats or crows or moths would carry the vampire off to wherever they wanted to be—at which point their body would reappear and all would be fine and dandy.

The general idea was *not* that, upon turning into bats for the first time (standard for a vampire—Leo would have preferred crows, but never mind) a few of those bats would *fly away*, thus leaving the unfortunate GRIMWALKer missing her right leg.

A phantom scream echoed in Leo's head as she ducked behind a store of firewood. Looking down, she saw that through one hole in her shorts poked a perfectly normal, gray leg. Through the other hole was a gnarled wooden fake, too bumpy to pass as a real limb, but at least it bent at the ankle and the knee. Dad had done the best he could. He wasn't exactly a prosthetics engineer, but he *was* Lord Dietmar von Motteberg, and he had his fancy lab equipment to work with.

Leo had been a baby of barely fifty vampiric years at the time of her accident. Ever since, she had been certain she would never GRIMWALK again, *ever*, nevernevernever for the rest of her unlife, cross her heart and hope to die again. She preferred her body parts attached to the rest of her. She didn't care how much anyone might tease; going without the GRIMWALK might be childish, but being grown-up wasn't everything.

When you were sworn off the GRIMWALK, you had to take matters into your own claws. After years of roaming the Dreadwald, Leo was (mostly) very agile, no matter how many legs she had. The townsfolk were blissfully oblivious as the young vampire slipped through the narrow roads of Otto's End, following the shadows.

Leo kept low beneath the covered windows, scuttled down gloomy alleyways, and flitted from chimney to chimney. Her cape billowed like wings in flight as she ran up the side of the clock tower. If anyone were to spot her, they may think they'd seen a giant bat creature.

It was a quarter to four. The autumn wind was crisp, wafting through Leo's hair. Perched above the number twelve of the great clock face, she stared out over the slumbering town. Her pupils contracted into slits, zeroing in on an old building that skulked on the outskirts.

*Bingo!*

The orphanage.

Leo had been here before, scouting out Otto's End, planning her meal and the best route of escape afterward. Usually, she would avoid being anywhere near a human (or any variety of Living folk, for that matter) but the occasion called for special preparation. She had spent nights covertly watching the townspeople, peering in windows and through cracks in the walls. According to her research, one way to avoid a Suspicious Death was to choose a target who would go down easy; for example, someone smaller than herself. Another child, for instance, of which the orphanage had plenty.

Leo took a flying leap, her cape spreading out to glide her safely down to the ground.

St. Frieda's Home for Unfortunate Children was a ghastly place. She could tell even from the outside. It was a colorless prison with barred windows, creeping weeds, and a perimeter fence topped with wire. The iron gate at the foot of the driveway promised doom to all who entered.

Eyeing the rusty letters atop the gate, Leo felt the lump rise in her throat again. She had lived in a sinister castle for all her unlife, and yet this place felt so much worse, especially from up close. Colder, somehow. Her insides writhed like a nest of agitated snakes.

She brushed the squirmy feeling aside. Now wasn't the time for nerves. Letting the breeze guide her, Leo darted up the bank, taking cover in the shrubs. She circled around to the back of the building, sticking close to the crumbling wall. Dust was chalky in the air—

"Ah . . . AA*CHOO*!" Leo sneezed before she could pinch her nose. Strictly speaking, her body didn't have to breathe, but it was a leftover habit from her Living days.

The orphans should all be in their beds. From what Dad had said, having nabbed an unlucky victim or two from this very place before, they slept in a long dormitory that could house ten children at a time. But then, he wasn't exactly an orphan whisperer.

If Dad was right, there would be plenty to select from. Leo could take her pick.

The question was: Which would she choose?

# 4
# The Missing Orphan

Leo's belly had become a rumbling pit as she approached a barred window. In further preparation for her birthnight, she hadn't eaten for more than a month. Her long black tongue curled inside her mouth. She swallowed saliva as she pulled herself up to peer inside the orphanage.

As luck would have it, she had stumbled across the dormitory on her first try.

It was a lengthy room, befitting Dad's description, with narrow metal beds and thin mattresses. The peeling wallpaper was a dull, grimy color. There were no curtains on the windows and so the moonlight trickled freely in, casting a bright shard across the tiled floor.

Out of the ten beds, nine were occupied. The children were huddled beneath their sheets.

The tenth bed, however, was empty.

Someone definitely slept here, Leo thought, spotting the faded pink blanket. It was pulled back in one corner; the owner had crept out of bed at some point that same night. On the pillow sat a ragged teddy bear, looking back at Leo with its button eyes.

"Where have you gone?" Leo mumbled aloud, as though the missing orphan might answer.

Even if she managed to wake one child without alerting the others, there was no getting through the bars here. There had to be a better way in. Squinting up at the building above her, Leo craned her neck backward and . . . *Aha!*

Two floors up, a circular window was not only unbarred, but slightly ajar. Welcoming lamplight streamed from inside.

Her wooden foot thunked off the gray brick as Leo scrambled up, clambering onto the ledge above her. She shimmied up the drainpipe, as easy as climbing a tree, feeling the small victory buoy her. Could her sister do *this*? Leo doubted it.

The room behind this window was quite different from

where the orphans slept. It was cozily furnished, with a posh writing desk, a wardrobe made of heavy oak, and a four-poster bed with its curtains drawn. Everything about the place was lavish, from the velvet drapes to the gilded armchair in the corner. . . .

Leo gasped, not quite believing her luck.

In the chair, bare feet swinging beneath her, sat a small human girl.

She was grubby and unkempt and wearing a tattered nightgown that reached down to her scuffed knees. Her face was round and rosy-cheeked, full of the stubborn vitality of youth, but her expression had all the seriousness of the most severe grown-up. The girl stared stonily at something in her lap. Papers, Leo realized. They were illuminated by the stubby candle that burned inside a lamp, balanced on the arm of the chair.

Leo reached for the round window, but her clawtips stopped short, pushed back by an invisible wall.

It was open. Any other creature would have been inside and feasting already.

Then she remembered:

*The first Vampiric Law. The Vampire will not enter uninvited.*

Leo could almost hear her sister giggling. It had been so long since Leo had ventured out, away from the castle and away from the forest, that she had forgotten about rule number one.

It had to be now. If she only believed in herself . . .

*"Pssst!"* Leo hissed, summoning the power of her Vampiric Will: the hypnotic force that would let her control any Living creature she chose. *"Hey! Hello?"*

The human girl whipped around. She had hazel eyes that looked greener in the light of the low-burning lamp. Her gaze met Leo's own from across the room and stuck there, as if she was unable to tear it away. Her hand vanished into the pocket of her nightgown, gripping something tight.

"Oh . . . hello . . ."

*"Come to the window,"* Leo ordered with as much Will as she could muster.

The Living girl slipped down from the armchair, sending paper fluttering to the floor. Her grubby feet moved of their own accord, carrying her over to where Leo was crouched. Her face, full of determination only moments before, was now blank and glassy-eyed. She was a puppet pulled by its strings.

Leo might refuse to GRIMWALK, but her hypnotism skills weren't too shabby. She had practiced inflicting her Will on birds and squirrels in the Dreadwald—not that they had done anything more than bounce around in circles, since their heads didn't have a great deal of room.

But this girl . . .

This human girl . . .

*"Do you have something you want to ask me?"*

The girl fought against Leo's psychic hold. Even though she didn't physically move a muscle, Leo could feel her pulling on the edges of her mind.

*"Human,"* Leo intoned, trying again, *"do you have something to ask?"*

*It's working!* she thought with an exhilarated rush. If only Mum could see her now!

"Ah . . . uh . . ." The girl shook where she stood. Her toes curled like she was thinking about running, but it was too late. "Would you . . . would you like to come in?"

Leo studied her meal as she squeezed her long body through the window and into the room. She had never planned to look too closely at her chosen human, or to spend any time talking. But the girl had a nice face, Leo decided—she was probably very kind. She had a gap between her front teeth and long brown hair that was knotty and unbrushed but kept out of her face with a headband. One elbow was crusted over with a purple scab; perhaps she played outside often, like Leo did. But there was something else about her—something intriguing.

The girl looked like someone Leo might have known in a century long past. Perhaps she reminded Leo of an old friend, in some part of her mind that had fallen asleep over the hundred years between her human life and her existence as a vampire. Truthfully, she remembered very little of her Living days.

*"What's your name?"* Leo asked. It had been a hundred years since she had last talked to a REAL HUMAN—what was the harm in a little conversation? She kept the Will up, as exhausting as it was, in case the girl tried to escape.

"Minna. Well, Wilhelmina. But everyone calls me Minna."

Leo stared.

*"My name . . . is Eleonore,"* she said slowly, though she didn't really know why she bothered replying. *"But everyone calls me Leo. I like it better. Eleonore is too fussy."*

Minna made a jerky half motion that might have been a nod, had she been able to properly move. Her eyes trembled like they wanted to dart around in their sockets, possibly looking for a way out, but Leo kept up her controlling stare.

*"You have something in your pocket,"* she said. *"What is it?"*

"It's mine."

Leo frowned down at her. There was a sliver of rebellion in Minna's voice; Leo would have to try harder.

*"Give it to me,"* she commanded, thrusting out her hand.

It was . . .

Leo blinked at the object as Minna obediently passed it over.

A dagger?

It was indeed a dagger, though it was shaped more like the tooth of some great beast. Its blade was sheathed in a leather pouch that felt warm in Leo's palm. There was an ancient inscription on the handle, almost too worn to make out, but in a language Leo couldn't have understood anyway. She hadn't seen writing like this in any of her books.

Looking up, Leo realized that her Will had broken, but she was unconcerned. The Living girl called Minna was backed uselessly up against the wall. She had gone even paler than before and seemed to be sweating, judging by the tang of salt in the air.

"Where did you get this?" Leo asked. It certainly wasn't the kind of thing that human children would ordinarily play with. Minna was, what, twelve years old? She didn't seem that much older than Leo—or, older than Leo had been, when she first died.

"That's none of your business!" Minna said, sharp and hushed.

"I think I will decide what's my business, but thanks anyway." Leo was used to rudeness, thanks to her sister. "This dagger looks very old. But— *Ow!*" She jumped as the point nicked her palm.

The blade had been polished sharp, sharper even than Leo's teeth. Despite the aged handle, the cutting edge was so fine it could have been made yesternight. Stained now with Leo's inky blood, it looked even deadlier.

Leo huffed, watching her wounded hand heal. The skin knitted back together in seconds, leaving only a thin black trail. She wiped it on her shorts.

"Yeah, I think I'd better keep this," she decided, tucking the dagger into a hidden pocket in her cape.

Minna clung to the wall. "Who *are* you?" she whispered urgently. "What are you? You can't just . . . you can't just come in here and—"

"Is this room yours?" Leo interrupted, looking around more closely. It didn't seem like a child's room. Where were the toys? Where were the books or the things for drawing? There were mounted animal heads on the wall—a fox, a boar, a proud stag with branching antlers—but Minna didn't seem the type to enjoy hunting. If anything, she was probably a vegetarian. She looked a bit like a scared rabbit.

Leo drifted to the desk. It was cluttered with the same boring-looking papers Minna had been studying, each full of complicated numbers. There was an opened letter still gummed with waxy crumbs from its broken seal. Something, something, *bill of ownership*, blah, blah, blah, *transfer of property . . .*

"You could use some actual books," Leo pointed out helpfully. "They would be more fun to read than . . . whatever this is."

"Please, keep your voice down. . . ."

It was only making it harder, her looking at Leo like *that*. With *those* eyes. With the PLEASE-DON'T-EAT-ME eyes.

*"Enough,"* Leo said, shaking off her hesitation, summoning her Vampire Will once more. Her empty belly twisted. *"This is taking way too long. Come here, away from the wall."*

She knew what she had to do. It was straightforward, wasn't it? Bite and drink. That was the way of the vampire. It was how she would complete her Waxing Moon and become as awesomely appalling as Mum.

Leo looked down at the orphan called Minna, an ordinary child. She would be easy to overpower, with or without hypnosis.

Faintly, Leo considered that it was a shame. In another world they might have been friends. In reality Leo's number of friends totaled a big fat ZERO.

That was, *actual* friends that were her age or thereabouts. Friends that weren't animals or castle staff or Dad (since he wasn't exactly an eleven-year-old girl). There *were* the children of the other noble vampire families, but they lived in the far-flung corners of the world and Leo hardly ever saw them.

Leo had often wished for another kid to play with. They didn't have to be a girl as well—she would settle for a boy. As long as they laughed at her jokes and liked to build hideouts.

No matter how tough a child might be, a hundred years spent playing alone could be . . . lonely.

“I’m sorry,” Leo said, “it’s just that, this is the vampire way. I’m a von Motteberg. The daughter of Sieglinde von Motteberg. I know that probably doesn’t mean anything to you, but . . . I’m really sorry. And I have to eat you now.”

Something beastly was taking over. Leo’s skin became tough and leathery. Her teeth lengthened, protruding out of her mouth.

“I’ll make it quick. It will be over before you know it.”

She felt her back extend, her spine standing out in a series of pops. Her arms and legs felt longer. In fact, she felt impossibly taller all over, having to fold further in on herself to bring her jaws to the human’s neck. Beneath her clawed hands, Minna’s shoulders felt as breakable as a bird’s bones.

“This isn’t my room,” Minna was pleading, somewhere far away. “Please, Leo, I sleep downstairs, w-with the others. This isn’t my room. . . .”

Leo opened her eyes. Minna wasn’t looking at her. Rather, she was looking past Leo’s shoulder, over at the bed.

The bed, where the curtain was slowly, gradually drawing back . . .

Minna’s sigh rattled her ribs.

“It’s *his* room.”

# 5
# A Fiery World

After that, there was confusion.

"Leo! LEO, please!" Minna uttered a moan of despair, struggling to pull free from Leo's claws. Leo let her go, her hands falling slack. Instinct pulled her back into the shadowy corner of the room, folding herself smaller.

She felt as though her head was submerged. Her body too—her movements were slow and sluggish, battling against an unseen tide. She was transfixed by the figure on the bed, swinging its powerful legs free of the covers. . . .

The Orphanmaster.

Dad had warned her about this man.

*Tread carefully, Eleonore. St. Frieda's is the ideal place for a young vampire's Hunt, but you must avoid the Orphanmaster at all costs. He is an EVIL man. Far more evil, in fact, than your mother—who, as you know, is a wretched creature spat out by the Underworld itself. I'm not exactly a captain of the Royal Guard, but I know that the man at the orphanage does not have a virtuous soul. . . .*

Leo had imagined a monster, but the human in front of her looked almost like any other. He was tall and broad, with gray hair and wiry sideburns. His mouth was thin-lipped and his ears were perhaps too large for his face, but nothing Leo would have looked at twice. He wore pinstriped pajamas, like the ones Dad preferred during the daytime. But beneath his bushy eyebrows, the man's eyes flashed. In an instant he bared his brown teeth and yellowed gums. Spit flew as he stared straight at Minna. . . .

"YOU again!" he snarled. "What are you doing up here? I see your week in the basement wasn't enough to change your tune." Looking around the room, he noticed the disheveled papers strewn across the floor. "Oh. I SEE. Poking your nose where it doesn't belong! I should have you locked up, you wicked little imp!" The Orphanmaster jabbed a thick finger, advancing forward a step. Any impression of him being an ordinary human vanished at once.

"I'M the wicked one?" Minna bit back. Her hand flew to the pocket of her nightgown, now empty, and her eyes widened a fraction. Of course, she no longer had her weapon.

"Do I need to remind you," the Orphanmaster continued, his oily voice lowering dangerously, "what would have happened to you all without my kindness? Without my food? Without my roof? Would you have everyone cast out onto the street? You SELFISH girl!"

Leo bristled. She couldn't move an inch, frozen as the fiendish man smirked at Minna.

Humans were scary.

The Orphanmaster swung out a meaty hand and snatched at the air. Minna ducked, scampering aside. Her attacker laughed, whirling around to follow, then his eyes locked on where Leo was braced in the corner.

His face slackened in surprise. For a long moment, neither of them moved.

Then, as deliberately as a spider descending on an entangled fly, the Orphanmaster's mouth split into a grin.

"And *what* are you?" he breathed. Behind him, Minna was floundering, looking from the vampire to the human man and back again. She didn't know which beast to root for.

Then her mind was made up.

*Run!* she signaled to Leo, gesturing frantically to the window. Leo glanced away, looking for her escape for a second too long—

"No, no!" The Orphanmaster laughed, far too close. One thick-fingered hand knotted in her cape, and the other grasped Leo's shoulder roughly. "I insist—stay a while! You've only just arrived!"

Leo gasped, shaken in his grip. Where her cape had twisted around to bare the gray skin of her shoulder, something was sizzling—but, no, it *was* her skin, it was her flesh, burning beneath the rings the Orphanmaster wore.

*Silver!*

*The third Vampiric Law. The Vampire will not touch the purest silver.*

"A VAMPIRE!" The Orphanmaster stared with rapt fascination at the rising steam. "I was right! An actual bloodsucker. I can hardly believe it—but here you are!"

Leo kicked blindly out at her attacker. The Orphanmaster fell back as her wooden foot sunk into his stomach, sending him sprawling.

Minna was by the door, leaning on the frame to keep herself upright.

"Leo! Look out!"

The Orphanmaster bellowed, outraged, lurching forward. He swung Leo around, hurling her across the room and into the desk. More paper scattered. Something crashed to the floor and splintered: a painting behind glass, now broken into shards.

It was a portrait of a human woman, her eyes smiling behind a bouquet of tulips. Leo glanced at her for a split second, before instinct took over and urged her to run.

Scrambling away, Leo reached for the handles of the wardrobe to help her stand. Her heart pounded like a war drum. Her ears were full of static and her shoulder stung where the silver had seared her skin. In the doorway Minna was now a blur. Leo couldn't focus on anything but getting out—

"Where do you think YOU'RE going?"

A cruel hand yanked her back by the right leg. The wardrobe doors were pulled open, making the heavy cupboard rock dangerously. Leo twisted, leaving deep gouges in the floorboards as she was dragged. She snarled her most fearsome snarl, pushing down her terror to fix the Orphanmaster with a matching glare.

*"Human,"* she growled with the full force of her Will. *"Stop. You will let me go."*

Still holding her by the wooden ankle, the Orphanmaster paused.

His eyes glinted with gleeful malice.

"Oh? Well, this does take me back!" He chuckled to himself, as though he had thought of something funny and was pleased with his own wit. "I have to admit, I never dreamed I would see the likes of your kind again. Isn't this a *treat*? You know, I once knew someone who would have had a WONDERFUL time dealing with you!"

*"Let go! Let me go!"*

"Your parlor tricks won't work, vampire. Not on me!" Spit flew as the Orphanmaster leered down at Leo, his brown teeth bared. "You're as empty-headed as the rest of them—these sniveling rodents we call children and spend all day worrying about. Do you want feeding too? Clothing? Do you need somewhere warm and dry to sleep?"

Leo's foot was coming loose. She could feel the brace start to slip where it was attached to what remained of her thigh. The Orphanmaster didn't seem to notice.

"A *child* will never get the best of me! I'm in charge here! This is MY house!"

Summoning all her might, Leo surged upward. She gripped the Orphanmaster's shoulders tight, sinking her claws in. She hunched her gangly body, and her powerful jaws gnashed inches from the man's nose.

She wouldn't die here. Not tonight.

Minna was gone, vanished into the hallway. *Good*, thought Leo. Let her go. To take an evil life was better than taking a good one. She coiled above her prey, teeth snapping furiously as she fought back, cornering the Orphanmaster against the wall. She was far stronger than any human, no matter how big they might be.

Later, looking back, she wouldn't be certain precisely what had gone wrong. Maybe they knocked into the armchair. Maybe it was the Orphanmaster's thrashing arms. Maybe it was the lingering force of Leo's Will, with nowhere to go, blasting out in a shockwave that rocked the whole room.

Minna's forgotten lamp seemed to fall in slow motion. It tumbled over and over in the air. Inside, the candle flickered ominously.

Bouncing on the floorboards with a metallic clank, the glass door of the lamp sprang open.

With a *whoosh-crackle*, the fire caught.

Otto's End had seen a great many fires in its history. The houses were crowded close together, with thatched roofs and wooden beams that made excellent kindling. The tiniest spark could trigger the most monstrous blaze.

St. Frieda's Home for Unfortunate Children was set apart from the rest of its neighbors, isolated on the edge of town. But in that room, high above where the townsfolk slept blissfully on, it was as though the *whole entire world* was suddenly aflame.

There were very few things that Leo was truly afraid of. She was afraid of losing her other leg to a botched GRIMWALK. She was afraid of Mum. She was most definitely afraid of the Orphanmaster now.

Leo hadn't known that she was afraid of fire.

"God preserve me," the Orphanmaster rasped. "What have you done?"

They were both rooted in place, frozen mid-fight. The Orphanmaster was on his knees. Leo was halfway up the wall.

They both watched helplessly as the flames formed a fiery carpet. It spread before their astonished eyes, reaching greedily to catch at the bed, at the ruined desk. The wood blackened and smoldered in an instant. A smothering smog filled the room.

The air began to shimmer with rising heat. No matter how much she wanted to, Leo found that she couldn't avert her stare. She didn't notice the Orphanmaster's grip close around her right ankle.

There was a snap as Leo's brace pulled free, her leg slipping loose and falling away.

Looking down, there it was: the prosthetic Dad had made for her, hanging limply in the human's hands.

"My leg!" cried Leo. "That's—*aargh!*" She was tossed to the floor. The heat rose to greet her, flames licking at her clothes, at her skin. Leo rolled away, cringing when something sharp sliced into the point of her elbow. A splinter of the glass, she realized with a chilly rush.

There was no time to dwell on it. The Orphanmaster circled her like a hungry shark. He was panting heavily, sweat clinging to his brow. His grin was utterly triumphant; he thought that he had won. He held the leg up over his head like a barbarian club or a woodcutter's axe.

Or a stake.

"Enough! This is it, vampire!" he declared, the orange flames reflecting in his mad eyes. "The END OF THE ROAD for—"

With every last ounce of her strength, Leo kicked out. She had no plan, not really. All she knew was that she *didn't want to be here*, she didn't want the Orphanmaster *anywhere near* her. Leo's heel caught the brute in the chest, her whole body a striking snake that snapped out with all its fury.

The Orphanmaster toppled backward, staggering, clutching the fake limb. His hairy feet skidded on the floorboards. His trouser leg was set alight as he went.

He flew into the open wardrobe with the force of a falling tree and hit the back panel with a resounding THUD. The doors banged closed.

The wardrobe wobbled once, twice on its unsteady feet, swaying with the impact.

Then with an earth-shattering slam, it fell forward onto its face, trapping the Orphanmaster inside.

# 6
# Home

The sky opened and released a torrent of rain.

On the driveway of St. Frieda's, nine bewildered orphans looked on as the building was engulfed in a ravenous inferno. There was Walter and Karin, Paul and Edith. There was Hermann and Hilde, the twins. There was August and Ilse and Wolfgang. Bustling through the gate was another figure: the town's ageing priest, Father Pavlov, stumbling as his feet caught in the robe he had haphazardly flung on over his pajamas.

The flames roared and spat, smoke pouring upward to mingle with the night sky. The grayest prison had become the brightest bonfire.

No one noticed the tall shadow appear from out of the circular window, silhouetted as it dropped down to the charred ground.

No one saw the girl called Leo as she fled for the safety of the Dreadwald.

She'd had the fright of her young unlife. Leo had been screamed at, hurled across the room, and her leg had been stolen. She had almost *perished in a fire* and—to top off the whole sorry situation—she had FAILED her hunt. The weight of the human girl's dagger in her cape pocket was a somber reminder.

She hadn't managed to take her first human.

Her parents would be so disappointed, not to mention FURIOUS. *Every von Motteberg passes on their first try*—that's what Mum had said only yesternight. No exceptions. No excuses. A do-over was a terrible embarrassment, and if Sieglinde had already informed the Council that Leo had passed . . .

What would come next, Leo dreaded to imagine. She couldn't think of any other von Mottebergs who had wrecked their first Hunt. They weren't on any of the family records, but there had been thousands of ancestors through the ages, surely they couldn't *all* have passed? Perhaps the vampires who failed had just . . . vanished.

Perhaps someone had MADE them vanish.

Bloody tears rolled down Leo's chin and dripped from the end of her nose, streaking her face with black. She staggered and stumbled through the forest, hopping on her remaining foot, every step a drawn-out agony. She felt as though she really *were* on fire; her muscles burned and her bones throbbed, and the silver-wound on her shoulder hadn't yet healed.

If the Dreadwald had been angry before, it was quiet now. Branches parted for Leo as she went, guiding her back to Mount Moth. Raindrops filtered down through the leaves, but not a single one plinked onto her head. Luminous mushrooms lit the mossy track. Leo's night vision was reasonable for her age, but it was hard to see with leaky eyes and a broken heart.

At the foot of the mountain the forest gradually began to give way. Only a few of the more stubborn species of tree remained, clinging to the mountainside as the ground became steeper and steeper. A stone path snaked to the summit, dotted with shrines to old gods.

To any Living thing who might be looking on, the three peaks of Mount Moth stretched up into the rainy sky, wreathed in cloud. The snow-tipped points formed an icy crown, as though the Dreadwald itself were a queen.

To the vampires who lived there, though, there were not three mountain peaks at all.

There were only two.

The third was Castle Motteberg. It was protected by complicated wards: spells to repel intruders and to camouflage the building from Living eyes. To the humans of Otto's End, it appeared as just another part of Mount Moth. But to Leo, it was an immense gothic fortress, with jutting towers and slitted windows. The stony walls—crisscrossed with climbing vines and studded with spiked gables and stained glass—soared impossibly upward to their pointed peaks, higher and higher until they seemed like they could pierce the moon itself. Hideous gargoyles loitered in the alcoves, glaring out at anyone who might dare approach.

It was sanctuary. More importantly, it was home.

Leo choked back her sob of relief as she came to the water. The mountain lake surrounding the castle was fed by a natural spring where it bubbled up from underground. Connecting the land to the castle entrance was a grand bridge: the only way in and out by foot, unless you were to leap from a window. Faceless statues of vampire men and women—Leo's ancestors—stood guard at intervals. Their empty faces felt especially judgy in the rain. With no canopy to shield her now, Leo was drenched.

Halfway along the bridge, equally pelted by rain, a knight clad in iron armor was waiting. Her gauntleted hands were clasped around her sword, which she held dutifully in front of her. The crimson plume of her helmet drooped and the raindrops pinged off her plating, but she didn't flinch. She could have been a statue herself, if Leo didn't know better.

As Leo approached, the knight lifted her head solemnly, regarding the girl through her visor.

The sword clattered onto the flagstone.

"Ohhhh, Miss Leo!" the knight cried. "Whatever happened, child? I was worried sick about you, stuck here waiting—I would have come with you, you know, had you only said the word!"

"Marged, please," said Leo tiredly. "I told you a thousand times: I had to go alone. No butlers allowed on the Hunt."

"I'm your *nanny*," the knight corrected, gently taking Leo's smudged face between her massive hands. "Miss Leo, you poor thing. You're filthy! And, oh . . ." She gasped, helmet tilting down to look at Leo's feet. Or her foot. "Where . . . where is your leg?"

Leo sighed. "Burned to a sizzle."

"Pardon me?"

"It's inside a wardrobe, in a house on fire."

Technically, the leg was in the hands of a human, inside a wardrobe, in a house on fire. Fortunately for Leo, Marged didn't demand further explanation. She was too busy mumbling to herself and turning Leo's face this way and that. Her giant metallic thumbs touched the dried black tears that smeared Leo's cheeks.

Leo batted her hands away. "I'm *fine*," she insisted, trying to stop her voice from wobbling. Fretting was what Marged did best—but it wouldn't bring Leo's leg back. Nor would it undo the terrible mistake she had made that night. "Mum will have arrived at the Council by now, won't she . . .?"

Marged patted her on the head. "Oh, little one. I know she would have wanted to be here. She will be back in a few nights at most—and she's probably choosing you the perfect birthnight gift right now! Have patience."

Marged always called her *little one*. She had done so ever since Leo was actually little. Now she was almost as tall as the knight but hadn't lost the silly pet name.

"Can we go in?" Leo asked to change the subject. The thought of having to face Mum was making her feel light-headed. "I'm soaked. You're soaked."

But Marged didn't budge. She was a stubborn old gal. Perhaps it was the tear smudges, but she appeared to notice something as she peered into Leo's face.

"Did you . . . ? Have you eaten?"

Leo shifted on her remaining foot.

"Miss Leo . . ."

Marged had this annoying way of *knowing* when something was wrong. For a moment, Leo considered telling her everything (about Minna, the Orphanmaster, the FIRE) if only to unburden herself of the smothering weight on her shoulders.

But what could Marged do? She was only a butler, after all. She couldn't turn back time. She couldn't wave a hand and change a failed Hunt into a successful one.

The fewer people who knew about the fiasco, the better.

"Marged, let's go inside. Everything's fine."

She didn't look convinced, but it was hard to tell beneath her metal attire. Marged gave a whistling sigh and scooped up her fallen sword. Clanking after Leo, the two of them made their way back across the bridge.

Midway across the lake, the stone sagged down into the freezing water below; the bridge only reached so far, having been partially destroyed in an epic battle at the castle gates, long before Leo's time. The metallic groan of heavy chains announced the lowering of the drawbridge, like hungry jaws opening to beckon them inside. At least the castle still recognized her as a von Motteberg. Part of Leo had been worried it wouldn't open up.

Castle Motteberg was as eerie on the inside as it was on the outside. Leo's and Marged's footsteps echoed through the grand foyer, the sound soaring up to ricochet off the high ceiling. Braziers glimmered and flags bearing the family emblem, a winged insect in flight, hung on the walls. Beside them was a faded banner that declared HAPPY BIRTHNIGHT, LEO! It had come unstuck in one corner, slumping sadly.

On the plus side, Emmeline was nowhere to be seen. Less happily, there was no sign of Dad either—probably still buried in his work. He tended to lose track of time when he was immersed in one of his projects.

"It's . . . it's great." Leo tried to smile, though her insides were slumping like the banner. "Thank you, Marged."

Marged's plume bobbed enthusiastically. "Ah! But there's more! If you follow me, I've put on quite the spread—it is a very SPECIAL OCCASION AFTER ALL!"

In the dining room the long table was laid out with a complicated display of party food. The centerpiece was a spiraling tower of eyeballs.

"Your favorite—the popping kind!" Marged exclaimed. "It was quite the head-scratcher, how to get them to stand up like that—but there are so many things you can do with those little wooden sticks! Look here." With a flourish, she picked up a brass platter of skewered sausage-shaped snacks. "*Cocktail fingers.* I hear they are all the rage right now! Sadly, the dungeon didn't have quite so many fingers still attached this time, so I've had to use a few toes, but I'm sure they taste much the same. Then there's blood jelly, blood pudding, blood trifle, blood mousse, blood brownies, plasma pie—of course that's also made of blood—"

"Wow," Leo interrupted, feeling suddenly queasy. It was so much. She could always count on Marged to go above and beyond.

She was also filthy and exhausted and very much wanting to crawl into bed and sleep.

"Actually, M-Marged—this is lovely, but I think I'm ready to turn in," she said, looking up at the knight. "After all, I'm just so f-full, from my Waxing Moon, so." She twisted her cape in her hands. "I'm not sure I can eat another bite."

It didn't feel good to lie. And poor Marged really had made such an effort. Leo felt sicker still as Marged's helmet tilted thoughtfully, and then a metal arm wrapped around her shoulders to give her a reassuring squeeze.

"Okay, Miss Leo. Let's get you off to bed now; you've had quite the night."

*CLANK! CLINK! CLUNK!*

Marged rattled dutifully behind as Leo hopped past the library, past Dad's laboratory, then past the plush parlor with its dusty china and crystal chandelier. There was an enormous portrait of Emmeline over the mantel, done up as usual in fancy frills and looking smug. She was flanked on either side by a proud-looking Mum and Dad. Lady Sieglinde had commissioned the image shortly after Emmeline's completion of her own Waxing Moon, during which she had eaten the Otto's End milkman.

The climb to the western tower where Leo slept was even more exhausting than usual. Each hop on her remaining foot was like trudging up Mount Moth again. Leo hung her head.

"Here," said Marged kindly as they crested the top of the stairs. "Now wash your face before you get yourself to bed. You're as grubby as a mudskipper! I'll be right back."

Water splashed into the sink in the bathroom Leo had all to herself. Marged called it the *lady's powder room*, but Leo didn't keep any powders in there. She scrubbed her face, shivering as the freezing water trickled down her neck. By the time she was finished, the basin was cloudy with black blood from crying her heart out.

Lifting her head, Leo stared into the mirror.

*The sixth Vampiric Law. The Vampire will possess no reflection.*

It had been difficult to get used to, not being able to see herself. Leo had kept the mirrors covered for her first few years as a vampire, since watching her clothes float around without her body was all a bit unsettling.

It was daft to her that she even had mirrors in the first place, but then, everything in her room was antique and inherited from her ancestors. Nowanights it didn't unnerve her quite so much, but she still kept the mirror covered with her own drawing of what she *thought* she looked like, based on her portrait. For old times' sake.

Leo pulled the plug and watched the dirty water swirl away.

Her bedroom was her third-favorite place—after the Dreadwald and the library—because it was where she kept her treasures.

She had her collection of fossils and her collection of weird rocks, and her collection of weird rocks that might have been fossils but she wasn't quite sure. She had her map of the Dreadwald, which she herself had painted onto her wall. It was a giant mural that spanned all the way from the door to the window. Mount Moth and Castle Motteberg and the mountain lake were all marked, as was Otto's End and the (now former) St. Frieda's orphanage. That would need updating soon. She had her personal bookshelf, crammed with exciting reads such as *The Survivor's Guide to the Wilderness* and *One Hundred Poisonous Potions and How to Brew Them* (there was a second volume for antidotes). There was also her well-loved copy of the *Encyclopedia Silva*—but even that couldn't cheer her up now.

Clanking on the stairs signaled the arrival of Marged, who clanged across the floor to place something down on the bedside table.

As she peered from the bathroom door, Leo's stomach clenched with painful longing. It was a simple cup of blood, invitingly red. Just how she liked it. Next to it, a small plate was piled high with popping eyeballs.

"For when you are ready," said Marged. "Since you really haven't eaten, have you?"

*Caught.* Nothing got past Marged for long, like last week when she had thwarted Leo's attempt to smuggle a family of newts to the dining table. . . .

Feeling Marged's gaze on her, Leo walked over to the bed and sat down. She took a sheepish mouthful of blood. Her belly was instantly suffused with warmth, but the rest of her felt stubbornly cold.

"Thank you." Leo paused, wiping a smear of red from her lower lip. "Hey, Marged?"

"Hmmm?"

"Are you . . . What . . ." The words stuck painfully in her throat, but she forced them out. The cup was in danger of shattering within her grip. "What are you going to tell Mum and Dad?"

Marged was quiet for a long moment. Stiffly, she took a seat next to Leo, smoothing down the bedcovers with one gauntlet.

"Miss Leo . . . when you were small, I took an oath that I would always protect you. No matter what, I will always do what is right for you, until the night I am released from this world."

"Hnnnngh . . ." Leo groaned, like she always did whenever Marged went all deep and meaningful. It was so embarrassing. "Marged, I *know* that. . . ."

"Perhaps," Marged returned slowly, "perhaps . . . Lady Sieglinde doesn't have to know. Or Lord Dietmar."

Leo blinked. Was she imagining things? Marged (strait-laced, stuffy Marged who loved rules more than anything else in the whole universe—seriously, she would MARRY rules if she could) would lie for her? And to *Mum* of all people?

"But what about the Council?" Leo fretted aloud. "They'll think I've already passed by now. And Mum's pegged to be the next Head! It's meant to be her BIG CHANCE, now that Lord Ayman is out of the running. She'll be FURIOUS if I ruin it for her. . . ."

Marged's sigh echoed inside her helmet. "The Council rules that every young vampire must complete their Waxing Moon. That's all." She placed a comforting hand on Leo's arm. "Little one. You are an excellent vampire. You are strong, like your mother. But not everyone can get everything right on their first try. Including the Hunt."

"Von Mottebergs do," Leo pointed out miserably. What about this was Marged not understanding? Perhaps it was because she wasn't a vampire herself.

"Well then, you will be the von Motteberg to do things your own way. *Try again*, Leo, when you feel you are ready. You will complete the Hunt. All Lady Sieglinde has to know is that it's done; that is what's most important to her."

Leo still wasn't convinced. Mum had been totally clear: there were certain EXPECTATIONS when you were part of this family, and a perfect Hunt was one of them. But perhaps . . . if she could try again as soon as night fell tomorrow, she could complete it before Mum returned and realized what she'd done. . . .

It was dishonest, part of her insisted. But wouldn't Mum be so PROUD of her for a job well done? Perhaps, when Sieglinde was Head, she might let Leo tag along and see a real-unlife Council meeting for herself, to kickstart her own career as a feared and respected vampire. . . .

She was still silently arguing with herself, when she was interrupted by Marged suddenly and gracelessly tumbling off the bed. Her metal bottom hit the floor with an almighty CRASH, not dissimilar to the sound of an upended tray of utensils. She gave an *oof!* of surprise as her helmet toppled off her shoulders, clattering away across the bedroom.

Where her head should have been, there was nothing. An empty space. The helmet was much like the chestplate and the gauntlets and the spiked greaves, which were all hollow too.

The knight—the suit of armor—crawled after her helmet, feeling her way across the floor. When her gauntlets found it, she twisted it back into place.

"Clumsy me!" chimed Marged cheerfully. She pushed herself upright while Leo rolled her eyes. "So typical. Now, Miss Leo, be sure to have your supper before you go to sleep. I won't have you wasting away. Don't you think on that Waxing Moon for one minute longer. It will all come right, you'll see."

Leo pulled on her pajamas and toppled down onto the mattress, coiling her battered body beneath the blankets. Her eyelids were already heavy and she felt weak all over. Some vampires, like Mum and Dad, preferred to sleep in their coffins. But Leo didn't like to be shut in or feel like she couldn't escape. She drew the blanket up to her pointed chin, her tired body beginning to give in to the healing sleep it needed.

Sieglinde would be home in just a few nights, Marged had said. Everything "coming right" on its own seemed desperately unlikely—but Leo's exhaustion was catching up with her. The frantic buzz of her brain was quieting, becoming foggier and foggier. Any plan for a secret second Hunt was slipping away from her.

Marged went for the bedroom door, pausing only to straighten Leo's dressing gown where it hung on a brass hook. She couldn't resist fussing.

"Um . . . ," Leo called after her, and the armor paused in the doorway.

"Yes, little one?"

"Good day, Marged," Leo sighed, defeated.

"Good day, Miss Leo," Marged replied. "Sleep well."

In the dwindling dark, something awoke from the ashes of the Otto's End orphanage.

Not that it remembered St. Frieda's—not at first. Nor did it know who it was, or indeed *what* it was. All the Something knew was a peculiar pain deep inside, an ache in the lungs that would be healed by a breath of cool night air. . . .

But, try as it might, the breath was not forthcoming.

The something collapsed into the cinders, its mind awhirl. Memories swam, fading in and out. No one was coming to help.

Alone. Afraid. Suffocating into eternity.

Its mouth cracked open in a silent scream.

# 7
# Daymares

That day, Leo slept like the dead. The dead-dead.

The sun rose over Mount Moth and drifted across the pale autumn sky. It dipped down and hid again, and still Leo slumbered on. The yellow orb appeared and vanished twice more—and, on that third day, Leo dreamt.

She dreamt of a garden, vibrant with sweet-smelling tulips. It was at once strange and familiar, like a memory that had been deeply buried. She could hear birdsong and the gentle scratching of a paintbrush on canvas. A calm breeze ruffled her hair.

Then an unholy scream, and she was plunged into murky

nothingness. The garden was gone, replaced by a frantic thudding that made her ears pound. It was suddenly hot, much too hot. Every way she turned was a scorching wall. She tossed and turned and sweated.

A face emerged from the gloom, pinched and papery. Its mouth cracked open to reveal rancid brown teeth, hateful eyes flashing . . .

The Orphanmaster.

"NO!" shouted Leo, hurtling upright. The room spun, blurring around the edges, and Leo clutched at her sore head. "Ow ow ow ow . . ."

Gradually, unhurriedly, her vision settled. Leo peeked through her fingers. She was in her same bed, in her same bedroom, with her same books and drawings and treasures. Relief washed over her.

But there was one thing that was not the same at all.

Perched at the end of her bed was a pale figure.

"Waaagh!" Leo scrambled back against the headboard, waving her long arms to ward off the intruder. But the figure didn't move—except for the curious tilt of its head as it stared right back at her.

"Well!" said the ghost sulkily. "Took you long enough! I thought you were going to sleep forever. I suppose vampires really *are* lazy."

It should be mentioned here that, traditionally, vampires and ghosts do not get along.

There have been countless bloody vampire–ghost WARS throughout history. The battles could last for nights on end, resulting in a vast number injured and even more dead (and dead for a second time, which was hugely inconvenient).

The ghostly finger of blame pointed squarely at the vampires—the very same vampires that had *created* the ghosts through their unusual eating habits. The ghosts were none too happy about becoming lunch. Being drained of all your blood and then coming back as a vengeful spirit could easily ruin your entire week.

On the other hand, the vampires argued that the whole situation was highly dramatic. The ghosts should get on with it and stop all the wailing and chain-rattling. After all, it was the vampire way to drink the blood of the Living, much as a predator animal must catch its prey to survive.

*The seventh Vampiric Law. The Vampire will consume the blood of the Living, thus sustaining their immortal unlife into eternity.*

As you can imagine, this suggestion had not gone down well with the Ghostly Guild, and so their never-ending struggle with the Vampiric Council had begun.

Leo, being only one hundred and eleven, had never been

in a battle . . . unless you counted the fight at St. Frieda's, which she was doing her best to forget about. But that had been with a human, not a ghost; in fact, Leo had never encountered a ghost before. Or, at least, she didn't think she had—not until the thing at the end of her bed appeared.

"G-g-g . . . ," gurgled Leo, clutching the headboard for dear unlife as she stared her immortal enemy in the face. She stopped short, looked them up and down, and then rubbed her eyes to make sure she wasn't seeing things.

"Wait . . . Minnow?"

The ghost puffed up like an angry cat.

"WHAT? *Minnow?* It's Minn*a*, Minn*a*! The least you could do is get it right, considering that you MURDERED ME!"

Leo was having trouble processing this information. But there was no doubt about it: the Living girl called Minna was sitting on the end of Leo's bed, now looking . . . rather less Living than she had before. In fact, the last time they had met, Leo remembered her being very much alive. It was clear that something had gone disastrously wrong in the meantime.

Minna was—there was no nice way to say this—Minna had never looked worse. She was almost see-through, and her whole body was cast in a milky-white color. Her long hair drifted around like she was underwater. Her eyes were blank holes, through which a bright light glowed. She still had her chubby cheeks and gappy teeth and tattered nightgown, and if it weren't for those, Leo probably wouldn't have recognized her.

Aside from these changes, there was one other difference between the Living girl called Minna and the ghost girl called Minna.

The last time Leo saw her, Minna most definitely hadn't had a metal poker piercing through her right shoulder.

"Um . . ." Leo stared. "You . . . you have something . . ."

She gestured weakly to her own shoulder.

Minna looked down at herself. "Oh. This?" With her left hand, she pulled the poker out in one smooth motion, like she was unsheathing a sword. The metal bar gleamed the same white as the rest of her, separate but still somehow part of her body. Its end was tipped with a wicked double prong.

"What happened?" Leo asked, her eyes warily tracking the movement of the poker as Minna swished it this way and that. "When I saw you back there, you were fine. Well. Maybe not *fine*, but you didn't . . . You weren't . . ."

"Skewered?" Minna finished for her. She frowned as she recounted the memory. "I was coming to help. I didn't want that . . . that *monster* to win. I grabbed this from the fireplace downstairs, since you pinched my dagger. Thanks again for that, by the way. . . ."

"You were going to stick the Orphanmaster with it?" Leo felt a bit faint. From the way Minna was waving the poker around, she definitely knew how to use it.

"I was." Minna gusted a heavy sigh, making her body waver like a dying candle. "I slipped. I was on my way back and I suppose I must have lost my footing. I fell aaaaaall the way to the bottom and . . ." She jabbed the poker in the air. *"Splutch."*

"Splutch?" Now Leo really did feel faint.

"Oh, don't be a baby! It didn't hurt, not really! The undertaker thinks I hit my head on the banister, which would explain why I don't remember anything much. After the fire, they buried me, then I came to track *you* down. It's more annoying than painful. You know. BEING DEAD."

"I see," mumbled Leo. "You know, Minna, you're not the only one who's dead. I'm dead too. Have been for ages."

"Yes, but *I* didn't kill *you*, did I? There's a difference!"

There it was again: the accusation.

Leo *hmmm*ed, squinting at Minna. "But you said you fell down the stairs?"

"I did."

"And hit your head and got stabbed with that thing from the fireplace?"

"I did."

"I didn't chuck you down the stairs. I didn't stab you." This was all feeling a bit unfair—and if there was one thing Leo couldn't stand, it was unfairness. Unfairness was one of her least favorite things, along with dusting the gargoyles, scrubbing stains from the goblets, and cleaning Castle Motteberg's many swords and shields and great battle-axes on Armory Night.

Minna's blank eyes flickered. "You really don't know, do you?" the ghost girl said.

"Know what?"

"Humph. Maybe it's easier to show you."

Turning her head to the side, Minna sucked in a deep breath, right to the bottom of her lungs. Her chubby cheeks bulged. When she exhaled again, she blew out a long stream of black smoke.

"Oh . . ." Leo wafted the smoke away. Her nose tickled. "The fire. You died in the fire?"

Minna didn't reply. She bent her head so her long hair obscured her face, and unflinchingly slid the poker back through her shoulder.

"Minna," Leo asked again gently, "did you die in the fire?"

"Technically, I breathed in a lot of smoke. So they think." Minna fixed Leo with a sour look. "Smoke from the fire started BY YOU, so don't assume you're off the hook! And, more to the point, you stopped me from killing him properly—PERMANENTLY. If it weren't for you, stealing my dagger, the Orphanmaster would be gone. My friends and I would be free!"

Leo stared. Somehow, the defenseless girl she had met at the orphanage seemed very different from the ghost sitting in front of her now.

"W-wait—what?" She gasped as Minna's words finally sunk in. "You were going to KILL him?"

"I would have, if I had to! Don't look at me like that. *You* were there to kill too, weren't you?"

"I . . . well . . . yes, b-but . . . !" Leo shook her head. "But . . . that's different. And you wouldn't have been free at all! Don't you get it? A man like that—it would have been a Suspicious Death. The other humans would have come after you. They'd have formed the ANGRY MOB!"

"You think I don't know that? That was why it was only my *backup* plan. He was never supposed to wake up; I was being stealthy before YOU came crashing in!"

The papers, Leo remembered. Minna had been poring over boring-looking papers when Leo had arrived at the window. "What were you doing there, then?" she asked. "What was your first plan?"

"That"—Minna turned her nose up at her—"is none of your concern. But it's one thing to wake the Orphanmaster while I'm trying to save my friends. It's ANOTHER THING entirely to steal my dagger and get me killed!"

"I didn't know!" Leo protested. "I didn't mean to! I was only there f-for my Hunt! It's the vampire way." She held up her clawed hands. "When you've been a vampire for a hundred years, like me, you take on your Waxing Moon and you *have* to hunt a human. The Vampiric Council says so! I didn't . . . I didn't know that you had a mission too!"

But Minna didn't seem to care about that. "It should have been easy," she muttered. "I'd have . . . you know." She drew her finger across her own throat, making Leo gulp. "It would have been over before he even got out of bed; he wouldn't have even seen me. No Orphanmaster. No ghosts. It would have been better for everyone."

That had been Leo's plan too. An easy kill—clean and simple and delicious.

How catastrophically wrong she had been.

"He was a horror." Minna's mouth twisted and so did Leo's heart—she had only ever heard that particular word associated with MUM. "He would make us scrub the whole orphanage, top to bottom, over and over, instead of going to school. Books were not allowed. Playing was not allowed. He kept us fed on cold gruel and water, and *that's* if we were allowed to eat that day at all. Some days, nothing."

"R-right, but, you don't have to worry anymore since he's—"

"AND we were only allowed to bathe once a week—three at a time, in the freezing tub," Minna continued, not listening. "He never called us by our names, not unless we were in trouble, or when he was gloating or making one of his stupid speeches." Her baleful scowl made Leo shiver. "I was going to fix everything. I was going to find our way out, before he could REALLY ruin our lives."

Minna's ghostly eyes were like lamps in the dark, huge and damning as they caught Leo in their beam.

"But there you were, at the Orphanmaster's window," Minna continued bitterly. "You HAD to poke your vampire nose in and now I'm *stuck* here as a ghost—and so is he."

Leo clutched her blanket tighter. The voice from her nightmare echoed in her ears. Not just one ghost, but *two*? She was in trouble. She was in trouble beyond imagination. If Mum found out . . .

She must have misheard. There was no way this could be right.

"Sorry, what?"

Minna sighed heavily, as though she considered Leo to be particularly dense. "You ROASTED THE ORPHANMASTER IN A WARDROBE. It's not difficult to comprehend! He became a ghost, just like I did."

A horrible chill was spreading through Leo's body, spreading out from a spear right through her heart. Her fingertips felt numb, as did her lips when she touched her hand to her mouth. "Y-y-you've SEEN him, then? The Orphanmaster's ghost?"

"I can *sense* him," Minna told her grimly, and Leo believed every word. Minna's white gaze pinned Leo in place, piercing her with the intensity of her stare. "A ghost doesn't just . . . doesn't just appear out of nothing—he *remembers*." Minna swallowed. Her face pinched, a look of desperation coming over her. "We have to fix this! You don't know him like I do—he'll be ten times as bad as he was in life! We can't let him run around, wreaking destruction. He'll be after me, and he'll be after YOU too! Don't think you're safe up here in your castle!"

With that, Minna began to rise up. Her hair whipped around her furious face. Her voice reverberated through her misty body, growing louder and louder.

"I have UNFINISHED BUSINESS! He's out there, getting stronger, and it's only a matter of time before he's awake for real and proper! I cannot rest until I remove him from this world!" Minna loomed closer until they were a breath apart. "You really messed up, Leo! You messed up, big time!"

"All right! All right! I'm sorry!" Leo cried, crawling backward up the wall. It was fortunate that her room was so high up, where no one could hear her scream. "I'm sorry, Minna! I get it!"

*"Leo von Motteberg!"* Minna boomed, her voice reverberating as though it came from a hundred Minnas. *"I am going to hunt the Orphanmaster. I will take my revenge. I am going to stop him from hurting anyone ever again! I am going to complete my mission, so I can finally be at peace!"*

The windows rattled and the curtains twisted and the bedding began to float. Paper blew around the room in a whirlwind. Over on the desk, the *Encyclopedia Silva* slammed open, pages flipping madly. Leo cowered, hands over her face.

*"And YOU,"* Minna thundered, *"are going to help me do it, VAMPIRE!"*

# 8
# The Library

After Minna's rage had calmed, the two girls stood in the middle of the bedroom, high up in the western tower. They faced each other across the floor.

*Wow,* Leo thought to herself, going clammy all over. *This is real.*

*A ghost. In my bedroom.*

*Minna the ghost wants me to help her take out the evil and now entirely Undead Orphanmaster.*

There was one, very slight issue.

"This whole 'killing a ghost' thing . . . ," Leo began, swallowing down the queasy feeling in her throat. "It's great and all—excellent plan, really, complete genius—but . . . where do we start?"

Minna (floating serenely now and mercifully no longer trashing Leo's room) shrugged her see-through shoulders.

"Well, seeing as I've only been a ghost for three days," she said curtly, adjusting her hairband, "I was rather hoping *you* might have more of an idea! I came to you for a reason—you're a vampire, aren't you? A vampire of Castle Motteberg?"

*How do you even know about the castle?* Leo wanted to ask, but she had a feeling she was better off not knowing. How many other ghosts out there knew about her family? And . . .

Her brain stopped and started, like an engine stammering back to life. Steam might have come out of her ears, but her eyes had blanked out and she couldn't see anything.

"Three . . . th-three . . ."

"Leo?" Minna's face swam into view, her expression somewhere between concerned and annoyed.

*"Three days?"* Leo squeaked out, flopping back onto her bed. She covered her face with a groan. "Minna. What do you mean, you've been a ghost for three days?"

"What sort of a question is that? We've been over this; you barged in through the window, you woke the Orphanmaster, then—"

Leo tuned out, letting Minna have her rant. Her mind curled up in a small, distant part of her brain, far away from her ears. Had it really been three days since her Waxing Moon? Had she been sleeping for three whole days—WASTING TIME—while Sieglinde was away with the Council?

If Marged was correct, Mum could be on her way back by now. She could be returning to a daughter who had failed her Hunt. And, even worse, a daughter who had managed to make such a mess of it, she had created two GHOSTS in the process.

This was unfathomably bad. If Sieglinde flew in and spotted Minna and the Orphanmaster battling it out, her fury might bring the whole castle down to rubble. Ghosts? On HER property? Woe betide whoever had been foolish enough to let them in!

That was, if Mum wasn't *already* back from her trip . . .

"What's going on with you?" Minna was asking when Leo peeked through her fingers. "So you slept for three days; it's not such a big deal. I think the Orphanmaster will still be piecing himself together, seeing as he was a lot older than me. He has a lot more memories to sort through."

"That's the way it works, is it?" Leo replied numbly, her head still full of moths and teeth.

"Who knows," Minna bemoaned, floating down next to Leo on the bed. "Who knows how any of this is supposed to work? I thought maybe *you* would have a clue, being a vampire. A CREATURE OF THE NIGHT." She looked sideways at Leo, suddenly suspicious. "You are . . . a vampire, aren't you?"

Leo blinked. "O-of course I'm a vampire," she said. "But vampires and ghosts are very different beasts! I don't really know, er, much of *anything* about ghosts at all! I'm only one hundred and eleven!"

Minna shrank smaller. "Really? Nothing?" Leo nodded. "You've never killed a ghost before?" Leo shook her head. "Oh, bother. I guess my rotten luck hasn't died. Trust me to end up with the only vampire in the world who doesn't know how to fight ghosts."

Leo wanted to argue. She couldn't possibly be the only vampire out there who hadn't fought a ghost. And she *had* fought a human of the large and scary variety, which was equally as brave! But Leo didn't fancy starting her ghostly experience by arguing with Minna. Minna was scary too. A lot scarier than she had seemed in the Orphanmaster's bedroom.

"How . . . how do you know about all this?" Leo asked, suspicion creeping in. "About vampires and ghosts? I didn't think humans knew much about us?"

"The Orphanmaster had books," Minna said curtly. "Lots of books, bound in leather, in an old trunk under his bed. Locked but . . . Well. Let's just say I took care of that."

"Without him knowing?" Leo wasn't sure if she was appalled or impressed.

"He was none the wiser. I got curious one day, when we were sweeping the floors upstairs, so I went ahead and took a peek. I thought it was weird that he had such an interest in vampires. I thought they were make-believe. Until you."

Leo cleared her throat, but the lump there stuck tight and wouldn't budge. She remembered how the Orphanmaster had recognized her, back at St. Frieda's. *Parlor tricks*, he'd dismissively called her Vampiric Will. He hadn't been afraid at all.

Could he have been a vampire hunter? It was unlikely—no hunter had dared venture into the Dreadwald for centuries, according to Dad.

"There must be ghost powers that you've already worked out, though?" Leo changed the subject, puffing a thin, nervous laugh. "Let's think positive! I mean, maybe the best way to learn about ghosts is to *be* a ghost!"

Considering this, Minna chewed the inside of her cheek.

"I've already figured out the walking-through-walls thing," she admitted finally. "Oh, and I can make myself invisible, but I'll definitely need to practice more."

"That's cool!" said Leo, trying to be encouraging.

"And I can move stuff around too, if I concentrate really hard. But even that isn't much help for fighting another ghost, is it?" Minna's face took a turn for the dejected again.

*This girl.* Leo stared in disbelief. Minna had mood swings to rival Emmeline, which was saying something.

"Hey . . . hey, don't be sad!" Leo reached out to touch Minna on the arm. Her claws went harmlessly through the ghost's skin, with the same chilly rush as dipping her hand into the freezing mountain lake. She snatched it hastily back. "Uhhh, look, it's fine—you've only been a ghost for, what, a few nights? I still have vampire powers I'm not quite . . . um . . ."

She thought of the GRIMWALK.

"I'm getting there," she lied.

Minna sniffed wetly. "Wonderful! Good to know!" She wiped her face on the back of her arm and then balled her hands at her sides. "But . . . what now?"

"Well . . ." Leo thought for a moment. There was one place she could always turn to, when she was in a bind. "I bet the *Encyclopedia* will have something!"

Yes. That was it.

How had Leo not thought about it sooner?

"The what?" Minna drifted curiously behind as Leo scampered to her desk.

"The *Encyclopedia Silva*! It's the best book in the universe. It has loads of information on the Dreadwald and all the creatures in it."

"Including ghosts?" asked Minna.

"Let's see."

The *Encyclopedia* was an ancient book. Leo liked all sorts of books, new and old, but there was something extra-specially amazing about this one. This book was wise. It had never let her down. Maybe it would even get her out of this terrible jam she found herself in—trapped between the twin perils of her mother and the Orphanmaster.

It was already open after Minna's outburst, showing a black-and-white picture of *Atropa belladonna*, or DEADLY NIGHTSHADE. It was in the D section, but they needed G for ghost. Leo's black tongue stuck out between her fangs as she leafed through the pages.

*Gardenia*, *garlic* (blergh!), *geranium*, *ginger*—no, too far . . . Ah, there it was.

***GHOST***

*(Woooeus Spookeus)*

*A spooky specter with supernatural abilities.*
*The ghost is a Living creature who isn't*

*Living anymore. Hates vampires. Likes creepy old houses, spidery attics, smelly basements, abandoned churches, and so on. Another favorite hangout is graveyards at midnight.*

*Ghosts are usually ex-humans, since humans tend to have too much going on and a lot of UNFINISHED BUSINESS, which is how ghosts are born. If you die angry . . . you could become a ghost. So WATCH OUT!!!*

Leo turned to Minna with a *ta-da!* sort of gesture, but Minna didn't seem too convinced.

"Is that it?" Minna asked, somewhat snottily in Leo's opinion. "I thought you said it was the best book in the universe?"

Leo didn't like Minna scoffing at her beloved book. Not one bit.

"No, that's not it! There's more!" she protested, turning the page.

There, right at the bottom . . .

*What to do if you encounter a ghost:*

*1) Hope that they are friendly!*

*2)*

Stunned silence fell over the room. Leo cleared her throat, sure she could feel her stomach sink all the way to her toes and through the floor. Her face burned a darker gray.

"Oh," said Minna politely. Then, somewhat less politely: "Oh! Isn't that SOOO helpful! I suppose there didn't need to be a second tip, since the first was such SHREWD advice!"

"All right, all right . . ." Leo was regretting ever mentioning the *Encyclopedia.*

"Hang on," said Minna, making things worse, "*you* wrote this, didn't you?" She lifted the page, an action that seemed to take a lot of effort, since her hand was only mist or secrets or whatever it was that ghosts were made of. The paper was slightly less yellowed than other pages in the *Encyclopedia.* It had been carefully fixed in with the swanky book glue Dad used to restore old books in the library.

"There's really useful stuff in here!" insisted Leo, wanting to defend her prized possession. "But I thought it couldn't hurt to add things that were missing. After all, the writer died a long, long time ago, so of course there will be stuff that they can't write about."

Specifically, she meant L. Hinterblatt, one of the greatest explorers and intrepid foresters that the world had ever known. It was a name that commanded respect, though apparently not from nosy ghost girls.

"So you added entries yourself?" Minna flicked curiously through the book. "What else have you put in, then?"

With a heavy thud, Leo slammed the *Encyclopedia* closed. She stroked the leather-bound cover in a private apology. "It doesn't matter!" she squeaked. "Besides, you're right, there's not much on ghosts."

An idea flickered somewhere in the back of her mind. It was small and dim at first, but became brighter and brighter, like the moon rising over the horizon.

Leo gasped. "We should try the LIBRARY; I bet Dad will have something! He has books on everything else."

There would be *something* that could save her in there. Some nugget of ghost-killing information she could use—hidden away in one of the places Mum NEVER set foot. She was always far too busy to visit the library. It was the perfect place for Leo formulate the plan she desperately needed. . . .

"Wait here!"

In a flurry Leo grabbed for her shirt and shorts and cape. Yanking open her wardrobe, she groped blindly for her spare leg (it wasn't as comfy as the one she had lost, but it would do). Arms overflowing with her things, she hopped into the bathroom. There was no time to waste. Minna bobbed up and down, bemused.

"What, so your dad will just hand over whatever we need?"

she called after Leo's retreating back. Maybe she wasn't used to grown-ups being much help after living with the Orphanmaster.

"He'll be too busy to notice, like always. Don't touch my things!"

The bathroom door banged shut.

Then it banged open again.

"ESPECIALLY my book. I shall know!" Leo brandished her spare leg threateningly.

The door banged shut once more.

The archives at Castle Motteberg were a labyrinthine maze of shelves, packed with books on every subject imaginable. There were books on botany and books on animal classification. There were books on lock-picking and astronomy and pirate history—all subjects that fascinated Leo deeply.

Of course, she suspected that they even had books that weren't to her taste, but she had yet to waste her time on those. You would need a million years to read every book in the archives.

That was the name Dad gave the place, anyway. You had to say *the archives* with a nasally sort of tone, to sound really intellectual. To get the proper effect, you had to hold your nose and pretend you were wearing a starchy shirt done up all the way to the top button. Bonus points if the shirt was brown.

Leo thought that *the archives* sounded far too uptight and

uninteresting. She much preferred to call the room by its real name, the one that suited it the most. The LIBRARY.

The library was a cave of magic and intrigue, full of all the riches of the imagination. In an instant she could be transformed into a scaly dragon, or flung to a faraway land, or sent back in time to when now-extinct beasts roamed. When you were (mostly) all alone and (sadly) friendless, the escapism of a book was difficult to resist.

Fizzing with anticipation, Leo cracked open the arched doorway to usher Minna inside. She cast a furtive glance behind them, ears pricked for Emmeline or, even more fatally, Mum. Minna gave her a funny look, but didn't ask. She bobbed aside and then simply floated through the wooden panels. When she emerged on the other side, though, she gasped.

Stone steps beckoned them down into the chamber, which had been built deep enough to accommodate the soaring bookcases, each as tall as any Dreadwald tree. The candlelight changed color according to whatever sort of science Dad was working on lately; tonight it was the murky green that Leo liked best. She looked slyly sideways at Minna, pleased to see that the ghost was finally as awed as she ought to be.

"It's nothing, really," said Leo, faking modesty. "I'm sure there are better libraries out there, but this is ours. It's . . . you know. Cozy."

Above them, the ceiling was painted in a tremendous scene that spanned the entire length of the library, depicting a battle between the vampires and their enemies. Goblins, ghouls and giants, banshees and sirens, a lone centaur wielding a golden bow . . .

No ghosts, though, which Leo had always found strange. Maybe the ghosts were invisible. Either that, or the artist really *did* hate them.

Minna, revolving clumsily, was taking it all in.

"It's . . . Leo, it's so . . ."

"Yeah. I come here every night. You get used to it." Leo smiled smugly. "But stay close. It's easy to get lost if you wander off."

They snaked between the stacks, winding down the narrow passageways. Minna's flying skills, it turned out, were shaky at best; a few times she vanished behind the dusty shelves, appearing again with a scowl and a body full of floating dust, her long hair tangled in her face.

All their reference books on science and magic were coded, and Leo paused to rifle through a box of cards that contained the topics and their locations. She concentrated, pinching her tongue beneath her teeth.

The subject they needed was one she had never sought out before.

❋ ❋ ❋

GHOSTS, as it turned out, was right at the back of the library, deeper than Leo would usually explore. It gave her a funny feeling, somehow. . . .

"Leo!" a voice piped up as a distant rumbling, scraping sound echoed off the stony walls. "Do you hear that?" When Leo snapped around, Minna had inched closer to her, her translucent body flickering as another grinding thud made her flinch.

Leo shook herself. "Ah!" she said, flashing her fangs. "It's fine, don't panic! The bookcases just like to take a walk from time to time."

"The . . . bookcases?"

A few stacks away, more dust flew up in a fat cloud, and the rumbling ceased. Minna's tense frame relaxed, and when she turned, Leo saw her take her hand off the poker spearing her shoulder.

It took a while to reach their destination. Leo led the way, guiding Minna deeper and deeper into the guts of Castle Motteberg. At one point she thought they had come to a dead end, but some searching revealed a hidden mechanism that revealed a rotating bookcase, which revealed another tight pathway. The back of the library was dark and musty. Even the books themselves were spookier too, worn with age and covered in cobwebs.

Leo bit back a yelp when they turned a corner and almost bumped into the foot of a long ladder.

Precariously balanced at the top, nose buried in an open book, was a familiar face.

"Dad!" Leo gasped, and was almost blinded by a bright light when Dad turned abruptly. He reached up, fumbling for the lamp he had attached to his headgear. He flicked a switch and two layers of magnifying lenses pinged off his goggles, allowing him to squint down at her.

"Eleonore?" Dad clung to the top of the creaking ladder, wobbling with the gigantic book balanced on the globe of his belly. His eyes were huge behind his goggles. "Oh! It's unusual to see you this far into the archives."

In fact, Leo seldom saw Dad at all, but she didn't correct him. Dietmar von Motteberg, lord by marriage to Lady Sieglinde, was almost always buried in his research.

He was also the opposite of his wife in almost every way. Shortish where she was tall. Round where she was angular. Meek and mild where she was . . . well, Mum. Dad occasionally gave solid advice, but most of the time he seemed more like a forgetful owl than a vampire.

Leo coughed. "I'm finding ideas for . . . for a story I'm working on."

She knew that she was a terrible liar. She wouldn't have

even attempted to fib, if not for the fact that Dad was an equally terrible *listener* when he was on the job.

"That's nice," Dad replied distractedly. He glanced back at his book and then down to Leo, as though he would rather be reading but was trying to mind his manners. "Well. Be careful down here, won't you? It can be a bit treacherous on your own."

"Ah, but I'm . . ." Leo stopped herself. When she peered behind her, Minna was nowhere to be seen, having hastily flown into one of the bookcases. Her ghostly skills were all right in a pinch. Leo breathed a sigh of relief. "I'll be careful, Dad."

"Right, right, that's good. . . ." Dad was already looking back at his book. "Well, I'm not exactly a bestselling author, but I'm sure you'll find some inspiration."

"I hope so!" A thought came to her, dragging her optimism like a stone to the bottom of the lake. "Erm . . . I don't suppose you've spotted *Mum* about tonight, have you?"

"Your mother?" Dad blinked, not quite looking up from his page. "No, my dear, hasn't Marged told you? Sieglinde is running late—the raven arrived yesternight. Unusual for her to write ahead . . . They must have made a real *pig's ear* of things at the Council."

Council affairs were usually tedious and took time to

resolve. From what Sieglinde had told her, there was much debating (and monologuing, boasting, swaggering).

Leo sucked in a breath, tasting ink and old paper on the back of her tongue.

"How . . . how long do you think she will be?"

"Hmmm . . . perhaps a few nights more," Dad mumbled, his eyes darting back and forth over the paragraph in front of him. "I wouldn't have thought long; it seems her patience with that place is wearing thin. . . ."

Mum wasn't here.

Mum was held up with the Council.

*Thank the stars!*

Leo looked up at her father. He knew a thing or two about time being precious; he was easily the busiest person she knew, always working on some project or another. He had become so tangled up in his work lately, he had started leaving himself notes to remind himself of when and where to be. Dad's curly hair was standing on end more than usual tonight and he was now humming quietly to himself.

It had been an age since they had spent any time together, any proper time, doing fun things. Leo had taken Dad into the Dreadwald three years ago, hoping to build a new hideout with him, but he'd touched some ivy and developed a weird rash and had to come home. He did his best and was always willing to give dadly advice, but he was always looking at his pocket watch—especially when he was in study mode.

"Hey, Dad?"

"Hmmm?" Dad didn't look up.

Leo took a deep breath. "I lied, before. I'm not here on my own, I have a ghost friend."

"Oh, that's nice. . . ."

"Yep. We're going to find a book on ghosts so we can fight an evil man who I accidentally killed a few nights ago."

"Yes, good, that's really good. . . ."

Dad wasn't listening. He scratched absently at the back of his neck, already sunk deep into his work again. Stuck to his elbow was a small square of parchment:

*To Remember:*
*Frog gelatin*
*Quartz powder*
*Take vial off boil after two hours*
*Eleonore's birthnight*
*Alpine bristle-moss*

Leo sighed.

"Love you, Dad."

"Yes? What? Ah. I love you too, Eleonore."

# 9
# How to Kill a Ghost

"Now *this* looks more like it!" Minna cheered, rubbing her ghostly hands together.

The book in front of them was as hefty as it was old—older than Leo, older than the *Encyclopedia*, probably older than your grandma. Blowing away the thick layer of dust, Leo reared back when a shiny purple beetle leapt from inside the book's spine. It was so quiet this far into the library—in the deepest and darkest and spideriest section—she could hear every tip-tip-tap of the beetle's tiny feet as it scurried for cover.

In gilded lettering the front of the book read:

*THE GHOST-HUNTER'S COMPANION*
*For the Tracking, Trapping, and Banishing of Specters, Spirits, and Apparitions*

They hoisted it to a low table (or, rather, Leo took the book's full and considerable weight as it slipped through Minna's hands). Two lumpy, overstuffed armchairs sat either side of the table. Leo perched in one, bracing her elbow on the table to heave the *Companion* open.

The two girls bent over the time-worn pages, heads together.

"Huh," Leo said.

"Huh," Minna replied.

The book was entirely handwritten in muddy ink that had faded in patches. Worse still, the author was more interested in being fancy than legible. The writing looped and spiked in a way that made Leo queasy. It might as well have been written in an entirely new language.

Leo looked at Minna. Minna looked back at Leo.

They both gave a resigned sigh.

It would take some deciphering.

Killing a ghost, as it turned out, was not a matter of simply biting them. Nor was it possible to stake or stab a ghost.

Or shove them off a cliff, or drop a piano on their head and squash them to death.

Upon creation of a ghost, they would bring with them a Spirit Anchor: an item to glue them to the world of the Living. The Spirit Anchor was usually the last thing a ghost touched before death—meaning that, if you were about to tuck into a banana when you died, that banana would haunt you for the rest of your unlife. If you were for some reason holding a hilarious rubber chicken, that rubber chicken would become your eternal companion. If you were on the loo and holding a roll of toilet paper . . . you get the picture.

A ghost could only be banished by destroying their Spirit Anchor, thus shattering their connection to reality and effectively killing them (for a second time).

But these items, existing in the limbo between the realms of the Living and the Undead, were not easily broken.

In fact, the *Companion* gave a whole list of conditions that needed to be met.

"Oh, pox and pustules!" Leo complained, flopping back in the armchair. "Really? I'd figured it wasn't going to be easy, but isn't it a bit much?" Perhaps part of her had still held the thin hope that the GHOST PROBLEM might be resolved on its own, that Minna and the Orphanmaster might . . . move on to wherever ghosts went next.

No such luck.

Minna ignored her, delicately lifting a page with intense concentration. The paper was so thin you could see the candlelight through it. *"Elements for the dispatchment of Spirit Anchors and banishment of their spirits,"* she read aloud. *"Salt. Sulfur. Smoke. Twice-blessed water. The glow of a sunrise. A weapon of intent."*

She looked down at her shoulder, where the glimmering poker stuck through.

"So this is my Spirit Anchor, then," Minna said, pulling the metal rod free. She studied its pointed tip. "That's why it came with me."

Shying away from the poker, Leo remembered something.

"But wouldn't it have made more sense for . . . you know . . ." She rummaged in her cape, finding the tooth-shaped dagger she had taken from Minna back at St. Frieda's. "Shouldn't your Spirit Anchor be this? I mean, you were going to use it, weren't you? If I hadn't pinched it."

Minna sniffed. "Well, I suppose it *would* have made more sense, but it obviously doesn't work that way!" She waved the poker, swishing it like a sword. "This was the last thing I touched before I died. Of course it has to be this."

The dagger looked accusatory now. Leo's mouth drooped sadly.

"You keep it." Minna sighed, looking completely fed up. "It was just something I found while I was sweeping the drive. I can't take it with me, can I? I'm still angry with you, since it was completely your fault that I died at all, but there's nothing we can do about it, is there?"

"I know."

"Then don't give me that look!"

"What look?"

"The sad-puppy-in-the-rain look." Minna fixed Leo with a stern glare, wagging the poker at her. "We have work to do! For one thing, we don't know what the Orphanmaster's Anchor actually is."

Leo's right leg itched. Or the place where Leo's right leg *used to be* itched. She touched her spare prosthetic thoughtfully.

"I know what the Orphanmaster's Spirit Anchor is!" she blurted.

"What?"

Leo gripped the edge of the table. "Minna! It's my leg! The Orphanmaster has my leg!"

*Have you gone quite mad?* Minna's face said. Leo leapt to her feet, the armchair screeching backward. On the towering shelves around them the dusty books juddered in place as though disturbed by the motion, rippling all the way up to the distant ceiling.

Both Leo and Minna paused. They stared up at the shelves and then at each other as dust floated down.

"I'm never going to get used to that," Minna commented. "The bookcases, I mean. I don't know how you live here and manage to get any sleep."

Leo shook her head. "No, no, that was weird. That's not a walking bookcase. It was like a . . ."

A shiver, maybe.

The girls stayed very still. Mercifully, so did the books.

"Perhaps it was Dad?" Leo thought aloud. "If he's gone back to the lab, it . . . it might be one of his experiments . . . causing a disturbance."

"Right," Minna agreed somewhat dubiously. She shook her head as if to dispel an unwanted thought. "And your leg? What . . . Sorry, the Orphanmaster has your LEG?"

"He pulled it off when we fought. He had it in his hand when he . . . before he . . ." Leo rubbed the back of her neck. She pulled a fluffy clump of dust from behind one ear. "You know. Met his end."

"In the wardrobe," Minna said flatly. "On fire."

"Yes. That." Leo cleared her throat. "But the important thing is: we know what we need to find. Salt, sulfur, and smoke. Twice-blessed water. S-sunrise." She stammered a bit over that one and moved swiftly on, counting the ingredients off on her claws. "Weapon of intent—that's probably your *poker*, Minna, if you can fight with it."

Considering this, Minna lifted an eyebrow. "My Spirit Anchor is also a weapon of intent?"

"Intent means something you're determined to do, doesn't it?" As Minna touched a pale finger to the poker's point, Leo sank down into her armchair again. She leaned back to put a more reasonable distance between the sharp tip and her own vulnerable eyeballs. "I, er . . . I think, if anything can defeat a ghost, a proper GHOSTLY WEAPON is probably the tool for the job?"

"Well . . . I should think so." Minna nodded in agreement. She sheathed the poker smoothly back through her shoulder. "It's certainly always at hand."

Leo's sigh deflated her further into the misshapen cushions, watching as Minna leaned again over the *Companion*.

"Oh—have you seen this?" Minna pointed to the bottom of the aged page. "Here, look, a footnote . . ."

> *A Warning:*
> *Beneath the watch of the seventh sinking*
> *moon will a spirit's power be fully realized.*

"The seventh sinking moon . . ." Minna frowned.

"Maybe it's the *fully realized power* part that we should

worry about," suggested Leo. She gnawed her lip. "Does that mean . . . the Orphanmaster, he'll be . . ."

"Growing. In the dark."

"Like a poisonous fungus," Leo added, and then blushed when Minna snapped around to look at her.

"Wait—the seventh sinking moon!" Minna hissed, as though the Orphanmaster might hear them. "That could mean the seventh night. . . . He'll come into his full strength. He will be at his very worst."

Leo didn't like the sound of that.

"Well, so will you? I mean—not your *worst*, but . . . you have your ghost powers too. Maybe you'll be at your most powerful. To fight him."

Minna shook her head. "You don't know the Orphanmaster, Leo. Not like I do. He was evil even *before* any 'ghost powers.'" She drew herself up a little straighter, nodding grimly. "We need to act fast. If we have any chance of defeating him, it has to be BEFORE that seventh moon goes down. Whoever wrote this probably found out the hard way."

The sooner, the better, as far as Leo was concerned. If an old book said they had seven moons—seven nights—then she wasn't about to argue. The most important thing was that it was over and done with before anyone FOUND OUT. . . .

A pensive silence unraveled between them.

Judging by Minna's tight expression, she was thinking the same as Leo.

How many moons did they have left?

"My Waxing Moon—that night was the *first* moon," Leo said slowly.

"It's been three days since the fire." Minna turned her face to the faraway ceiling, as though she could see through it into the night sky. "So tonight is the fourth moon . . ."

There was a creaking sound overhead, like old leather being squeezed through a tight gap.

Minna was already looking up. "Watch out!" she cried as Leo shot out of her chair.

Where she had been sitting only a heartbeat before, a book bigger than her head came crashing down with an almighty THUD, sending the armchair flying backward. There was a sharp *crack* as one of its wooden legs fractured into splinters, skidding away across the library floor. The cushion split open, a fluffy wave of its goose-feather stuffing spilling out.

Stunned, Leo and Minna turned their eyes upward. The shelf above them was innocently still—with a large gap on the very top shelf that hadn't been there before.

Then, in unison, they stared down at the fallen book.

*DEATH AFTER DEATH*, its dust-smeared cover read.

Leo clutched at her chest, feeling her organs heave behind

her ribs. She thought for a moment that she felt a chill on the back of her neck, like a puff of icy breath.

"We should go," she wheezed.

The library door closed with a *creak-thunk*, the sound echoing away down the hallway. Leo huffed, hefting the *Companion* in her arms.

"Are you *sure* you can't help me with this?" she groaned, feeling as though the ginormous book might squash her, much like an ant trying to lift a mountain.

Minna hmphed. "Even if I wanted to—because a bit of heavy lifting is the LEAST you can do for me—I'm not sure I can!"

Her haughty demeanor had been quick to return. Despite the bite of her words, however, Leo couldn't help but notice that Minna was looking somewhat washed-out, as though her vibrancy had dimmed. Her otherworldly glow barely cast any light at all.

Leo was about to ask Minna if she was feeling all right, when something made her pause.

Her spine prickled.

"Hide!" She shuffled behind an ornamental suit of armor that could have been Marged's cousin, although this one was holding a long chain with a spiked ball on the end.

"What?" Minna's disembodied voice questioned; Minna

herself had vanished into the wood-paneled wall behind them. "What's wrong? What's going on?"

"No time to explain! Shhh!" Leo struggled into the small gap, fighting to squeeze the book in with her.

She had definitely sensed something. Something that cast a startling shadow up the wall when it flew past the candlelit braziers. Something that drew closer and closer . . .

"Leeeeeeo!" a lilting voice called.

"*Oh no*," Leo half whispered, half mouthed, hoping Minna alone could hear her. *"Don't. Move!"*

"I KNOW it's you!" the newcomer insisted, and Leo squeezed her eyes shut at the sight of the shadow looming menacingly large on the wall. "Who *else* has their feet in the mud and their nose stuck in a grimy book?"

EMMELINE. Leo held still, clutching the *Companion* to her chest.

"I know you're here!" Emmeline snarled, moving farther away down the other end of the hall. Something rattled—perhaps the paintings on the walls. "You can't run from me forever!"

*We'll see about that*, Leo thought. Peering out from behind the suit of armor, she saw a snatch of frilly lace as it disappeared around the corner.

"Phew . . ." Leo wiped her face with a handful of her cape. She juggled the book awkwardly as she all but fell out from her hiding place.

Minna emerged from the wall. "Who was *that*?" she asked, eyebrows raised.

"Oh, j-just my sister. No big deal, it's fine."

"Sounds as though she likes YOU a whole lot."

"She does! We're . . . not exactly on friendly terms at the moment, but she does." Honestly, with Emmeline, it was sometimes hard to tell. But all big sisters could be like that, Leo reassured herself. "We should hurry and get this upstairs before she comes . . . Minna? Are you all right?"

Next to her, Minna was looking fainter and fainter.

In fact, she had disappeared up to her waist.

"What is it?" Leo fretted. "Is it the Orphanmaster?" She would have wrung her hands, but her arms were full. The Orphanmaster was somehow snatching Minna away to another dimension where his dark power would be inescapable—

"Huh? No!" Minna rolled her eyes with weary resignation. "No, I'm . . . ugh, I knew this would happen . . . I've been struggling to hold my form for a while now. I have to recharge every now and again."

"Oh . . ." Leo nodded, halting her frantic dance. Minna really did look tired. "Um. You should take a break. I'll get this up to my room—we can always meet up first thing tomorrow and get started. When I've read more."

*When I've figured out how to keep Mum off our tail while we fix this*, she added silently.

Even fading away, Minna's glare was fierce. "Don't feel sorry for me!" she bit out. "I'm only three days old in ghost years! It takes some figuring out!"

"I-I wasn't!" Leo snipped back, from behind the book. "I wasn't feeling sorry for you at all! I know you can handle it!"

"Good!"

"Fine! Enjoy your sleep!"

"I will!"

"Okay!"

Minna's eyes were the last thing to fade, still glowering at Leo before they too disappeared.

Back in the safety of her bedroom, Leo heaved the *Companion* onto her desk with a sound a bit like *hrrrrrnk!*

Then she collapsed in a puddle on top of it.

"Oh," she panted, feeling her black heart pound and the blood rush back into her numb arms. "Never again." Her clawtips tingled. Her knee felt weak. It was a long way up to her room from the depths of the library, and the book really was monstrously huge.

Pushing herself up, Leo considered the book. Sat side by side it looked a bit like the *Encyclopedia Silva*'s big sister. But it wasn't only the size difference; the *Encyclopedia* had always given Leo a comforting feeling, like having a friend who is looking out for you. This new book gave her a sense of dread.

Four moons, including the one rapidly running out.

Four short nights to defeat the Orphanmaster and stop Mum finding out about the ghostly fiasco.

It didn't seem like much time at all.

*"Mmrowr!"*

Leo almost did a Marged and clattered to the floor, but caught herself on the back of her chair.

Crouched on the book, sparse fur sticking up like a grumpy toilet brush, was the ugliest creature Leo had ever seen. A hideous black cat, to be precise, with a squashed face and protruding teeth, spindly legs, and a crooked wire of a tail. It glared up at Leo with its one remaining eye. . . .

And began to purr.

"Button, you scared me! Look at you, sneaking up on me on me like that. . . ." Leo scratched the top of the cat's head, and its raggedy ears perked toward her. It bumped its nose against her hand. "Who's my vicious predator? You are!"

Button had moved in fifty-something years back, after Leo had found him wandering the Dreadwald as a kitten. He had lived here in the western tower ever since.

If you are thinking that fifty years is a very long time for a cat to be alive, you would be absolutely correct. Perhaps, living with an ageless vampire, some of Leo's immortality had rubbed off on him.

Dribbling happily, Button crawled into Leo's lap. He was at least half deaf, but never failed to sense Marged's clanking and clattering when she was on her way up the stairs. Button had a habit of making himself scarce whenever the suit of armor was around.

"Was it the creepy ghost girl?" she cooed, scratching around the scruff of his neck. "Awww, Button. Did she frighten you, tough guy?"

"She was certainly fearsome!" replied Button—only, Button couldn't speak, and therefore it wasn't Button who replied at all. The distinctive sound of an opening drawer met Leo's ears, but she didn't bother turning around.

"Rodrigo," she said, with deliberate calm. "We've talked about this. You need to stop listening in on me when I'm doing private things."

"Like talking to the weasel?" the voice asked snootily, and Button spat. "Okay—cat! I meant *cat*! Yikes . . ."

"Yes. I happen to like talking to Button." Leo soothed the cat, stroking up his twisty tail. "I'm . . ." She swallowed, feeling the lie burn the tip of her tongue. "I'm a g-grown-up now. Grown-ups need their privacy sometimes."

There was a tapping sound: feet creeping up over the lip of the drawer.

"You still sound the same to me. Like a girl who didn't really hunt a human. Like a girl who went running around the castle with a gho—"

The voice—Rodrigo—didn't have time to finish.

Button went flying as Leo stomped over to the chest of drawers. She yanked the top drawer fully open, winter socks spilling across the floor and littering Leo's bedroom like fallen leaves as she tried to dig Rodrigo out.

"Ah! *Ah!* No, Leo, mercy! Mercy!"

Eventually, there were no socks left. In the back corner of the drawer was a huddled brown lump, about the size of Leo's fist.

*"Rodri!"* said Leo fiercely. "You must never breathe a word. Not about the Waxing Moon. And CERTAINLY not about Minna. Do you understand?"

"B-but—"

"*Do you understand?* I swear, Rodrigo, I will feed you to Button myself!"

Behind her, the cat licked its chops.

"Yes! YES—I get it! N-not a word! You can trust me!"

Satisfied, Leo focused on calming thoughts. The night sky. The sound of birds. The cries from Mum's dungeon that meant dinner would be served soon. She could feel that her nightmarish form had started to take over, as it always did when she got upset. She breathed deeply, feeling her body shrink back to normal.

Inside the drawer, eight beady eyes blinked sightlessly up at her. Eight legs unfurled to match, tottering unsteadily. The spider muttered to itself under its breath, smoothing its downy hair.

"I never," grumbled the spider called Rodrigo. "I never. Back in Arg—"

"You aren't in Argentina anymore," Leo told him, exasperated. "You're in Castle Motteberg. In *my room.* And if you're going to live here, you have to be a bit more considerate."

"I have been a respectable roommate. There are no flies in here, you will notice."

Leo scooped up Button and floated to the bed, settling cross-legged on her pillow.

"And," Rodrigo continued, "there was the time I gobbled up all those annoying *other spiders* for you—you remember that?"

"Your brothers and sisters?"

"Mmm, yes, they were delicious." Rodrigo burped at the memory. "But my point is: Think of all the fun times we've had. No need for this hostility, not between roomies!"

There was a long silence, while Leo cuddled Button and Rodrigo tapped his eight feet restlessly. He cleared his throat, fangs clicking.

"So, ah, anyway . . . You . . . you're really going to fight a ghost, then?"

"That's right."

"Why?"

Leo paused at that. Why indeed?

Because if the secret escaped, even to Dad or to Emmeline or to Marged, then Lady Sieglinde would be the next to know. And if Sieglinde knew, then it would inevitably follow that Leo had failed her Waxing Moon. And if word got out that Leo, the youngest von Motteberg daughter, had not only failed but created two ghosts . . . two ENEMIES of the vampire world . . . Sieglinde would lose her spot on the Council and there would be no escaping the sheer FURY that would follow—

"It would take too long to explain," Leo said, shivering beneath her cape. "I just have to."

"Even though it's an Incredibly Bad Idea and even *I* know that, being a spider who lives in your sock drawer?"

"Yes, Rodrigo."

"Okay. Great. Okay. I was only checking, er, in case you had changed your mind."

Sometime later, when the sun had risen and Marged had been by to tuck Leo safely in bed, Rodrigo crawled down from his hiding place. He felt blindly around the floor, finding it littered with socks. For most of the year, they went untouched—it was only when the snow fell that Leo needed them, and only when she was cross that she threw them around the room.

Rodrigo shook his spidery head and set about collecting them up. They kept him warm in his drawer.

Speaking of warm, it was a little chilly in his room that day, even for the western tower. Rodrigo's furry body bristled and he shook himself briskly.

"Honestly, vampire girls . . . so messy . . . ," he muttered to himself as he worked, mindful of his roommate snoring softly in her bed. The last thing he needed was another earful, or for the DREADED CAT to be set upon him.

At first Rodrigo didn't notice the peculiar mist that seeped through the cracks in the floorboards, but then his taste receptors picked up a strange scent. It wasn't the musty books. It wasn't the coppery tang of the cup of blood on the bedside table. No—it smelled like burning timber, strong and woody, but the room remained ice-cold. DEATHLY cold.

He turned, unseeing as the fog swept around the room. Moving in a smoky stream, it flowed around the desk and the wardrobe and the foot of the bed, exploring the layout of the furniture. A thin, unsettling rasp made Rodrigo twitch; it sounded like someone (or something) was trying to draw a breath . . .

"Hello?" Rodrigo whispered. He clicked his fangs anxiously and scuttled behind the socks, as though they might protect him. "D-don't try anything! I'm trained in martial arts! All of them—including karaoke!"

There was no reply. The foggy cloud flowed away beneath the door that led to the stairs, continuing on its journey.

Leo mumbled in her sleep, tossing and turning against her pillow. Her long arm dropped to dangle off the side of the bed, her claws sending vibrations through the floor.

"No thank you!" Rodrigo hissed, spooked, his eight legs carrying him back up to his drawer and to safety. The rest of the socks would have to wait.

# 10
# Salt

The following night, another faint mist rolled into Leo's bedroom. It became brighter, clearer, spinning itself out until it formed two arms, two legs, and a head full of white hair, becoming Minna. Button yowled and launched himself off the bed, waking Leo from her vampiric slumber.

"You . . . *uuuwaaaagh* . . . really need to start visiting at a more reasonable hour." Leo yawned, peeling herself reluctantly from her pillow. She floated to the window, peeked around the edge of the blackout curtains, and inched open the emergency shutters. The sky was a dark amber and the sun was almost set.

"No time like the present," Minna said, her voice clipped. "The sooner we strike, the better our chance of catching the Orphanmaster off his guard, while he's still waking up. We're under the fifth moon, after all."

Leo scrubbed her hands down her tired face. "I wonder what the deal is with all these moons?" she pondered aloud. "The Waxing Moon for vampires. Seven moons for ghosts."

"Would you rather it be the sun?"

"Absolutely not!" And with that, Leo escaped into the adjoining bathroom to brush her fangs.

They would start small, she had already decided, since some of the items on the *Companion*'s ghost-killing checklist made her insides flip-flop. Better to start with something easy, something that didn't need an elaborate plan to retrieve, something right here in Castle Motteberg. . . .

Something in the castle kitchens.

Salt.

Salt was useful for all sorts of things—particularly spell-casting and brewing potions—but Marged insisted that it belonged in the kitchen, on account of it being an "excellent seasoning." Not that Leo would know, having lived on the blood of the Living for a hundred years. But apparently the salty stuff had a mysterious ability: in moderation, it made food extra delicious to mortals.

Finding the first item on the list in the kitchens would be like taking salt from a baby, or something like that.

"So!" Leo said thickly from behind the bathroom door, her mouth full of fangpaste. "Speaking of the sun—where've you been while it was up? Did you sleep all the way through?"

"You're awfully nosy for a vampire, aren't you?" came the reply.

"How many vampires have you met?"

"I've met enough."

Leo spat into the sink. The lingering herbal taste made her gums tingle. "I was only asking!"

"Well, don't!" said Minna tightly. She was in an even worse mood than yesternight. "If you must know . . . I was back in the town. I had to check in on my friends, to make sure they're all okay."

Leo paused. She looked down at the toothbrush; it was comically small in her long-fingered, clawed hand. She had almost forgotten about the other children, HUMAN children, who had been Minna's friends in her old life.

"Are they okay?" she asked, though the mention of them made her feel a pang of something that might have been jealousy. . . .

"They are. Or they're all still in Otto's End, at least—*temporary accommodation*, apparently." Minna huffed. "There's a weird atmosphere in the town, though, like something bad is brewing. There's something in the air and it's not the muck from the stables."

Leo hummed, swishing water around her mouth. She wondered absently whether she might have been one of Minna's friends, had she been human too.

"One thing about the fire . . . it's kept everyone together," Minna was saying. "Even if I'm not there anymore."

The memory of Minna sitting in the Orphanmaster's chair came again to Leo; she could picture her vividly that first time they met. Minna had been looking for something—searching all that boring paper for some sort of information.

That boring, very flammable paper . . .

"Why were you up there, that night?" Leo asked. "You never said."

There was silence from beyond the doorway. Then—

"There you go, being NOSY again when it's none of your business! We have a job to do, Leo—we should stay focused."

*"We have a job to do,"* Leo repeated to herself in a silly voice. *"We should stay focused. I'm Minna and I hate everything!"* Her long black tongue rolled out of her mouth and she crossed her eyes.

"I can hear you, you know!"

Leo gulped and yanked her cape over her head.

❋ ❋ ❋

Icy Minna still refused to defrost as the girls journeyed through the majestic Castle Motteberg, taking the hallways less traveled to avoid bumping into Emmeline again. They went on together, stonily silent, down the blustery gallery that wound through to the servants' wing. The arched window frames were empty, with no glass to protect the walkway from the elements, and the mountain air seemed to sing as it swept relentlessly through.

To their left, imposing spires pierced the night sky, surrounding the grand castle courtyard. To their right, a sheer drop down the mountainside drew the eye to the Dreadwald treetops. The forest lay in wait at the bottom of the cliff, stretching out like a vast leafy blanket all the way to the horizon.

Leo twiddled her thumbs. The breeze was insistent tonight; it ruffled her wiry hair, blowing the black nest into her eyes. She brushed it impatiently back.

Glancing sideways at her companion, she wondered if Minna was even the teeniest bit curious about the castle. It was certainly very different from St. Frieda's, or indeed anywhere in Otto's End. In fact, in Leo's opinion, Minna should be saying things like:

*"Oh, Leo, it's amazing!"*

Or *"Wow, your home so cool—and so are you!"*

But her guest didn't make so much as a peep.

Minna ignored the melodic whistling of the wind. She turned up her nose at the serpent-headed fountain that spouted water from its marble maw. She hmphed in an unimpressed manner at the flying buttresses that soared from . . .

Leo sniggered quietly to herself. Mum didn't like her giggling at the flying buttresses—the massive arches that connected the towers to their supporting columns. They made the castle look like a chained ogre anchored to the earth: a very intimidating image indeed. But, since they were named BUTTresses, Leo couldn't help snort.

"What are you laughing at?" Minna asked sharply, breaking her silence.

Leo coughed. "B-buttresses," she choked out, pointing weakly upward. Through the empty window frames, the foreboding peaks of the castle loomed above.

"Right. Hilarious. Are we almost at the kitchens?"

Leo cleared her throat. "We're close. This way!" She straightened her cape in what she hoped was a mature and businesslike manner. There was resistance at the hem; the wind felt almost as though it was trying to tug them backward.

They had arrived at the end of the gallery, where an iron door opened into the castle. Leo had barely touched the door handle when the gale suddenly started up again, shriller than before. The way it wavered back and forth, swelling and receding over and over, it sounded like a mournful groan. A human voice—or a not-so-human voice—carried on the breeze.

*"Ahhh . . . Ahhhg . . ."*

Leo stilled, her ears pricked.

*"Ahhhg!"* the voice moaned, more urgently now.

"Do you hear that?" Leo blurted, feeling her hair stand on end. "What *is* that?"

*"Ahhhh . . . Aaaagnes!"*

Leo flattened herself against the wall. Her claws screeched against the stone and her teeth tingled unpleasantly.

Minna's expression pinched. "We should hurry."

*"Agnes!"* wailed the wind. *"Agnes!"*

There was a gusty rush, an invisible wall of air that slammed Leo from the side. She yelped, suddenly blinded as her cape whipped up to wrap tightly around her head. Staggering, Leo's flailing arms caught the edge of something hard: the window frame, she realized with a sick lurch. She was pushed up against the side of the gallery, her clawtips puncturing the weathered wood, teetering dangerously forward into nothing.

If Leo stumbled, she would fall, and fall fast, with no time to unfurl her cape and glide. The eastern side of Castle Motteberg caught the worst of the storms that came from the faraway sea, and the stonework beneath the gallery had become crumbly and unstable.

"Leo!" she heard Minna cry out, her ears muffled by the cape. Leo's feet scrambled for purchase—the wind was trying to force her up and over, through the frame, down to . . .

Leo spared a hand to wrestle the cape from her eyes and stared down at the sheer drop below. Her breath hitched, icy in her lungs. Far beneath her, the green sea of the Dreadwald treetops shuddered in alarm.

"Hang on!" Minna shouted. Leo could feel her at her shoulder, trying fruitlessly to grab her arm and pull her back, but Minna's ghostly hands couldn't find their grip.

"I'm trying!" Leo hung on for dear unlife. She wobbled, fighting for balance. Around them, the whole gallery creaked, its wooden structure groaning as though it might be blown apart. The wind screamed furiously against her, rising to a shrill whistle. . . .

Summoning all her strength, Leo shoved back.

Stumbling, she dropped to her belly and ducked down beneath the onslaught of the phantom wind, which bellowed as she scrambled for the door. Minna sailed above, her poker drawn.

Yanking the handle, Leo rolled into an equally cold passageway that was at least shielded from the bite of the wind. Little feet skittered: castle rats, running along the wooden beams above their heads. The door banged shut and, to Leo's immense relief, the whistling ceased.

For a long moment, the girls stared at the door. Leo was sprawled out while Minna floated above her. All was quiet.

"Is THAT a feature of the famed Castle Motteberg?" Minna asked with breathless sarcasm.

"No!" Leo's voice was equally thin. "No, it's really *not*! Minna. What WAS that?"

"What do you think?" Minna sunk solemnly down next to her, folding her legs. "You heard him. Obviously it's the Orphanmaster."

"How can we be sure? He wasn't like *that* when he died—he wasn't a . . . an evil twister!"

Remembering the shuddering books and how she was almost crushed in the library, Leo's gray face paled. From the look on Minna's face, she was thinking the same thing.

"It had his voice. It's him." Minna looked defeated in a way that worried Leo; the Minna *she* knew would snap right back at her. "He's waking up, as we thought."

"Er. Right, yes." Leo eyeballed the closed door, braced as though an angry ghost might come bursting through. She could taste copper, and realized her lip had split in the frenzy. She licked the healing skin. "He's, um, still taking his time, then. Compared to you, I mean."

*That* earned her a hard look. "I would suspect that not all ghosts are the same, Leo."

"I know! I know you're not! That's not what I'm saying!"

"Well, it sounded like it! And I hope you're not expecting ME to become a tornado or drop a book on your head!"

"No, I . . ." She clapped a hand to her own forehead. "Look, Minna, I just want to know—that was *definitely him*? He kn-knows we're here?" The thought made her knee quiver and her spine turn to mush.

"Yes. But we don't need to worry, not yet."

"We don't need to WORRY!?" Leo exclaimed. "Minna—he tried to throw me down the mountain!"

"If he *actually* had the strength to get you right now, a door wouldn't stop him."

Leo couldn't bring herself to feel too comforted by that. She frowned at her wooden foot, biting back a retort.

Instead, another question came to her.

"Who," she dared to ask, "is Agnes?"

A small crease appeared between Minna's brows.

"You know her?" Leo persisted, though her belly was starting to feel all twisted up. She had a terrible feeling that she was falling down a rabbit hole without an end, headfirst. "Is he looking for her? Is she in trouble?"

Gusting out a sigh, Minna drifted upright again. She

folded her thin, translucent arms across her chest, fiddling with her scabbed elbow. "No, I didn't know Agnes," she said finally. "But I *do* know that she was a better person than the Orphanmaster. She was his wife."

"His *wife*?"

"Yes. She died before I was born—she got sick and passed away."

Leo blinked. It seemed unthinkable to her that a man with such a temper could have been *married*.

But then, Dad was married to Mum, and they were as different as any couple could possibly be. One was a scientist, the other an ancient fiend with a ferocious appetite and dark power beyond comprehension. There really was a match for everyone.

"If Agnes had been at St. Frieda's," Minna continued, "things might have been different. You've probably realized that . . . the orphanage was NOT a good place to be. Not with the Orphanmaster in charge."

Leo nodded, though Minna wasn't looking her way. She appeared lost in her thoughts.

"Father Pavlov said Agnes was very kind. You know, patient. The type of person who wants to help you, not punish you. I used to think about her sometimes, but mostly . . . I thought about my parents."

"How long had you been there?" Leo asked quietly.

Minna paused.

"It was . . . six years," she said, as though she herself couldn't believe it had really been that long. To Leo, in her immortality, it felt like the blink of an eye—but it was probably half of Minna's whole life. Half a life spent with the Orphanmaster . . .

A shiver broke out at the nape of Leo's neck and then rolled down her back.

"I was five when Mum and Dad died," Minna said. She looked up, watching as a whiskery nose poked over the top of one of the beams. A fat brown rat watched them from above. "Since I was so little, I suppose I don't really remember a lot about that time," she admitted. "But I remember *them*."

"What were they like?"

"Hmm. They were . . . They were my parents." As Minna spoke, the brown rat was joined by six tiny ratlets, beady-eyed and noses twitching. "They were everything to me."

Leo understood. She fidgeted with the hem of her sleeve, scuffing her wooden heel against the stony floor. Her memory of her own life before she had become a vampire was . . . blurry at best. It had been a whole century ago, after all.

She knew, logically, that she'd had another set of parents once, when she was human. They had lived in a normal house, had normal jobs and normal lives. Leo had been a lot shorter and less alarmingly skinny back then too.

When she tried to picture them, it was like seeing a portrait that had been crossed out. She couldn't imagine their voices or their mannerisms, or even what their faces had looked like.

But they had been her parents, and that was enough. They had been *Mum and Dad*, before MUM—Lady Sieglinde—had chosen Leo to be her daughter for eternity. It was a great honor to be made a vampire. It was THE GREATEST of honors to be brought into a noble vampire family, even if Leo hadn't thought so at the time of the bite. Her memory of that night was hazy; a hundred years passing could have that effect. Now Leo liked to think that her first set of parents would be proud of her, after the initial shock of her death.

"I was on my own for a while, after Mum and Dad died," Minna was saying, pulling Leo from her thoughts. "Then . . ." She waved a hand as if to indicate everything that had gone wrong since. There was a lot of it, after all.

"I'm sorry, Minna," Leo said sadly. "I'm sorry that this happened to you."

"It doesn't matter now, so don't be sorry. It's pointless thinking about impossible things." Minna shook herself, all business again. It was probably the low light, but her glowing eyes looked shinier than usual. "We have salt to find. Come on."

Casting one last, uneasy look at the door, Leo found her feet.

This particular wing of Castle Motteberg could be described as "simpler" if you were feeling kind, and "damp and bleak" if you were feeling honest. It was where the servants had lived and worked, back when there were still servants to live and work in the first place. (Now there was only Marged. Mum had a nasty habit of snacking on the staff, so they never lasted long.)

It had been a while since Leo had visited the kitchens. Hanging around in the servants' wing was a surefire way to run into Marged . . . which was a surefire way to receive a nagging lecture about cleaning her bedroom.

Underfoot was warm flagstone. Ceramic tiles patterned with wildflowers lined the walls. The fire was crackling away, over which simmered a pot that smelled strongly of rosemary, stirred by a wooden spoon rotating of its own accord. Marged was brewing something up—perhaps some sort of cleaning concoction—but as Leo peered cautiously around the room, she noted that Marged herself was thankfully absent.

"Here we are!" Leo grinned, trying to cover up just how much the Orphanmaster's unearthly attack had rattled her. "Let's find your salt!"

❋ ❋ ❋

More than an hour later, Leo was starting to think that perhaps they weren't so lucky, after all.

"Have you found it yet?" Minna called from inside a cupboard, her head stuck through the closed door. "This is ridiculous! The seventh moon will have already sunk at the rate we're going!"

"It *must* be around here somewhere." Leo pushed aside more jars and bottles, each filled with a questionable substance. There was a weird whiff in the air as all the different scents jostled to get up Leo's nose. She thought for a moment that she detected a hint of something dangerously unpleasant . . .

*The fourth Vampiric Law. The Vampire will not partake in the foul bulb, flower, or stalk of the garlic plant.*

. . . but thankfully it was just a rotten radish.

The crooked cupboards, crammed with pots and pans and more ingredients than Leo could name, were messier than her bedroom had ever been. She found herself in a huff—why was Marged always badgering Leo when the kitchen looked like this?

A peculiar sound interrupted her thoughts. It went a bit like *ssshhhink*. . . .

"Minna, have you found it?" Leo pulled herself free of the cupboard she had been searching, shaking cobwebs from her hair. She turned and came nose to ankle with a pair of see-through feet.

Minna hadn't found the salt.

In fact, she was floating next to Leo, staring up at something over the island countertop.

Slowly, deliberately, Leo straightened up. Somewhere outside, a crow's piercing call rang out. The moonlight cast needlelike shadows, streaking across the kitchen floor and up the back wall.

Hovering in the air in the middle of the room, held there by some supernatural force and pointing straight at Leo and Minna . . . was a swarm of sinister-looking knives.

Chef's knives, paring knives, table knives, a serrated bread knife, a cleaver from a butcher's block, and a pair of kitchen shears—they quivered with evil intent, trembling in anticipation.

"Look out!" Leo threw herself sideways into Minna, falling through her transparent body and sprawling to the floor. Whipping around, Leo gasped as the knives shot straight through Minna and . . .

*Shunk!*

*Ker-thunk!*

. . . they embedded themselves deep into the cupboard door behind her.

Minna blinked, frozen for a breathless moment. Then she clutched her chest and looked down at herself, at her ragged but intact nightgown. The blades had gone harmlessly through her and out the other side. They were sunk deep now into the wooden cupboard, which had cracked all the way up to the countertop.

*The Orphanmaster?* Leo thought, her mind awhirl. She hunched down, goosebumps roiling over her skin and . . .

"LEO!" seethed a furious voice, and a shadow shot up from the floor like a cork from a bottle. "Really? Frogspawn? FROGSPAWN? What—did you think I'd forgotten, worm-meat?"

Tiny feet alighted on the counter, tottering unsteadily. The little figure stuck its chubby arms out to balance, wobbling forward to glare down at its prey.

Leo peeked up over the counter's edge.

It was a young girl. No more than a toddler in appearance, around two years old. She had angelic blonde curls tied with a ribbon, and wore a white dress that was ninety-nine percent lace and frills. Her feet were clad in matching booties. The spattering of freckles across her button nose made her look like a child's doll—or, they would, but her eyes were actually a demonic red, and she was visibly sniffing the air for blood. . . .

"Emmeline!" Leo squeaked out, jerking upright. She grinned from ear to ear. "Fancy seeing you here!"

The toddler tossed her head. "Yeah, fancy that—the FROG-SPAWN, Leo! I told you to stay *out* of my room, you dis*gust*ing toad!" The voice, coming from such a small body, was not small at all. In fact, it would better suit a moody teenager. And Emmeline's moods were truly legendary; not even Minna's grumpiest grump could best them.

Leo was beaming so widely, her jaw twinged. "Ha ha ha!" she tittered, even as her DANGER senses went haywire. "Yeah, that was such a funny joke, wasn't it? A joke! Harmless! A joke between sisters!"

"A joke? A *joke*! Do you know how long it took me to scrub slime out of my hair?" Emmeline demanded, clenching her fists. Embedded in the cupboard door, the knives juddered ominously.

"Um . . . ah . . ."

"Well, it . . . it was . . . it was a long time, okay? A REALLY LONG TIME, slug-features!"

Leo could believe it. Being forever trapped in a two-year-old's body, Emmeline's motor skills weren't the best. Coordinating her stubby limbs was troublesome, which was why she relied so much on her telekinesis. Controlling water, though, wasn't one of her specialities. It was too slippery or something.

"I warned you," Emmeline said. "I warned you that the

next time you would regret it. And now here you are . . . with a . . ." She paused. Her long eyelashes fluttered in a slow blink.

She looked straight at Minna, as though noticing her for the first time.

"A . . . ghost?"

"Emmeline," Leo said, raising her hands in a "now, now" sort of way. "It's cool. This is Minna. She's all right. There's no need to—"

"Oh! OH! You are IN FOR IT!" Emmeline crowed, viciously pleased. "Wait until Mum comes home! She's going to absolutely *crucify* you!" She clapped gleefully. "I can't wait. This is too good! What will she do? Oh—OH! Maybe she'll bury you alive, or slather you in honey and throw you into a bear's den? Perhaps she'll hang you from the tallest spire and wait for the sun to come up!"

"Yes!" Leo agreed. She inched sideways, away from the knives. "Yes—Mum will be so angry, won't she? Furious, I bet. Worse than the time you knocked over that vase." Emmeline hissed and Leo stumbled to correct herself. "I mean—the time *I* knocked over the vase! And it fell into another vase, which fell into *another* vase, which fell into the statue of Lady Motteberg the Third, which knocked that antique tapestry into the fireplace. . . ."

Emmeline's crimson eyes narrowed, but Leo kept going.

"Best to leave everything to her, Em. I'm sure she will want to deal with it all herself." She made eye contact with Minna, nodding deliberately. "So we'll grab what we need really quickly, and *be on our way* for now, since it's best to wait for Mum."

A beat behind, Minna's mouth opened.

"Yes!" she squeaked. "It was so lovely to meet you, Emmeline, but we really should be going."

"Wasn't it?" gushed Leo. "Wasn't it so nice?"

"So nice!"

"It really was!"

"WAIT A MINUTE!" Emmeline declared. "You're not going anywhere! Just because Mum will want you for this"—her nose wrinkled—"*ghost* thing, don't think you're getting off lightly! You'll still GET IT for the frogspawn!"

"I hear frogspawn is really good for hair," Leo said weakly, clutching the counter behind her. Out of the corner of her eye she noticed the knives start to shudder again. "Makes it soft and healthy!"

There was a deafening crunch as the knives splintered free of the cupboard door. Leo leapt in horrified surprise and Minna disappeared almost completely into the wall, her pale face peeking out.

"I'LL SHOW YOU *SOFT AND HEALTHY*!" Emmeline roared.

All the kitchen cupboards slammed open at once. The air crackled with psychic energy. Pots and pans flew, crashing across the floor and clumsily upward, sucked into an invisible updraft. They were followed by plates and bowls and utensils, whizzing across the kitchen in a deadly dance.

Leo ducked under a flying saucepan, narrowly missing the cleaver as it came careening toward her.

"Minna!" she cried, flattening herself against the wall to avoid a speeding teapot. "Minna, the salt!"

The ingredients were beginning their parade, joining the rotating storm. Emmeline hovered in its epicenter, fingers outstretched as though conducting a bizarre orchestra. Jars and bottles, spices and herbs and dried fruits, a moldy hunk of bread, unidentified powders and paper packages of stinky origin—they all came pouring out.

Minna's head poked tentatively farther from the wall.

"Min— *Ack!*" Leo was jerked downward by a phantom grip on her arm that slammed her into the countertop. The room spun, blurring, and then a jar of white granules flew past her face in slow motion. . . .

*Salt*, she thought dizzily, watching it go. Then, more clearly, *Salt!*

"There it is!" Leo cried.

Emmeline's hold was formidable, but it wasn't perfect. Leo yanked herself free, turning cartwheels in midair. She grabbed for a large pot as she stabilized herself, jamming it onto her head like a makeshift helmet. She clutched its lid, using it as a shield to deflect a smelly string of onions.

"I see it!" Minna shouted, bursting fully from the wall. She swept through Leo in a freezing rush, making Leo's skin break out in goosebumps.

Emmeline went into temper tantrum mode, clutching at her ringlets. Her jaws opened wide—too wide—in a shrill scream. A crack splintered up her cheek where her skin had gone cold and hard, like porcelain. She looked nothing short of nightmarish when she was this worked up; the last time they fought, Leo had seen her head spin all the way around. The sight had haunted her ever since.

"HOW!" Plates smashed, ceramic shards flying. "MANY!" A wooden spoon bounced off Leo's pot lid. "TIMES!" A meat fork flew harmlessly through Minna and hit the wall with a reverberating twang. "HAVE I TOLD YOU!" A bag of flour exploded like falling snow.

"Emmeline! Stop!"

*"STAY OUT OF MY ROOM!"*

"I get it! I get it!" Leo yelled, cowering. She gave a floury cough. "Gack . . . blergh . . . I . . . I'm sorry! What about Mum—you were going to wait for Mum, weren't you? She can't punish me if I'm already dead! Again!"

Emmeline's red eyes sparked. "A few extra holes won't hurt!" She must have really despised the frogspawn—which made sense, since she'd reacted similarly to pond scum beneath her pillow the other week. . . . "Besides, Mum will be AGES yet! Dad said to give her at least another few nights. That's plenty of time for you to heal up before she gets her CLAWS IN YOU!"

Behind her, Minna snatched at the jar of salt, but it went straight through her reaching hand.

"Any time now, Minna!" Leo called.

"It's not—*blast!*—as easy as it looks!" Minna swiped again, to no effect, struggling to stay on course. "Oh, fiddlesticks!"

The salt was flying back around again, caught on the mad carousel of telekinetic power. Looking back over her shoulder, Leo could see it coming. Emmeline shrieked with rage, fangs bared.

In a risky move Leo leapt up higher, pulling the pot off her head.

"Catch it, Leo!" cried Minna.

"NO! NO, NO, NO! You don't play *fair*!" screamed Emmeline.

Leo stretched, her shoulder protesting in its socket as she

reached as far as she possibly could, bending her arm behind her and over her head—

*BAM!*

Somewhere, in a private corner of her mind, an imaginary crowd bellowed their appreciation.

She scooped the jar out of the air.

# 11
# Hollowhome

As always when Emmeline was on the warpath, there was only one place to go.

Salt in hand and the twin weights of the *Companion* and the *Encyclopedia* heavy on her back, Leo hurried through the Dreadwald. Every step felt cumbersome and her left leg had started to wobble not long after they had left Castle Motteberg, but the fresh night air and the comforting crunch of leaves urged her on. She managed a weary smile as a squirrel went scuttling for cover, an acorn pinched between its teeth.

"Where are we going now?" Minna complained, flying behind her while Leo sweated and struggled. Minna swooped unsteadily from side to side, struggling to fly in a straight line when they were crowded on all sides by the Dreadwald trees. Leo glanced over her shoulder in time to see Minna swerve hard to the left and then disappear into a thorny bush.

"Are you okay?" Leo called.

Minna re-emerged, irritably plucking away the twigs that had become trapped in her ghostly body. Her blank eyes rolled back, tracking the trajectory of a red leaf as it traveled up through her skull. She reached in through her forehead and snagged it.

"Peachy," she replied, in a way that told Leo that she wasn't *peachy* at all. If anything, she would be something sour—perhaps a lemon. "Surely I don't need to remind you that we're against the clock? There isn't time to waste! The Orphanmaster—"

"I know, I know . . ." Leo suppressed a shiver. "Look, Emmeline will be in my room *right now*, trashing the place. We need somewhere safe to regroup, to work out what comes next." Even though she'd stashed her most important things beneath a loose floorboard, she couldn't risk Emmeline finding the books—not when they were so vital to their mission.

At least she could put one foot in front of the other without falling over. She dreaded to think what might happen to her beloved *Encyclopedia* if Minna was the one carrying it. . . .

"My flying is FINE, thank you!" Minna snipped, making Leo startle. She hadn't meant to think that out loud. "You should worry about yourself!"

"Sorry!" Leo said quickly. "For what it's worth—I've always wanted to fly."

Minna frowned. "Flying isn't a vampire power? But . . . your sister . . ."

*Is lucky*, Leo thought to herself bitterly. *I can't fly without the GRIMWALK.*

"Some vampires can fly," she explained, picturing Mum floating ominously over her coffin. "But it's not . . . my *thing*. I bet it's so cool being able to zoom around in the air! I'm jealous!"

Though Minna was grumpily silent, her face was slightly less peeved than before. The nearby caw of a hooded crow made her jump and she cast a wary glance at the dark trees around them.

"THIS is your idea of safe?" She wrapped her arms tightly around herself. "The forest again, really?"

It was almost as if . . .

"Aw, *Minna*, I didn't know you were afraid of the Dreadwald!" Leo teased.

"I'm not *afraid*. I just . . ." Minna gulped. "I have common sense! And a lot more of it than you, apparently!"

Leo felt a bit bad for her.

"It's . . . not so horrible, honestly," she said, noticing a young sparrow alight on a mossy log. It chirped as they drew nearer, tilting its head curiously. "Look! Would you look at him? He's adorable. He loves it here, see?"

In an instant the barbed vine of a carnivorous plant whipped out and snatched the bird. There was a squawk and a puff of feathers, and it was gone.

Minna's pallid hue turned somewhat greener than usual.

"Not another word," Minna warned, glaring mutinously. "I don't want to hear it!"

On the branches high above them the Dreadwald leaves whispered, and out of the ground, thick roots bulged to make footholds for Leo as they came to a steep bank sloping down to the river. She hoisted the books higher on her back and began her descent.

It was the beginning of the River Mothling, born from the spring high up on Mount Moth. Here it was barely more than a stream, but the trees still parted respectfully for it. The water was beautifully clear and cool. Leo hopped over the jutting rocks, feeling them beneath her bare foot where they had been worn smooth and shiny.

"Ugh!" Minna's voice startled her; Leo pinwheeled her arms for balance before the heavy books sent her toppling into the water. She looked around to see Minna staring down into the stream, her legs tucked up beneath her.

Rising from the pebbled bottom was an oily, inky slick. It was unlike any of the various Dreadwald slimes Leo had ever seen. Perhaps it was some species of weird black algae, gathering around the stepping-stones. Globs of it flowed off downstream, drifting away in the water.

"Nature is revolting," Minna bemoaned.

*Yes*, Leo privately agreed, because that was how she liked it. But this . . .

She straightened up, her gaze following the path of the water along the bank of the stream. The weeds there had blackened and shriveled, their leaves rolling up. The grasses too had turned a deathly gray; when Leo ran her hand gently through them, the dry blades broke off between her fingers.

"It's like a poison," she mumbled, scanning the nearby trees for any signs of decay. So far, they appeared to be their usual selves. But if this stuff spread any further, it would mean trouble. If it was already in the water . . .

"Hang on. I've seen this before," Minna said suddenly. "In Otto's End." She crouched as low as she dared, inspecting the slimy mass. A greasy bubble rose and popped, making her rear back. "Ick. It was all over St. Frieda's when I went back to check on my friends. There were globs of it growing on the walls in town too."

Leo looked down at the earth, envisioning it contaminated by rot. Her heart kicked into life (or an imitation of it), making her breath quicken.

"The Orphanmaster's work?" she whispered.

To destroy the forest was unforgivable. Leo felt her eyes start to burn.

"I think so," Minna said. "What else could it be?"

Leo swallowed. She took a deep breath.

"Let's keep moving." She turned away before Minna could see her face. The thought of anything bad happening to the Dreadwald made her feel sick to her stomach. The forest was her home away from home. Even if Lady Sieglinde found out about the ghosts, even if the Council found out about Leo's failed Hunt . . . there was no way Leo could let anything bad happen to this place, and THAT meant putting a stop to the Orphanmaster as quickly as they could. Clomping determinedly ahead, Leo sniffed hard, drying her eyes on her shoulder.

Her heart lifted as they came to a familiar path: one she had walked countless times over. Just being here made her feel suddenly invigorated, like anything was possible.

It led to her best, all-time-favorite, MOST AMAZING SECRET BASE.

"Here we are!" Leo announced. She trudged to a halt, allowing a little spark of pride to lift her spirits. She had never showed this place to anyone, though she had imagined bringing a friend here many times before.

They had arrived at one of the most ancient trees in the Dreadwald, mercifully free of the terrible rot they had spotted in the stream. It was gnarled and knobbly, with silvery bark that looked almost like stone. Its autumn leaves were a sunny yellow: a welcome sight, since every winter Leo would look up at its bare branches and privately worry that the old girl had finally given up. But, as striking as it was, there was one other trait that set this particular tree apart from the rest of the forest.

Even for the Dreadwald, the tree was *impossibly massive*, as thick as any of the castle turrets and almost as tall. Around it, the neighboring pines shied back, leaving a rare clearing. If there was such a thing as the Queen of Trees, this would be it.

"It's a tree," Minna said flatly—or tried to, because her look of awe somewhat ruined the sarcastic effect. She tipped her head back . . . back . . . back . . . until she was almost floating horizontally, taking it all in. The angle unbalanced her and she had to do a clumsy backflip to right herself.

"A large-leaved lime tree, to be precise!" Leo said, her mood lifting at Minna's shock. "Shall we?"

The base entrance was half concealed behind a gargantuan protruding root. To the casual observer, it was a dark cavity in the tree trunk, completely ordinary and easy to miss, if you didn't know what you were looking for.

Leo knew what she was looking for.

It was narrow—barely wide enough for Leo to scoot through, as though it was made especially for her. She had to free the books from their tangled straps and ease them past one at a time, turning them at an angle to fit around the bend. Minna, though, flew right on through, and then they were both inside.

"Welcome," Leo announced, "to Hollowhome!"

"Hollow . . . what?"

"Hollowhome! Or HH for short," Leo said quickly, sensing she was losing her. "If it's easier. My home in the hollow. You're very welcome here!"

Minna stared.

"Make yourself comfy!" Leo said to fill the silence. She busied herself by pretending to inspect the salt jar, letting her guest take it all in.

Inside the monster tree was a monster cavern, more than roomy enough for a base. Furthermore, it was sheltered and dry and strategically placed between Castle Motteberg and Otto's End, making it perfect for stashing foresty things that Marged might "tidy away" at home. Or anything that Leo would mourn if Emmeline went on one of her rampages.

Leo set the *Encyclopedia* and the *Companion* down on a low table, made by herself a few decades back when she was really into whittling. She had strung up a hammock made from an old hunter's net, comfy on milder nights with its knitted blanket. Notched into the bark were footholds, leading up to a trapdoor above their heads, and then to a lookout platform among the branches. A family of friendly Dreadwald fireflies lived on the ceiling of the hollow, giving enough of a glow for even a non-vampire to read and to plan.

"Emmeline doesn't know about this place," Leo explained, pushing aside some of her clutter so they could lay out their ghost-killing kit. A knobbly mushroom, dried out in the sun and half encased in mud, fell to the floor and bounced out of view. "No one comes here—except me. And, I guess, except for you now! You're my first visitor!"

Minna was silent, staring thoughtfully up at the winking lights above her head. The fireflies buzzed in greeting.

Leo shuffled her wooden foot. "Anyway! I figure it will be better to bring everything here, in case Emmeline figures out what we're up to. Or, you know, if she's in a bad mood and tries to smash everything to bits."

"Your little sister . . ." Minna settled herself above the hammock, folding her legs like she was meditating. "She's . . . interesting."

"Big sister."

"Sorry?"

"Emmeline. She's my big sister. Well! *Older* sister—I suppose I am quite a bit bigger than her, aren't I?" Leo perched herself on the table, pulling her knees up. The wooden one creaked like a rusty gate. "But I can see why you would mix us up! She does look very young. She became a vampire about fifteen years before I did."

"Became a vampire?"

Leo leaned back on her hands. She had heard this story a thousand times over; it was Emmeline's favorite. "Yeah. Mum spied her in her crib, when she was MERCILESSLY PILLAGING a fancy-pants town somewhere across the sea. She spotted her through the window. Used her AWESOME VAMPIRIC WILL to hypnotize the servants into letting her in. And she . . . she knew that Emmeline was meant to be her daughter! So she did what she had to do."

"Chomp?" Minna guessed.

"It's a *bit* more complicated than that, becoming a vampire," Leo said, "but you get the idea."

Minna hummed thoughtfully. "So Emmeline is more than a hundred too. And she still looks like a baby. That has to be a pain."

"Oh yeah—she's pretty mad about it!" Leo said cheerfully.

"She'll probably grow some more eventually, like me. But every vampire is different. I'm like Mum: long and thin. Dad has stayed pretty much the same as he was when he was alive."

"So . . . Emmeline's always like that, then?"

"You mean crazy and out for blood? Most of the time, yes."

"Because you put frogspawn in her bed?" Minna wrinkled her nose, unimpressed. "*Why* would you do that?"

"*Technically* it was above her bedroom door. I balanced a bucket of it up there, and then when she walked through . . ." Leo flailed her arms, mimicking her sister's outrage. "Hah! Classic! It's an old trick, but still the best!"

Minna didn't seem to get it. "I think if you did that to me," she said seriously, "I would want to murder you too. And I would succeed." Her stare was unnerving.

"It's just a joke!" Leo said, flapping her hands. "Emmeline gets me *all the time.* I had a mouse trap go off on my toes as I was getting into bed last week. Ready to drift off for the day and then SNAP!"

"Ouch . . ."

"Luckily it was my prosthetic! But all the same, it's what we do, us sisters." To tell the truth, Leo was privately sure that sisters should do more than just death threats and destroying kitchens. She would have loved to do actual proper sister things with Emmeline—like making up secret codes or having races through the castle hallways. Maybe in another hundred years.

Leo leaned her chin on her knee, turning over a thought. Minna seemed more conversational now that they had the salt—what could it hurt?

"Do you . . . have any brothers or sisters, Minna?"

Minna paused. For a moment, Leo thought she'd gone and put her foot in it (the real one) but then Minna shrugged.

"No, I never had any," she said. "Unless the other orphans count?"

"They count if you want them to."

"Hmmm." Minna twiddled her fingers. Then she added, "I've always wanted a sister, though. A real one."

Leo snorted. "Would you like mine?"

"Let me think about that. . . . No, thank you!"

"Ah, but I insist! You can have her! Completely free!"

Minna, to Leo's astonishment, actually smiled.

"YOU would have to pay ME!" She laughed. The ghost called Minna . . . had a sense of humor? Leo couldn't believe what she was seeing.

She was considering asking Minna if she had been body-snatched, or whatever the ghostly equivalent was, when Minna spoke again.

"I wonder how the others are doing." She sighed, a faraway

look coming over her. "I wonder if the grown-ups are keeping them safe."

"You saw them," Leo reminded her, swallowing down the weird lurch she felt at the mention of the other children. "They're safe, Minna."

"I know. But with that . . . *inky stuff* lurking in town, it makes me wonder if the Orphanmaster is after them as well. He really did hate us, you know," Minna added.

Leo nodded. "He was awful to you. He treated you all terribly."

"And not only that. He . . ." Minna trailed off. She frowned at her own pale knees. "Never mind. Forget I said anything—you wouldn't understand."

"No—no, I will understand!" Leo hopped down off the table. She jumped up into the net hammock next to Minna. "Or, I mean, I will try my best. If you want to tell me."

As she exhaled a long, slow breath, a wisp of smoke curled out from Minna's mouth. It hit the ceiling and dispersed, causing the fireflies to crowd curiously around it.

"I . . . I don't know if I can tell you."

"You can trust me, Minna. We're in this together now."

"I just mean . . . It hurts. It hurts to remember." Minna looked sideways at Leo, her ghostly eyes glowing in the dim light of Hollowhome. "You must have things you don't like to talk about? Things you'd rather not keep bringing up?"

Lady Sieglinde's words echoed in Leo's head:

*No child of mine will ruin the Hunt!* Every *von Motteberg passes; no second chances! It's practically tradition.*

"I do," Leo said, slumping back against the cool bark of the tree. "I understand how you feel."

The difference was, she told herself, Minna would never understand her completely. Leo had been human once. She'd had a human life and felt human things, and Minna had been human too until a few nights previously. Minna, on the other hand, had no experience of being a vampire; she couldn't even BEGIN to comprehend the seriousness of what Leo had done. What it would mean for the Vampiric Council. What it would mean for Mum's reputation.

There was a chilly hand just above her knee. Minna's palm radiated cold, even though she wasn't actually touching Leo's skin.

"Leo," she began awkwardly, "I want to tell you, but it's hard."

"You don't have to."

"No, I . . . I just don't know where to *start*. . . ."

Leo didn't have the answer to that either. As she was about to say so, Hollowhome was suddenly cast in a bluish light, colder than the warm glow from the fireflies. She looked up, startled, to see Minna's expression mirroring her own.

"Oh no," she bemoaned. "What now?"

"M-Minna . . . ," Leo stuttered, pointing at her own head with a clawtip. "You . . . um . . ."

"What? Why are you staring?" Minna asked, unaware that an extra, radiant eye had opened right in the middle of her forehead. "Is there something on my face?"

# 12
# Honest Work (Mind Your Arms and Legs)

Leo shrank back in the hammock, unable to believe her eyes, as her beloved base was transformed by the ghostly light.

The rough walls became smooth paper, decorated with a repeating pattern of curled shapes. The hand-carved table sunk lower, becoming slimmer and more delicate. Leo's books disappeared, replaced by a crystal decanter with a long neck. There was an antique globe next to an enormous fireplace, which dominated most of the room. On its mantel stood a candlestick engulfed in melted wax. Everything was cast in the strange blue-white hue, as though encased behind misty glass.

All around her, the heads of various animal trophies sprang up on the walls: badgers, stoats, a hare with long ears. They reminded Leo suddenly of the grim souvenirs in the Orphanmaster's bedroom.

"Minna," she whispered, backing herself into the corner of the net hammock. "What's happening?"

"I . . . I . . ." Minna blinked—or, her usual two eyes blinked. The third was eerily staring, wide open and beaming out the otherworldly projection. "It's the drawing room. The drawing room at St. Frieda's."

When Minna drifted across the floor, an elegant carpet appeared around her bare toes, unfurling farther and farther to touch the edges of the room. Above her head, fireflies scattered in alarm; the ceiling warped and dipped down, spinning into a lavish chandelier.

"I can't believe it. This is *exactly* it. Before the fire—this is what it looked like. Except . . ." Minna whipped around, in time to see a tall-backed chair emerge next to the fireplace, a matching footstool at its feet. "Okay. NOW it's exact." She pinned Leo with a look of alarm. "Is it the Orphanmaster? Is *he* doing this?"

"I don't think so," Leo started weakly; the sight of the eye in Minna's forehead was somehow one of the more unsettling things she had seen over these nightmarish few nights. "I think m-maybe it's YOU, Minna."

"Me? Why would you think that?"

"Uhhh, well, it's . . ."

Leo never finished that thought.

Emerging from the floor was a spark of red light, barely the size of a hawk's egg. Leo choked. The orb paused in midair and levitated there, suspended by its own unearthly glow.

There wasn't time for shock. Around Minna's dangling feet, nine more lights—this time the same blue as the room—flickered to life. Minna jumped, floating upward so as not to accidentally kick them. Leo pulled her cape tighter around her, watching incredulously as the lights start to revolve, gently bobbing in place. They pulsed, sending shadows dancing across the walls.

"Oh, crumbs," Minna gasped. "I think . . . I know what this is! I *remember* this! This was the day before I died!"

"HAH!" the orb of red light roared as it flared up, shocked into life. It flew swiftly across the room, accompanied by an echo of heavy footsteps that made the room vibrate. Jostled in the hammock, Leo grabbed the wall for support.

The red orb settled above the tall-backed chair. There were two thuds and the footstool shook, its plush cushion denting beneath invisible boots.

"You're LATE!" the orb boomed. "To be expected, I suppose. Lazy, disobedient children never change . . ."

"You're right, Leo," Minna breathed. She was transfixed on the scene. "I think . . . this IS me. It's MY MEMORY. This all happened, not too long ago."

Leo hunched smaller, feeling a shiver crawl up her back. "Y-you were here?"

"We all were." Minna looked to the carpet, where the nine blue lights had begun to take the hazy, indistinct shapes of bodies. Children, certainly, HUMAN children—some tall and lean, others shorter or stockier. All of them were gathered around the armchair, hastily settling onto their knees. A few of them were already huddling together.

"Then," Leo began, her throat tight as she dared to peek at the red orb, "that's . . ."

Minna nodded tightly. "It's him. My memory of him, anyway." Behind her, the red silhouette of the Orphanmaster was growing, his broad shoulders filling the chair.

"I have some good news! Not that you deserve it," declared the Orphanmaster's voice. There was the sound of rustling paper, and the brisk snap of a wax seal. "But I've generously found a buyer for EVERY ONE OF YOU! My final gift to you: a good job. HONEST work!"

There was a pause in which Leo couldn't help but picture an oily, brown-toothed smile.

"Aren't you lucky," the Orphanmaster said, "that you have ME to take care of matters for you?"

"What's happening?" Leo hissed. She wanted to grab for Minna's elbow, though it would be pointless. Minna herself was suddenly stony-faced, glaring at the figure in the chair.

"He was going to sell us off."

"Here we are—now, LET'S SEE . . ." The Orphanmaster hummed smugly to himself. "Ah. Yes. Walter, to the logging plants. An excellent opportunity, my boy, so long as you don't mind splinters! And little Edith—YOU'RE off to pick fruit in the south. Long hours, but beautiful weather at the moment. Their summers run blisteringly hot, don't you know!"

"Sell you?" Leo didn't feel good about that.

"Hermann and Hilde, personal servants to noble lords and ladies in the city—separately, of course. I'm certain they will keep you busy scrubbing their boots. And, Paul, I thought you would make an EXCELLENT kitchen boy at the palace! Very prestigious. Luckily for you, the last servant ran afoul of the head chef and ended up in the soup . . ."

"That's terrible," Leo gasped. "H-how is this allowed?"

"There was no one to stop him." Minna drew forward, staring down the Orphanmaster's silhouette. "There was only us."

"No one? Not even, I don't know . . . What about the church? What about the priest?"

"Father Pavlov? He was clueless. And I doubt he could have done anything, even if he'd wanted to. The Orphanmaster is the kind of evil that only evil can fight."

"Now, who's next?" the memory mused. "Ah! Karin, my dear! Yes, there's a workhouse across the sea, perfect for a wiry lass like you. You'll be up and down a chimney in a jiff! Your lungs will be sooty, but at least you'll be strong. August, smeltery—mind the boiling metal! Ilse, factory floor—mind your arms and legs!"

"We knew we were done for," Minna said, now vibrating with anger. She drew her poker. Around her, the image of the orphanage drawing room had begun to splinter, cracks appearing in the walls. "We knew that he could send us anywhere, and he would get away with it. We would never see each other again!"

"Wolfgang, don't worry, I haven't forgotten you," the Orphanmaster chimed in, oblivious to Minna's glare. "I had the fortune of encountering a wonderful family in need of a new stable boy. The last one was trampled in a ghastly accident—can you imagine? I'm certain you will be just fine. And, Wilhelmina . . ."

Leo's black heart stood still.

"Of course, I couldn't leave out our beloved Minna. Now, where is it . . . ?" Paper rustled, deafeningly loud somehow to Leo's ears over the roar of her rushing blood. "Ah, here it is! Yes. SALT MINES. Hard labor, as they say—but it will surely be the making of you! A life underground, doesn't that sound exciting? What an adventure! What—"

There was a *whoosh* as Minna lunged. She stabbed her poker through the Orphanmaster's outline, right where his heart would have been and into the chair behind him. The light sputtered and died, fading into a red mist.

Around them, the shapes of the children leapt to their feet and disappeared. The furniture collapsed in on itself. The wallpaper peeled and rolled down the walls, crumpling into nothing.

In the time it took for Leo to wriggle to her feet, Hollowhome was back to how she remembered it, down to the confused fireflies now bobbling around the hammock.

Minna's poker clattered to the floor. The eye in her forehead closed tight and was gone.

"Minna!" Leo cried, making a grab for her as she slumped. Of course, Minna's shoulders went straight through her hands; Leo fell to her knees instead, trying to see into Minna's face through her hanging hair. "Oh, pustules, are you okay?"

"I'm . . ." Minna blew out a breath. Her eyelids drooped.

Her head seemed too heavy to properly hold it up, as though the pain and sadness of the memory were a physical weight on her. "Wow. That was really something."

"I can't believe you did that," Leo blurted, not sure if she was impressed or horrified. "That was some serious ghost stuff. And it all came from your . . . um . . ." Leo tapped her own forehead.

Minna frowned up at her. "My what?"

"Your . . ." Leo smiled queasily. Perhaps the third eye could wait. "Your *brain*, I mean. It's like I was really there—that was so cool." Her face fell. "And . . . also horrible. I had no idea. *This* is why you had all that paper, in the Orphanmaster's room that night?"

"Yes. We needed more information," Minna said tiredly. She groped for the fallen poker and pushed it back through her shoulder. "I don't know . . . I suppose I hoped that, if I could find out the exact details, we might have been able to somehow stop him from sending us away. The only power we really had in that place was that we were all together."

Drawing herself further upright, Minna gathered herself. "He always kept his letters on his desk, up in his room," she continued, her expression tightening as she recalled the details. "I knew it couldn't wait. So when everyone was asleep, I went to look for clues. And then . . . I met you."

"And we know where *that* got us."

"We do. It's what happens next that worries me," Minna murmured, to herself or to Leo, Leo wasn't certain. "The Orphanmaster always said we were his. To work until we dropped, to lock in a basement, to sell and send away. I don't think for a second that he'll be satisfied, not until we're all suffering. *Really* suffering."

"What . . . do you think he will do?"

"After he's through with you and me?" Minna's hands shook; she tried to steady herself on the edge of the table, but her fingers slipped through. "I don't know. What if he goes after my friends? He's got a hold over the town already, I could *feel* him there."

*And in the Dreadwald*, Leo thought, remembering the inky rot. She squeezed her eyes shut and tried desperately to think.

*You still have time*, she reminded herself. *We're on the fifth moon! The seventh hasn't sunk, and Mum won't be home for nights yet. Dad said so. Emmeline said so. You can fix this. Before the forest suffers, and before ANY MORE GHOSTS turn up at the castle!*

Leo gave herself a shake. She counted off the ingredients in her head.

Salt. Sulfur. Smoke. Twice-blessed water. The glow of a sunrise. A weapon of intent.

They had the first item on the list; the jar of salt was now stowed in a natural alcove in the tree. The fireflies bumbled over to inspect it, their lights reflected in the glass.

"Right, we need that sulfur!" Leo announced. She tapped the *Companion* where it lay open on the table. "We need to stick with the expert advice on ghost-killing and everything will be all right." She felt Minna's gaze on her as she briskly opened the *Encyclopedia*, flipping through to the S section.

"You know where to find it?"

"No," Leo admitted, "but *she* will." She stroked the book's pages lovingly. "Look—SULFUR. Can smell like rotten eggs. Naturally forms as a solid crystal. Found near . . . volcanoes . . ." Leo stood back, frowning. The Dreadwald wasn't exactly famous for its volcanic activity. . . .

"Ah!" she exclaimed, jabbing a finger at the ceiling in her excitement. "Dad's lab! He's bound to have some, for his science. He has EVERYTHING else, I'm not even kidding. It will be easy-peasy!"

Minna looked distinctly dubious. "Didn't you say that the salt would be easy too?"

"Yes! Well!" Leo cleared her throat. "Unforeseen sisterly circumstances. But this time will be different."

"Are you sure that your dad will be okay with you taking it?"

"You saw him back in the library. It'll be a breeze. He

doesn't usually care what I do." Even though she was trying to be reassuring, Leo felt a tiny pang in her chest. She ignored it, like she always did.

"Right." Minna bent closer to the *Companion*, examining their ghost-hunting list. "Well, as fun as it was meeting the INFAMOUS VON MOTTEBERGS, I think I'm going to sit this one out." Now Minna mentioned it, she was going a bit thin and wispy around the ankles; the projection of her memory really had wiped her out. "After I get some sleep, I want to scout ahead for the twice-blessed water. I don't suppose the church is one of your hangouts?"

Leo pulled an ill face.

*The fifth Vampiric Law. The Vampire will not gaze upon Holy artifacts.*

Minna sighed. "Okay, I didn't think so. Anyway. Tomorrow night is the sixth moon—I'll see if I can work out when the priest is likely to be fast asleep."

"Why? What are you planning on doing to him?"

"Leo, the water has to be *twice-blessed*—there's no guarantee that the stuff in the font will do. You might have to do your vampire thing, to make him bless the water again."

"My . . . vampire thing."

"You know," Minna continued pointedly, "like when you hypnotized me back at St. Frieda's."

"Ah. THAT vampire thing."

"And made me let you in through the window, so you could ruin my plan and burn down the orphanage and get me killed—"

"Right—yes, I get it, okay!"

Honestly, how long was Minna going to hold a grudge? One tiny little death and now Leo owed her the world.

When Leo stopped being affronted, though, Minna was actually hiding a smile.

"You're very easy to wind up, did you know that?"

"Hmmm. Thanks." Leo couldn't help but smile back. It was catching. "Well. You know, feel free to stay here. Only if you like." She swept an arm to gesture around the room, with its cozy clutter and firefly housemates. "Everyone needs a really brilliant secret base. I don't mind sharing HH with you—since you already know where it is. It would be a waste if you didn't stay."

Minna considered the offer.

"Am I . . . am I really the only other person to see this place?" she asked.

In another universe, one where they were still alive and didn't have an evil ghost of an evil man to hunt, Leo and Minna might have been normal girls.

They might, Leo thought to herself, have even been on their

way to becoming friends. But she was getting carried away.

"Yeah," she said truthfully. And then she tried to fib to play it cool. "I hang out somewhere else with my other mates. They get scared, this far into the forest."

Minna tilted her head, watching the fireflies. She looked faintly pleased, as though a happy thought had come to her from a life long gone.

"That's a shame," she said, starting to vanish. "I think it's quite charming, in its own way. Bye, Leo. Good luck."

"Sleep well, Minna."

A feeling of what might have been warmth lingered after Minna was gone, but there was little time to dwell. The laboratory—and the sulfur—was waiting for Leo.

She took one last look at the space where Minna had been, and then slipped away into the Dreadwald.

# 13
# Dad's Laboratory

Leo woke, curled up in her cape with a crick in her neck and a large and uncomfy copy of *The Sky at Night: A Compendium* for a pillow. She hadn't dared return to her room, in case Emmeline was still on the prowl. In the end she'd retreated to the library, but there had been little peace and absolutely no quiet. The bookshelves had been persistently rude all day, moving around to have noisy chats with their neighbors.

The moon rose over the castle, swimming upward through the reassuringly dark sky. Though no light could penetrate the library, Leo was keenly attuned to the movements of the sun and moon. The threat of being turned to boiling stone was never far away, setting alarm bells ringing at the merest hint of a sunrise. It was a vampire's most ancient instinct, apart from the thirst for blood.

*Mmm. Blood.*

She was thinking about how much she would love a cup (fresh and red, still warm was preferable, but she didn't mind it being reheated over the fire) when the telltale *clunk* of an opening lock echoed through the maze of bookshelves.

Leo's eyes snapped open, her narrow pupils expanding in the dark. Dad's laboratory was next door. In fact, there was an additional adjoining entrance through the scientific reference section, which housed all Dad's favorite go-to books. Both this and the main door were kept under lock and key—or a lock and a very specific spell that kept them barred until Dad was ready to use the space. The lab was only ever open when its chief scientist was in, which was bad news for any interloper.

Still—this way in, Leo figured as she approached, was safest; Dad might not even notice her. He might be busying himself at his workstation over on the other side of the lab, which was where he kept all his chemicals and mixing apparatus. Perhaps a distraction would work to her advantage? There must be something in the lab she could use. . . .

This wouldn't be quite as *easy-peasy* as she had reassured Minna.

Dad didn't let anyone else go into his lab, not even Marged. ESPECIALLY not Marged, after she had knocked over a bubbling flask that had dyed her armor bright pink for a month. There was no way that Leo could just waltz in and start poking around for sulfur.

She pulled in a long, deep breath that she technically didn't need, but it always made her feel calmer. One hand on the door handle, she paused.

*Come on, Leo. You can do this.*

She had to. She was running out of time. The sixth moon—she could hardly believe it had arrived so quickly—was weighing heavily on her mind. There were only two nights left to fight the Orphanmaster before he came into his true ghostly nature and, according to the *Companion*, unleashed powers yet unknown. Minna had seemed sure it would be a disaster beyond measure; the Orphanmaster's gathering strength was already terrifying enough.

Leo didn't have even the slightest clue what she was going to say if she was spotted in the laboratory. She didn't want to wind up suffering one of Dad's punishments; while Mum's fury was enough to turn a werewolf white, a night spent scrubbing burnt-on crust from the lab beakers also made Leo think twice.

It was a shame that lying wasn't one of her strengths.

In fact, lying, as every good girl or boy knows, is not a skill to be proud of. But in certain circumstances—certain *select* circumstances, such as going on a perilous quest to slay a ghost—it can be useful. Getting past Dad and into his beloved lab would certainly require quick thinking. Sadly for Minna . . . she had picked the wrong sister to help her on her mission.

EMMELINE was excellent at fibs, feints, and all kinds of deception. She played the role of the innocent baby so well, she could be covered in mud or blood or the ashes of a deceased ancestor, and *still* no one would suspect that she was up to cunning trickery.

Even worse, the key to Emmeline's success was blaming everything on Leo.

*It wasn't ME who got paint all up the wall and over that priceless painting of Great-Uncle Bertrand—that was Leo!*

*Leo smashed the priceless china!*

*Leo brought down the chandelier!*

*Leo was messing around in the armory and caused a landslide of maces and lances and deadly, deadly swords, ending in a falling battle-axe that chopped Marged's arm off!*

"Hey, Dad," Leo mumbled to herself, gripping the handle of the laboratory door hard. "Oh—this? Yes, I need it for . . . for a new salve I'm trying to make. For cuts and bruises."

She frowned. Okay, maybe not; cuts and bruises weren't an issue when your skin healed instantly most of the time.

"Hi, Dad. Hello, Dad. Yo—Dad. Just. Grabbin' some sulfur! It's . . . really popular with the kids now—"

"Leo, I really hope you're not planning on sneaking in there!" piped up a voice from somewhere on top of Leo's head, prompting her to leap backward in alarm.

She felt a rustling tickle as Rodrigo pushed his spidery face free of her wild hair.

"Rodri!" she admonished, craning her neck to try to shoot him a glare. Of course she couldn't see him, so she tried to make her voice as cross as possible instead. "Forget eavesdropping! You're actually spying on me now?"

"Not spying!" Rodrigo protested. Leo saw the tips of his hairy front legs, waving back and forth. "Not spying, just . . . checking in!"

"Are you sure? Because it looks like you waited here for me and then stowed away in my hair . . ."

"No! No, I had to lie low for a while. There was . . . you see . . ." Rodrigo twiddled one leg in a circular motion. "There was a tornado in the tower last night. My drawer was blown right across the room!"

"Hmmm. *Emmeline.*"

Rodrigo sniffed pitifully. "There was a big mess. Too big

for me. I decided to retreat and then I got lost and—BAM! Here you are! About to make a huge mistake! Again!"

Though Leo suspected that the story might not be the whole truth, she knew for certain that her sister had been on a revenge rampage. Thank the stars she had thought to save the books.

"This ghost business," Rodrigo continued, "it's going to land you in trouble! And what about me? Hmmm? Did you ever stop to think about old Rodrigo?"

"What *about* you?"

There was an affronted huff. "Where will I go? What will I do? If Lady Sieglinde finds out and turns you into dust—"

"Mum wouldn't turn me into dust!" Leo said, ignoring the part of her that wasn't *completely* sure. "Don't be so dramatic!"

"Well! I'm only saying—what I'm trying to say—what you need to realize, young lady, is . . . it's not only you who'll be up for the chop! I'll be homeless! Penniless! Not even an old sock to my name! Out in the forest with nowhere to turn . . ."

"Thanks for the sympathy!" Leo rolled her eyes. "Rodrigo, nothing will happen to you. Nobody knows that you live here. But I need sulfur from Dad's lab, or"—she dropped her voice to a whisper—"I won't be able to help my friend. And that's VERY IMPORTANT right now!"

"Wait—waitwaitwait*waitohnooo* . . ."

Rodrigo's voice became smaller and smaller as Leo grasped the door and pulled, a tendril of moonlight sneaking in across the library floor.

Even after so many years, Leo could count on one hand the number of times she had been in Dad's lab. And most of those times had been by mistake, back when she was a newborn vampire, still getting lost around the castle.

The sight made her fingertips tingle and her mouth feel dry. The laboratory was a stark white room, with a tall arched window that looked over the mountain lake. There was a permanent chill in the air and everything smelled chemically clean, as though the place had been thoroughly scrubbed only yesternight. But the most gripping thing about the lab, the thing that always made Leo *really* itch to explore, was Dad's equipment for scientific testing.

There was a station for analyzing elements and one for analyzing biological matter. There was a weird tube for looking at really small stuff, and another for looking at stuff that was really far away. There were vials and flasks and sharp tools for dissection—which was when Dad chopped something up to see what was inside.

Everything was, of course, precisely stored and neatly labeled in Dad's square handwriting. Leo had a feeling that Dad loved tidying almost as much as he loved doing research and investigating his theories. When you had all the time in the world (and your wife preferred to conduct her killer crusade across the world ALONE) your interests naturally became quite specific.

And there was no better example of tidiness than Dad's bank of specimens.

Around the desk where he sat to record his findings, the entire wall was made up of mahogany boxes. These compartments were attached to a complicated system of clockwork: cogs and pulleys that moved the boxes up and down, backward and forward, allowing easy access with the pull of a lever.

They each held a different treasure, from stones and crystals, plant matter and creatures preserved in resin, to butterflies and beetles pinned in their glass cases. This bank, Leo knew, was stupendously vast and extended far back into the wall; Dad owned at least one example of every animal, vegetable, or mineral he'd ever studied. And there were many of them—Dad had taken up his interest in science when he was a young vampire, having been a teacher in his previous life.

Leo was certain that Minna's sulfur was in one of these boxes.

"Lord Dietmar! I can smell him!" Rodrigo hissed, wiggling frantically in the general direction of the desk. Sure enough,

Dad was sitting in the high-backed chair, only his dangling feet visible as he bent busily over his work. The scratch of his quill echoed off the cold walls.

Crouched low so as not to be spotted, Leo crept into a shadowy corner.

"I see him," she whispered back. She had held the faint hope that perhaps Dad might be busy elsewhere, so she could get in and out unseen. But while he was at the desk, there was no chance of being stealthy.

That meant she would need a lie, after all. Leo gritted her fangs unhappily, feeling her stomach drop.

Unless . . .

Peering about, she zeroed in on a low shelf not even an arm's length away. On it a glassy orb caught the low light. A paperweight, she remembered, which had apparently once belonged to her second-cousin Hugo, before his death in a disastrous garlic accident.

"What are you doing?" Rodrigo asked. "What are you looking at?"

"Shhhh!"

It was shiny. It was sparkly. It was perfectly round.

It could be rolled across the floor of the lab, creating a distraction to draw Dad away from his desk.

"You can still change your mind, Leo," Rodrigo was urging

her. "There's still time; we can go back. Who even *cares* about a silly ghost girl? I mean, honestly . . ."

Leo shushed him again, snagging the paperweight from its iron stand, which was shaped like the talons of a bird. The orb was cool, cooler even than Leo's own Undead skin. She tested the weight of it in her palm.

"I'm not turning back," she replied. "So either you can help me, or you can leave."

Before Rodrigo could argue, Leo knelt down on the white tile beneath them. She would need to be gentle or risk shattering the glass, but it still had to reach the other side of the lab.

Slowly, painstakingly, she wound her arm back. She tested a few underhanded swings and tried to imagine the sphere's trajectory.

Then, with a slow *tunk-tunk-tunk-tunk-tunk*, Leo rolled the orb across to the other side of the room.

Over at the desk, Dad's curly head peeked out from behind his chair. His big eyes blinked apprehensively.

There was a muted tapping sound as the paperweight connected with the far wall once, twice, trundling beneath an old cabinet and out of sight. The floor must have been uneven, because the sound was uncannily similar to the skitter of tiny feet. Unseen and holding her non-existent breath, Leo looked slyly over to the desk.

Above all else—even above having unpredictable children in his laboratory—Dad despised VERMIN.

Rats. Roaches. Dad couldn't take it. His revulsion made him sweat. And living in an old, creaky place such as Castle Motteberg, he was often very much on edge. It was part of why he kept his lab so clean; the thought of there being something loose in his workspace . . . it would be too much to bear.

"Oh no . . . Oh no, no, no . . . ," Dad mumbled, rising from his desk. He wrung his pudgy hands in front of him as he wafted over to the source of the noise, far away from the desk. Leo almost felt bad for him—almost, since she had a job to do. She crept behind a taxidermy weasel. It was as dead as Leo was, and long since stuffed.

Crouched so low she was almost on her belly, Leo slunk across the room.

The desk made perfect cover; like most of the furniture in the castle, it was huge and solidly built. Leo could hear scraping from the other side of the lab, and someone huffing and puffing. Dad was trying to get at the phantom noise. She didn't have much time.

Examining the boxes, her heart sank. Bamboo. Bauxite. Barn owl. Brandt's bat.

Following the library's example, Dad's treasures were organized alphabetically, for ease and efficiency.

S for SULFUR wasn't even close. Leo frowned. She would need to activate the clockwork mechanism, which would definitely bring Dad running. She peered out from behind the desk to check on him.

"I know you're in here," Dad was muttering on the other side of the room. He had his back to her, shuffling around now on his hands and knees, clutching a pair of tongs like a weapon. "I *heard* you, you creepy-crawly— *WAAAUGH!*" Probably spooked by his own shoelace or the brush of his frilly sleeve against his wrist. "Aaah . . . phew . . ."

Leo shook her head. Confident she wouldn't be seen yet, she turned to the levers.

The switch she needed to pull was labeled with a tiny brass plate marked *S*.

*Go on*, it said, glimmering enticingly. *You can do it!*

Crinkling her nose, Leo stared the lever down. She had no choice, she knew; without the sulfur, there would be no defeating the Orphanmaster and no hiding this mess from Mum. If Leo couldn't find the vital sulfur here in the lab, where else could they turn? The more time that passed, the closer the seventh moon loomed. At this rate the Orphanmaster could attack again at Castle Motteberg, blast a great hole in a wall and drag Leo away into the night. After what had happened in the library and the gallery leading to the kitchens, Leo didn't doubt Minna's warning about his strength.

And if he didn't destroy Leo first, then Mum would surely finish the job when she found out. . . .

Leo gulped. She wound her clawed fingers around the switch. Dread filled the pit of her stomach, twisting and writhing. There was no way that Dad wouldn't notice this. She would have to be fast—faster than she'd ever been.

*"Leo, you useless rat-baby!"* the Emmeline in her head jeered. *"You'll never do it! You'll never do anything remotely right in your entire unlife, you—"*

As always, picturing adorable blonde curls and scowling eyes cured Leo's hesitation.

She pulled the lever.

# 14
# Sulfur and Smoke

There was a grinding *crunch-whirr* and a rumble so loud and fierce the whole room began to vibrate. From floor to ceiling the boxes were startled in their sockets, rattling madly, disturbed by the motion of the awakening mechanism behind them.

"What— Oh, *not again*!" Dad cried.

Ducking low, Leo slunk around to the other side of the desk, obscured from the rest of the room. In a beat Dad was back; he had a natural aroma of old books and powdery soap, and the scent was closer now than ever. Leo kept her head down—not that it really mattered, since Dad was in full Dad mode and highly preoccupied. . . .

She could hear him mumbling to himself, jiggling the offending lever, but it was stuck fast. Above them, the first box was snatched backward, disappearing into the mysterious chamber behind, and then the whole wall burst into a flurry of motion.

There was a landslide of boxes, juddering and jostling, sliding back and forth. One by one, they vanished back into the wall, and a nearly identical set emerged to replace them, though each now marked with a neat *S*. Leo cowered back, her black eyes bulging. She was certain that, at any moment, a compartment would jump free and clonk her on the head.

Fortunately, they stayed shackled to the wall, and after a long minute, the dust motes were floating down and the chaos was over.

Leo froze.

*S* for SULFUR was less than an arm's length away.

There was a grating cough. Leo risked a peek over the top of the desk. Dad seemed wary of the wall, standing well clear. It was for good reason.

For a long moment, neither father nor daughter moved. Then, slowly, as if approaching a cornered beast, Dad drifted forward a step . . .

*I'm sorry, Dad*, Leo thought.

In the time it took Dad to blink, Leo struck out with her wooden leg, kicking the wall of specimens as hard as she could. . . .

*SHER-CLUNK!*

A compartment shot out, setting off a shuddering ripple effect in its neighbors, and booted Dad soundly in the face.

*SHUNK!*

Another whacked him square in the belly.

*SHHHK!*

A final one thumped him somewhere quite rude indeed.

Dad wheezed something quite rude to match, staggering backward. He rolled into an agonized ball, clutching between his legs.

This was her chance. Leo offered up another silent apology. She was shielded by the desk as she slithered forward, flat against the tiled floor, and yanked open the box she needed.

There, nestled carefully inside, was a bright yellow crystal.

It was a more modest sample than she had expected, with jagged protrusions that looked like an odd flower or fungus. The color reminded her of the daffodils in spring or Hollowhome in autumn—but it was STRANGER than any plant, she decided. She could tell it was powerful just by looking at it. This sulfur was, without a doubt, one of Minna's ghost-killing ingredients.

Bracing herself, Leo reached in. She paused, her hand hovering just shy of her target. . . .

What if it was dangerous? Poisonous?

Watching through slitted eyes, Leo gingerly picked up the sulfur, first with only her clawtips. Her whole arm trembled.

*Got it!* She paused, waiting for searing pain or bubbling flesh or a flash of Holy light. But there was none of that—only the sulfur, sitting innocently in her hand.

Salt. Sulfur. That was two items down.

Leo allowed herself a toothy smile. Surely Minna would be pleased to be presented with this. And what would she say?

*"Oh, Leo, you are so clever and brave!"*

*"Well done for finding the sulfur! I wouldn't have known where to start!"*

*"You're the best, Leo!"*

*"You're a great fr—"*

"Incoming!" Rodrigo's hair bristled as he sensed the vibrations of movement. Crystal in hand, Leo crab-walked around the back of the desk. She watched Dad jerk unsteadily upright. He had gone somewhat cross-eyed.

"Time to go," breathed Rodrigo. "You have what you came for, don't you? Let's get out of here!"

But Leo didn't hear him.

Sometimes, when she was thinking REALLY HARD, her

brain tended to take over her ears. Now was one of those times.

Salt? Check. Sulfur? Check.

Smoke.

Leo knew how to create fire—in fact, she knew more ways than one. It was one of the first and most important survival skills of the forest.

But making a fire . . . under pressure . . . in a hurry . . . with the angry ghost of an angry man leering down at them . . .

A helping hand wouldn't go amiss.

Over on Dad's workstation, the one for experiments and testing chemical reactions, there was a box of matches.

"Oh, what now?" Rodrigo moaned. Leo crouched like a stalking cat. She eyed the matches. They would be ideal. Achieving fire would be simple—much easier than wasting time striking flint or rubbing sticks together. And where there was fire, there was smoke.

*One last thing!* Leo thought, hearing Dad stumble against the desk. Luck had been on her side so far. As long as Dad didn't turn around, as long as he didn't look up at the wrong time, as long as she *wasn't seen*, she could grab the matches and be out of there.

She took one step. Two. Three to duck behind a buzzing coil that crackled with energy. Four steps to creep past a twisty plant with long vines. Five to make it to the workstation, to the matches, then to freedom—

"Eleonore?" a voice croaked, and Leo paused.

*Oh dear.*

Rodrigo made a noise like a mouse whose tail had been stepped on.

Sulfur in one hand and matches in the other, Leo slowly turned to face Dad. She was in big, BIG trouble. *So* much trouble. The kind of trouble that would usually lead to the most pitiless of punishments from Dad, such as being GROUNDED FOR A DECADE. Why, oh why didn't she escape when she had the chance?

Dad's eyes were watering, though he was trying to hide it for some reason. His face had turned a dark gray. His nose was starting to swell as it healed. Leo, on the other claw, had gone as pale as Minna.

"What are you doing in here, young lady?" Dad demanded thickly. "And—what is that? What do you have there?"

"Dad!" Leo exclaimed, belatedly hiding the sulfur and matches behind her back. "Th-there you are! I've been looking for you!"

"I see," said Dad. "That's strange, because it *looks* like you were sneaking in here and helping yourself while I was . . ." He glanced down at himself, at the small black stain of blood on his lapel. "While . . . I was busy doing very important things! Scientific things!"

"Yes! I mean—I can see why you would think that! But I was actually coming to find you because . . ." Leo's mind whirled.

*Silver tongue, don't let me down!* she thought desperately.

"Because . . . ?"

"BECAUSE! You see, Emmeline . . . BORROWED THESE before!" Leo produced the sulfur and the matches, showing all her fangs in the brightest grin she could muster.

"Your sister borrowed them?"

"Yes! And I was RETURNING THEM for her, because she . . . is SO BUSY! You know what she's like—she completely forgot she had them!"

Dad frowned. "Really, now?" He rubbed his sore nose. "Is that . . . wait, that's my sulfur crystal. How peculiar."

"It's very peculiar!" Leo agreed fervently. "But, well, you know how she is! So mysterious! I'll put these back, while you clean yourself up. You'll have to soak that stain or it will never come out!"

Out of the corner of her eye, she saw Dad twitch. A stained lab coat was a disaster beyond measure.

"Y-yes, quite . . ." He scrubbed forlornly at the stain with his sleeve before he could stop himself, wincing when it only made more of a mess. "But—Eleonore . . ."

Leo, her back turned while she surreptitiously pocketed the sulfur and the matches again, looked guiltily over her shoulder.

"Emmeline never comes down here," said Dad thoughtfully. His gaze darted to the ceiling, back and forth as though he was assembling an invisible puzzle. "She says, well, she thinks that scientific pursuits are terribly dull! It seems strange to me that she would require such items for a project, given that she has never done so before, don't you think?"

"I . . ."

"And she has never been in the lab for long enough to know where these things are kept—at least, not with me around."

"Yes . . . that's . . ."

"It is quite the conundrum!" Dad's huge, owlish eyes turned on her, like the beam of a lamp in a dark room. Leo's heart lurched and sank. The consequences were coming and she was sure the list of boring chores would be longer than her arm. . . .

Neither got the chance to continue, as the hallway door slammed open.

*The Orphanmaster!* Leo bristled and leapt toward Dad, braced to defend them both before in clattered the clumsiest guardian angel—

"My lord!" Marged exclaimed, plume quivering with excitement. "My lord, pardon the intrusion—you must come at once! Lady Sieglinde is arriving! I anticipate touchdown in the next few minutes!"

The world stopped, turned itself inside out, and shrunk down until it was impossibly, microscopically small. The entire Dreadwald could sit on the head of a pin. Leo herself was barely the size of an atom, floating on through an endlessly echoing void.

*Lady Sieglinde . . .*

*Lady Sieglinde . . .*

*LADY SIEGLINDE?*

This wasn't right. It couldn't be—Emmeline had told her that there would be NIGHTS before Mum's arrival. In fact, Dad had said the same thing, back in the library.

"Mmm . . . ," Leo stuttered out, her bulging eyes swiveling to the window. "*M-m-m-m—*"

"Oh! Goodness!" she heard Dad's voice say, as though he was a mile away. "That's— Hmmm! How excellent! Yes, Marged, thank you for alerting me. Come now, there is no time to waste!"

Blinking hard, Leo tuned back in to see Dad ushering Marged out the lab door.

"You know, if you thought . . . I . . . I wasn't crying back there," his retreating voice was saying over the clatter of Marged's armor, out in the hallway. "I was dissecting a large rat and hit a main artery, you see. I'm not exactly a rodent surgeon. . . ."

In Leo's hand the sulfur crystal felt as though it was vibrating, but it was probably just because her whole body had begun to shake.

Because . . .

*No, no, no, no, no!*

In a flash Leo zipped to the window overlooking the lake, turning her face skyward. Sure enough, beyond the jagged turrets, a gray swarm had gathered, turning over and over in the air like a living, breathing hurricane. It was a thousand giant moths, their wings beating so powerfully as to cause an audible whirr. This was Sieglinde's GRIMWALK in action. Leo shivered to see it.

She could hear Rodrigo somewhere near her ear, ranting about "foolish children!" and "booking a one-way ticket back to Argentina, PRONTO!" but she couldn't bring herself to care. Even the matches and the sulfur, her prizes, her trophies to present to Minna, felt insignificant now. Leo stashed them safely in her cape, next to the dagger.

Over the bridge, across the water, the storm of moths needled toward the earth.

# 15
# The Great and Terrible Sieglinde von Motteberg

The family had gathered in the grand foyer, waiting pensively before the soaring double doors. Marged was standing at dutiful attention. Next to her, Dad smoothed down his lab coat and the tweed jacket he wore underneath. He fiddled with his pocket watch and adjusted the chain. He scrubbed both hands over his black-streaked cheeks and through his fluffy hair.

"Do I look okay?" he asked Marged quietly.

"Yes, my lord, very dapper," Marged replied to spare his feelings.

Emmeline, who was wearing her frilliest, poofiest dress for the occasion, turned to glare at Leo as she skidded belatedly in. Emmeline's scowl made her nose wrinkle and her lip curl menacingly. . . .

And then she smiled sweetly.

*Ohhhhh, this is bad*, Leo thought to herself, feeling as though she had swallowed a fistful of squiggling worms. She gulped and hunched down to hide behind the globe of Dad's belly. If Emmeline told Mum about Minna . . .

What would Leo say? Would she deny it—because "How absurd! Ghosts? Never heard of them!"

Who would Mum believe?

Beyond the stained-glass windows, distant thunder uttered a rolling growl. Flames wavered in their braziers as a menacing wind whipped up. Leo tensed, reminded of the attack in the gallery—but the bitter air just stirred restlessly, harmlessly around the waiting family.

Then came footsteps from outside, each like another stormy thunderclap. Leo felt the hair on her arms stand on end, then the fine fuzz on the back of her neck. She sunk her chin into her cape, the collar of which was now damp with sweat.

*Oh, pox, pox, pox—*

"Lady Sieglinde!" Marged announced, in case any of them could forget—or mistake Mum for a door-to-door saleszombie. Leo might have snorted to herself, had she any room to be anything but terrified because the doors were swinging open and—

Instantly, all the light was sucked from the room. A fog of familiar disquiet descended over them.

In stepped an arresting figure, pale as marble and equally as stony. She seemed to glide, graceful as she was gaunt. Her voluminous gray cloak was adorned with furs. Her silvery hair was swept back from her pinched face, sloping-nosed and pointy-eared, and her black bottomless eyes were narrowed in an expression of . . .

Barely withheld rage. Leo stole a glance from out of her cape—yes, *something* had definitely ignited her wrath and was boiling beneath her icy surface. This was BAD.

*Oh no.*

Did Mum already know about the ghosts? About Leo's failed Hunt?

Behind her, the doors banged closed, making both Leo and Dad jump. Marged's armor rattled. The sound echoed away off the bare walls, as if hundreds of doors had been slammed in rapid succession.

"Mummy!" cooed Emmeline in her best baby voice, flying forward with her chubby arms outstretched. "Welcome home, Mummy! I love you!"

In an instant Mum's icy face thawed.

"My darling girl," she purred, scooping the little body out of the air. "Hush, now. I have returned."

"I missed you so much, Mummy," babbled Emmeline, tangling her fingers in Mum's furs. She turned the adorable eyes up another notch. "I've been so lonely, stuck here by myself! Bored without you!"

It was no secret that Emmeline was Mum's favorite. Watching them cuddle, jealousy was a barb in Leo's heart. She felt especially gawky and unwashed now in her scruffy shorts and raggedy cape, with her knobbly knee and unbrushed hair. She had never quite fit into their portrait of an aristocratic mother and daughter.

"Night of my life," Dad ventured, also left out, "did you enjoy your travels? You're home early, is everything—"

"Yes, yes." Distracted, Mum bent to allow him one peck to her veiny cheek before she batted him away. "Dietmar—be a dear and draw me a bath. It has been a tiresome, not to mention IRKSOME, road. I am weary." She shrugged off her capacious cloak without turning to look, and Marged clanked dutifully forward in time to get a visorful of velvet.

Underneath, Mum looked especially bony in her high-necked dress, bedecked in milky opals. Leo couldn't help but see herself in Mum; Leo was tall and thin too for her age. Maybe in a few more centuries they would look completely alike. She had inherited Sieglinde's monstrous gene through her bite.

Maybe it would be enough to save her.

Maybe Mum might forgive her mistakes. She hadn't disowned her on sight, at least. That was a good sign.

"Mum," Leo choked out, "I'm glad you're back too."

Mum didn't seem to hear her. She bounced Emmeline, making her giggle. "Be sure to add some of those bath salts, Dietmar—you know, the lilac ones? The *favor* from Lord and Lady Ecker." She absently combed her pointed fingers through Emmeline's hair, fiddling with her curls.

Emmeline's smile only grew broader as she stared slyly at Leo, showing her tiny fangs.

"Mum," Leo tried again, "I really need to talk to you." If she could get in there first, perhaps to distract Mum before Emmeline could—

"Yes, Mummy," Emmeline chimed, practically wriggling with excitement. She shot Leo a gleeful look, full of daggers. "Such a lot has happened since you've been away!"

Mum finally snapped around to look at Leo, like one might react to an irritating noise. Beneath her scrutiny, Leo felt as insignificant as a mosquito.

"Ah. Leo," rumbled Mum. Her pupils contracted to hungry slits. "Of course, my child. Your Waxing Moon."

Leo had Mum's attention now.

The stare was hypnotic, twin abysses beaming out from

Mum's papery face. Or were they pulling her in? Leo was trapped by those eyes, forcing her to stand ramrod straight.

"Yes," she said, feeling stupid and small, and tried to ignore the sneering face Emmeline pulled at her from beneath Mum's chin. She tried to muster up her groveling apology, but somehow the words wouldn't come.

"And?" enquired Mum. "What do you have to tell me?"

"Yes, Leo," Emmeline echoed, menacingly sugary. "What do you have to tell Mummy?"

"I . . . I . . ."

Behind Mum, Leo caught Marged's eye—or, she caught the space where Marged's eyes would have been, if she had any.

In the tiniest, teeniest movement, so slight that Leo almost missed it, she saw Marged shake her helmet.

Leo wanted to be honest, she really did. The weight of her secret was stifling, heavier than the *Companion* and the *Encyclopedia* combined, as though she'd fallen headfirst into a sucking swamp and couldn't pull herself free.

And now Mum was toying with her, she had to be, like a spider rolling a fly in its sticky web. Her greatest fear was coming true. Sieglinde probably already *knew* about the failed Hunt, she *knew* about Minna and the Orphanmaster, she *knew* how much of a disappointment Leo was—

"Oh, come on, girl. Spit it out," Mum growled.

Leo said nothing, her mouth hanging stupidly open.

Mum tossed her head. "The Council have made the mistake of the century," she snapped with a gruesome grimace, unable to hold it in any longer. Veins bulged at her temples and spit flew as she snarled. "You all might as well know! Lord Ayman is still the head—and, I mean ONLY a head. An underling found it in a locked chest, sunk to the bottom of a lake. They're working to recover the rest of him, but he inSISTS he's fit to work! In the end I had to come home or I'd have done something regrettable. I couldn't suffer those fools for a single night longer!"

None of the other von Mottebergs breathed a word. No one dared. Dad was wringing his hands. Even Emmeline was stunned, still held in Mum's arms. She had gone a funny color from where Mum was inadvertently squishing her.

"A vampire with NOTHING BELOW THE NECK," Mum continued, fangs gritted and veins standing out on her forehead. "The head of the Vampiric Council! What a joke! It was SUPPOSED TO BE ME!"

Mum had no idea, Leo realized with a dizzying rush of relief. It was the *Council* that had drawn Mum's ire; she was none the wiser about what had happened while she was away. Leo's heart soared. Her fists trembled at her sides. Her stomach flip-flopped like she had taken a tumble down the western tower stairs.

But.

"Go ahead, then," Mum said testily. She relaxed her grip on Emmeline, who made a noise like a leaky balloon. "Have YOU made me proud, at least?"

"I . . ." Leo knotted her hands in her cape, shrinking herself down. She heard Marged's armor creak. "Well, I . . . yes . . . Yes, I did, Mum."

There it was. She'd done it. She'd lied to Mum.

A thin, wheezy noise escaped her before she could stop herself; she disguised it as a cough.

Emmeline snorted in disgusted amusement. Above her head, Mum looked down her long nose at Leo.

"You completed your Hunt? You took your first life?"

Unseen behind one of the looming pillars, something stirred. A head full of floating, snowy hair peeked out, framing a chubby face. Minna clutched her poker cautiously.

"I did, Mum," Leo lied. "I made you proud."

Mum's smile was more like a grimace, lined with twin rows of nightmarish teeth.

"Humph. Good. As I knew you would." Mum's hand was a crushing weight as she graced her with a rare pat on the head. There was a muffled, spidery squeak. "Even if the Council is chaired by FOOLS . . . it is good to know that my daughters are deserving of the family name."

There was a lump in Leo's throat. Emmeline's red glower promised mutiny—later. Leo would suffer for her secret.

"Yes," she croaked.

Outside, a pitter-patter against the windows announced the arrival of rain.

"Well!" Mum looked about herself, arching a thin brow. "Dietmar—why are you still here? The bath won't run itself, I'm sure. Are we all to stand around until dawn?"

And, as it always was with Mum, that was that.

"Leo! Leo—wait!"

Up Leo flew, around and around the spiraling stairs of the western tower. Minna gave chase, following her up to her bedroom at the very top. It was the same bedroom, they found, that had been thoroughly and mercilessly trashed.

Pausing in the doorway, Leo stared at the mess.

Her desk had been knocked over, paper torn and strewn across the room. There wasn't a single drawer that hadn't been emptied. Clothes littered the floor. Even her mattress had been upended, slumped against her map-mural wall, bedsheets falling like the petals of a wilted flower.

Looking at the destruction, Leo felt . . . not much of anything at all.

Her mind was too full.

"Leo, you . . . Oh . . ." Minna poked her head through the wall. "Oh, golly . . ."

"It's fine," Leo said wearily. "I already knew about it. And it was my fault, really—I shouldn't have pranked Emmeline." Then, bare toes sinking into the carpet of clothing, she trudged into the adjoining bathroom and shut the door behind her.

*Well, that was a disaster!* she thought grimly, sinking onto the edge of the bathtub. She wanted to slip down the plughole into oblivion. Part of her knew she'd been lucky—extremely lucky—that Mum had believed her lie . . . so why did she feel so bad about it?

Leo drifted over to where her reflection had once been, to the scribbly self-portrait she'd pinned over the mirror. Its fearsome face snarled back at her.

"As soon as this is over," she told not-Leo, "as soon as this is all done . . . you're gonna do it for real. You're going to hunt a human, for real and proper."

She hadn't been brave enough to tell Mum the truth. There was no helping that now. But she could still take her lie and *make* it the truth, and then everything would be okay. If she could just complete her Waxing Moon . . .

Maybe next year, Mum might even remember a gift for her birthnight.

Touching her face, Leo's fingers came away wet and inky. She sniffed hard. She needed to be brave; their ordeal was FAR from over. It was funny—embarking on the Hunt at the Waxing Moon had felt like the end of the world only a few nights ago. Now, as well as solving *that* problem, she had a far worse obstacle to overcome. The Orphanmaster was out there, growing stronger by the night.

After gathering her resolve, Leo re-emerged from the bathroom to find a half-tidied room and a busy ghost.

"You're back," said Minna, dropping the sock she had been holding. Or, rather, it flopped through her hands and onto the floor. "Oh, bother. I really thought I had that one."

"You . . . you're picking things up?" Leo turned in an astonished circle; she could actually see the floorboards. "You can *move* stuff again! That's progress."

"The Orphanmaster isn't the ONLY one getting his powers," Minna said. "I need practice, though. This mess is kind of ideal for this, isn't it?" She looked down through her hazy legs and feet, where there was still a nest of scattered clothing, though definitely less than before. In among the tangle the green sleeve of an old jacket poked out.

Leo felt her face darken. "Don't worry about all this," she said quickly, scampering to bundle up her things. She snatched up a pair of striped underpants, blushing harder. "It's my job to sort it—you really don't have to. We should get going to the church; the twice-blessed water is next!"

"Let me help you."

"No, no . . ." Leo flapped her hands.

"Leo, I've already put half this stuff away," Minna grumped. "Don't be so silly. And it's barely midnight—Father Pavlov won't be asleep yet. I watched him last night, he's a total night owl. We want to wake him from a *really deep sleep*, to give your hypnotism the best chance of working!"

"Yes, but—"

"Besides, tidying up is helping me to test my ghost powers. You DO want to help me, don't you?"

There was no arguing with that. Leo was increasingly beginning to feel as though she wasn't the boss even in her own bedroom. She sighed and started to help.

"How was Otto's End?" she asked to distract herself, gathering up more clothing. She tried not to flinch as she watched Minna scoop up another sock.

"Grim." Minna looked worried. "The rot has spread further—it's all over the houses where my friends are staying. No one knows what's going on. Everything feels . . . uneasy."

Leo straightened up. A thought came to her. "D-do you think the Orphanmaster is targeting your friends specifically?" she fretted. "Is that why the rot is growing there?"

"Who knows. I wouldn't be surprised. He really did hate us; in the end, the only thing that *might* have made him happy was the GOLD he was going to get from selling us." Rolling her eyes, Minna bundled two socks into a ball, even though one was black and the other gray. "Even then, we weren't worth a lot."

"He won't be seeing a penny now," Leo reminded her.

"True. But it's what he'll want INSTEAD that worries me. . . ."

It worried Leo too. What chance did a small human have against a vengeful ghost? A petty part of Leo might not have been totally sold on the idea of Minna's other friends, but that didn't mean they deserved to have anything bad happen to them.

And the Orphanmaster, Leo knew, was practically crawling with badness.

"He won't have the chance," she reassured Minna. "We'll find that Spirit Anchor and destroy it before he can do anything else."

The two girls worked together, putting everything in its rightful place. They stood the desk up again and righted the mattress, setting it back on the bedframe that was now missing one of its posts. Her back to Minna, Leo slid the threadbare green jacket back onto its hanger, tucking its matching sash and belt around it.

Unfortunately, it didn't go unnoticed.

"What is that, by the way?" Minna asked, rather nosily, in Leo's opinion. "Are you some sort of vampire forest scout?"

"No, no—it's nothing."

"It doesn't *look* like nothing. All your other clothes are black or gray."

"It's just something I found, a long time ago. It doesn't even fit me. I don't know why I kept it, really."

Leo shut the wardrobe doors, safely sealing the human-size jacket—and the memory—away from prying eyes.

Rain splattered on the roof tiles, sluicing down the window-pane in miniature waterfalls.

Leo flopped heavily onto the bed, exhausted. There wasn't long to rest before they would have to make their way to the church. Adopting her usual thinking pose, her head dangled off the edge and her legs rested up the wall at crooked angles. Perhaps being upside down satisfied the bat in her blood. She turned the yellow sulfur crystal over and over in her hands, considering it. Peering closer, the wobbly reflection of her bedroom floor stared back at her.

They had the salt. Now the sulfur—that and the matches in her pocket would make smoke. No problem. They were well on their way to being fully prepared for their hunt.

In another unlife Mum might have been PROUD of her.

As it was, Lady Sieglinde was downstairs—deep downstairs, in her quarters, soaking in the copper tub with the fancy salts from Lord and Lady Ecker. She didn't know how brave Leo had been, nor did she care to know. . . .

"It looks . . . It's not quite what I expected, somehow," Minna commented from above Leo, interrupting her gloomy thoughts. Minna's chilly hair flicked Leo's chin as she floated curiously closer.

"Me neither. It's definitely the real deal, though—I can tell." Leo gripped the crystal harder, letting its pointy peaks press into her skin. She could feel its subtle thrum reverberate down her arm. "We're almost ready, then? We nearly have everything we need!"

A thrill shot through her, equal parts excitement and alarm.

Minna nodded. "We do. You should know, I practiced my ghostly combat in the graveyard too." She drew her poker and darted across the room, stabbing it into the air. "*Yah!* Our WEAPON OF INTENT! The Orphanmaster won't know what hit him!"

Feeling queasy, Leo tracked the movement of the poker, her eyes trained on the pointy end. "Ah, yes, great . . ."

A snort. "You should brace yourself. The church is all empty and echo-y at night." Minna grinned. "Oh—and full of all sorts of stuff I'm sure you won't like."

"It's not that I don't *like* the church," Leo protested. "It's more that it doesn't . . . agree with me. Gives me a bellyache."

"Well, we'll set out in a few minutes and hang around just long enough for you to hypnotize the priest. He'll be fast asleep by the time we get there. We'll need that second blessing for the water." Minna spun in a slow roll, reminding Leo suddenly of a sausage on a human barbecue, though she didn't dare say it. "Then on to find your leg. The Orphanmaster's Spirit Anchor. Hopefully it will still be at the orphanage—we should start there."

"I, uh, I have this too, by the way." Leo had worked hard too; she didn't want to be outdone. She fished the matchbox from her cape pocket. "Thought they might make the smoke thing easier."

Minna's eyebrows went up. "Ah! Yes—good idea!"

It wasn't quite the adoring praise Leo had envisioned, but it would do. A tiny, pleased smile tugged at her mouth. Then . . .

"We kind of *do* make a great team, don't we?" Minna said, completely unaware as Leo lit up like a bonfire.

"Yeah!" Leo squeaked. "Yeah, I suppose we kind of do!"

Minna laughed. It was a bright, breezy sound; it fit her, somehow. "Vampires really are full of surprises!" At that her smile turned downward and she looked serious again. "Hey . . . I meant to say—I mean, about your mum . . ."

Creeping up from nowhere, there was that black hole feeling in Leo's chest, tight and sharp. She looked up at Minna, still upside down.

"It's fine, Minna, really."

Minna pinched her lip between her gappy teeth. "It didn't seem—"

"We should be off to the church," Leo cut in, heaving herself up. She busied herself with adjusting her cape, pocketing the sulfur and the matches again. "Keep going while we're ahead, you know?" She didn't turn around. She knew her face had gone blotchy.

"Of course," Minna said. "I'm sorry. I . . . I shouldn't have said anything. It wasn't my place. I'm not one to really talk about parents."

The truth was, having a friend be actually *concerned* for her was so far out of Leo's experience, she didn't know what to do. She'd never had this conversation with anyone, not even Marged.

In a blink, Leo twisted her wiry body around. She found herself abruptly nose to nose with a startled ghost girl.

"I'm sorry," Leo blurted. "You can ask me anything!"

"It's okay—"

"No, I . . . I want you to know. You told me about the Orphanmaster, didn't you? Or you showed me, back in HH."

It was a long time since she had talked about her old life, blurry as it was. Her *actual* life, back when she had been ALIVE and eleven years old and very much human. It was hard to explain Lady Sieglinde without thinking about that time; after all, it was Mum who had ripped Leo from her old existence and turned her into a vampire.

Leo cleared her throat. "I did . . . I had another mum, once, a really long time ago. But THIS mum—she's all I have now, since the night she chose me. She's very old, and very powerful, and more than a bit mad. Which means that sometimes she's . . . she's . . ." She shrugged helplessly. "She's like you saw back there."

Minna hummed. She thought for a long moment, and then said, "She ignored you."

"She did."

"That . . . must have been hard."

"It's always the same," Leo said with a shrug. "I'm used to it. She has a lot on her mind, so it's hard for her to focus on the little things."

*Like me*, Leo added silently.

"What do you mean, a lot on her mind?" Minna frowned. "You mean, like this Queen of Vampires thing?"

"Head," Leo corrected. "Head of the Council."

"Right, right."

"It's easier to let Mum focus on what she wants. Once she gets this kind of obsession—like taking control of the Council—there's no distracting her, trust me." Leo shook her head. "It's locked down in her secret brain vault. Nothing can get in her way."

"Not even her family?"

Leo shot her a grave stare. "You would have a better chance of moving Mount Moth," she said seriously. "Things will only be worse, now that Mum hasn't become Head this time around. She'll be in a bad mood for another TEN YEARS, I bet. Last time she missed out on the headship, she got so steaming angry that she triggered a massive earthquake. Sinkholes for miles, apparently, on the other side of the continent. She'll have forgotten I even *exist* by—"

There was a faraway BANG, like a door being blown open far below them. The sound ricocheted up the spiral stairs, accompanied by a whoosh of air being pushed up the tower: the arrival of something flying at speed toward them. . . .

"Minna!" Leo gasped.

"One step ahead of you," said Minna.

When Leo turned, she was already gone.

With a noise loud enough to rival one of Dad's lab explosions, the door to Leo's room slammed open. In the doorway Emmeline fiddled daintily with her frilly collar.

"Hah! I knew you'd be up here!" she crowed, flying in to land on the floorboards. She tottered on her chubby feet, her silk booties wrinkling around her little toes. "HIDING, are you?"

Leo sighed. "Hi, Em."

"Hi, Leo!" Emmeline cooed, worryingly pleased with herself. "Your bedroom is looking good! Shame about the bedpost—but other than that, it's good as new!"

*Oh, not right now!* Leo groaned inwardly. Glancing over at the wardrobe, she thought she noticed a thread of white hair poking out.

"What do you want, Emmeline?" she asked. They had a priest to catch! There wasn't time for this!

"Oh, nothing much." Emmeline waved a pudgy hand. "Just thought I would come to check on my *favorite* little sister!"

"I'm your only sister."

Leo didn't like where this was going.

"True," Emmeline allowed. Her brows lifted gleefully and she took a stalking step forward. "You know, I thought it was so INTERESTING what you said to Mum downstairs."

"Well," Leo said, starting to sweat, "it's been an interesting few n-nights! With Mum being away and all. I needed to catch her up."

"About your Waxing Moon?" Emmeline's smile widened a fraction. "It WAS your birthnight not so long ago, after all."

She didn't give Leo time to reply before she sighed wistfully. "I remember when I was one hundred and eleven. That human who delivered the dairy . . . he was delicious. Did your human scream?"

"I . . . uh . . ." Leo could feel the wardrobe watching her. "Yes? A bit, maybe? It was all over so quickly. I don't remember a lot of the details—"

"That's convenient, isn't it?" Emmeline interrupted her. She had backed Leo up against her desk, drawing closer and closer. "Because it seemed to ME that maybe something FISHY was going on."

"I'm n-not the biggest fan of fish—"

"Seemed that PERHAPS," Emmeline finished victoriously, "you FAILED your Hunt and didn't want to tell Mum the truth!"

The room was silent. Emmeline's chest heaved and she was wild-eyed, like a cat slamming its paw on a fluttering sparrow.

Leo laughed, high and desperate. "What? Failed?" She shook her head. "Oh. No, no—that's not true, I definitely passed. Don't know where you're getting *that* idea from . . ."

"I know your lying face. It looks a bit like . . ." Emmeline pushed out her lower lip in a mockery of trembling fear. "You're a TERRIBLE liar, and that was one whopper of a big fat lie!"

Emmeline took off with a bound, flying up until she could look Leo in the face.

"I did you a *favor*," she said bluntly, so close that Leo could feel her breath on her chin. "I didn't tell Mum about your creepy little ghost friend—because I'm actually a good sister."

"Right. And NOT because you wanted to torture me forever?" Leo crawled back onto the desk, leaning away.

"I said I was a good sister, not a perfect one!" A tiny finger wagged an inch from Leo's nose. "Now I'm wondering what YOU are going to do for me in return."

"What?"

"You really are so thick, aren't you, grubling?" Emmeline huffed, as though talking to Leo was a huge chore. "It's MY TURN to scrub the armory this year. Who wants to be stuck with stuffy old Marged, polishing for hours?"

*Oh no.* Leo had completely forgotten about Armory Night.

She put on her most convincing smile. "I'm sure it won't take you long, Emmeline—"

"I *know* it won't take me long!" Her sister smiled right back at her, pronouncing every word carefully. "Because *you're* going to do it for me!"

From inside the wardrobe there was an urgent THUMP.

"A-actually, Emmeline, I can't tonight."

"Can't?" Emmeline pursed her lips. "I see. You're busy." She turned and wafted over to the door, an air of casual indifference coming over her. "I'm sorry, I didn't realize you had plans tonight. I'm sure Mum will be TOTALLY CALM when I tell her all about your failed Hunt, then. I bet she'll be very interested to hear about your GHOST FRIEND too. I wonder what she'll do to *her*?"

*Oh no . . .*

In her pocket the ghost-killing ingredients were ready to go. Father Pavlov would be soundly asleep. Minna was here, waiting for her . . .

"So you understand." Emmeline sniffed. "You're going to clean the armory for me. Right now, actually—Marged is waiting. There's a bucket with your name on it."

The wardrobe rattled again.

There was no way that Minna would have Leo's help in fighting the Orphanmaster . . . if there was no Leo around at all. If Emmeline blabbed to Mum about the Waxing Moon and about the ghosts, her fate would be sealed.

"Off you pop, then!" Emmeline said cheerfully. "Best make a start. You'll be scrubbing gauntlets into tomorrow!"

*Please wait for me, Minna.* Carefully, so as not to be caught, Leo reached into her cape when Emmeline's back was turned. Dropping the sulfur crystal and the matchbox onto her bed, they bounced harmlessly on the blanket.

Hearing a final, betrayed thud from the wardrobe, Leo followed her sister out of the room and down the tower.

# 16
# Invasion

The cloth squeaked over the tarnished surface of the shield, again and again until the irritating sound had made a permanent nest in Leo's brain. Her elbows ached and she ground her fangs miserably.

Squeak!

*Pox!*

Squeak!

*Pox!*

If her vampiric face could be reflected behind the grime, Leo would have seen morose eyes and a line of worry crossing her brow. She was barely halfway down the armory and the sun was already up. Much like the rest of Castle Motteberg's insides, the armory was sealed against the deadly light. But unfortunately, meeting her second death wasn't Leo's foremost concern.

The sixth moon had sunk. There was only one more left before the Orphanmaster would come into his true ghostly power. Minna was out there on her own and they were running out of time to banish their foe . . .

*And I'm stuck here!* Leo scrubbed harder, baring her teeth. Her cloth was smearing the grungy coating on the shield, rather than lifting it off. The bucket clanked annoyingly against her wooden foot, water sloshing inside.

The armory was a long underground chamber, lined from floor to ceiling with all sorts of old family heirlooms and artifacts. Every single one of them had been used in battle by Mottebergs past—from the suits of armor (of which there were one hundred complete sets) to the swords and pikes and great double-handed axes. The fancy shield Leo was currently working on was not only enormous, but the grooves and notches around the family crest were tricky to clean. She didn't even have Marged to help her; the knight had vanished hours ago, in a panic about the state of the ransacked kitchens.

There was only Leo and that squeak. *Squeak*, *squeak*, *squeak*, and now the rattling of a suit of armor from farther down the chamber—

*What?* Leo whipped around. Her narrowed gaze followed the long line—each suit dutifully stood as though they were the Royal Guard itself—all the way to the end of the room.

By the door, the final suit of armor was shaking.

It clanged noisily as the chin of the helmet (known as the beaver) struck the top of its metal breastplate—over and over, as though someone inside was caught by the sudden urge to dance, or was choking on a chunk of brain sausage.

The convulsing tremor was catching; its neighbor began to shake too, making a sound not unlike Marged running at full pelt. Then the armor next to it began to tremble, and the next, coming closer and closer to where Leo stood. Leo had never known them to do this before; this wasn't Motteberg magic at work. Something was very, VERY wrong indeed.

Leo gasped as the bucket was upended by her clumsy step backward, water spilling out. The cloth fell forgotten from her grasp. She nearly leapt out of her skin when something wriggled inside the pocket of her cape—

"Not again!" Rodrigo bemoaned, poking his sleepy face out from her pocket. "Honestly, you vampires, what do you have against PEACE AND QUIET?"

Leo took off at a run, making for the other end of the chamber. Her heels slammed on the polished floor. "Rodrigo?" she panted disbelievingly. "You're still here?"

"Of course I am! Where else would I be, after what happened to our room? Do you think I WANT to get squished?" The spider clicked his fangs in what might have been a tut, crawling along Leo's arm and up her neck. He was oblivious to their peril as he settled comfortably in her hair. "Leo, what's all this racket about NOW?"

"It's . . . uhhhh . . ." Leo had come to the far wall—DEAD END—skidding to a halt. Behind her, the tremor was moving like a wave, infecting the armor at an alarming pace. Gauntlets clanged and helmets rolled, crashing to the floor. Leo had to shout to be heard over the din. "No time to explain! Just . . . hang on!"

She needed to think fast. Scale the wall, maybe, try to run *up and over* the menacing armor and get to the door. Whatever was doing this, it certainly wasn't friendly. There were too many sharp edges in the armory for Leo's comfort.

Her foot lifted, about to make the leap onto the wall, when the deafening clamor suddenly stopped. All at once, the suits of armor fell silent, slumping where they stood. A falling axe embedded itself deep into the floor with a final CRUNCH.

Leo froze too.

There was *something in her hair*, she realized, with the sort of dread that trickles down your back and pins you in place, unable to do anything.

Something . . . *moving* in her hair.

Something that wasn't Rodrigo.

"AAAARGH!" a voice burst out, and then eight legs were extended in midair as Rodrigo backflipped off Leo's head and onto the floor.

"INTRUDER! INTERLOPER!" the spider bellowed, scuttling blindly away. He was pursued by . . .

A ghostly hand, leaping from Leo's hair and skittering across the armory floor. Leo bit down on the collar of her cape to contain her belated scream, her nerves leaping beneath her skin. Five thick fingernails scratched on the floor and the hand's ragged pinstripe sleeve flapped behind it. Its misty form was tinged a furious red, WARNING-red. The sight of once silver rings, cast now in their translucent glow, made Leo clutch her shoulder. She knew those rings all too well.

It was the hand of the Orphanmaster.

"YAH!" Rodrigo shouted, turning ninety degrees and striking out at nothing. His fangs clicked. "Begone, fiend!"

Shocked into action, Leo's legs moved before the rest of her could catch up, jolting her to run after them. What chance did a blind spider stand against an evil ghost? "Rodri, behind you!"

Rodrigo yelped, fleeing to the wall and then up it, the fine hairs on his legs gripping the stone. The phantom hand was close behind, lumbering after him.

"HELP ME . . . Don't— *Aaargh*!" Hindered by gravity, Rodrigo had slowed. A step behind, Leo took a flying leap onto the wall, clambering up with nimble ease.

"*LEO!*"

"I'm here!"

The room tipped, and Leo felt her belly slosh as they scrambled onto the ceiling upside down. Now that she had caught up with them, she wasn't quite sure what to do. The sight of the disembodied hand, insect-like in its movements, made her spine tingle. It leapt forward, grabbing hungrily for its still screeching prey, its horrible fingernails scraping. Rodrigo did a frantic lap of the ceiling, followed by the hand and then Leo.

"Now! It has to be now!" Rodrigo squealed.

"What do I *do*?"

"I DON'T KNOW—something! Anything! SQUASH IT!"

Pushing off with her foot, Leo threw her body forward. She felt a chilly rush through her hands and up her arms, spreading like fractals of ice. She gasped, and then the frost was in her lungs, filling her chest.

"Leo? Did you catch it?"

She was flipped, the armory spinning as she tumbled head over heels, and then the hand of the Orphanmaster slammed over her eyes, its ghostly hold pinning her against the ceiling.

Leo grasped the ragged sleeve, pulling fruitlessly as her vision began to cloud over and the chamber was obscured by a red mist. Her stomach lurched with a falling sensation. Her head felt full, as through her ears had been packed with cotton.

The suits of armor vanished. So did the fallen axe where it was sticking up out of the floor. Rodrigo, scuttling uselessly down the opposite wall, disappeared too behind a smoky veil of nothingness.

*"Agnes! Agnes!"* a familiar voice wheezed. It was close, TOO close, and the breathless echo rattled around Leo's skull.

Leo thrashed, legs kicking out, but found that she couldn't budge. Her free hand dug her claws hard into the ceiling beneath her.

*"Agnes!"* the voice—the Orphanmaster—insisted.

"No!" Leo cried. "She's not here! Agnes isn't here!"

There was a long silence. Blind, unable to feel anything but the grip of the icy fingers over her eyes, Leo stilled. The crimson fog enveloped her from all sides. What *was* this?

Then . . .

*"You . . . ?"* the unearthly voice rumbled.

"Yes," she rasped. "It's me."

*"Wil . . . helm . . ."*

Wilhelm? Did the Orphanmaster mean . . . Wilhelmina? Through her panic, Leo remembered that Minna had said Wilhemina was her full name. A fancy, too-long sort of name, just like *Eleonore.*

"Minna's not here! She . . . she's somewhere no one can find her!"

Leo really hoped she was safe at Hollowhome. The last time she had seen Minna, she had been flying into the wardrobe to avoid Emmeline. And they hadn't exactly parted on good terms . . .

*"Wilhelm . . ."*

"No . . . I *told* you—"

*"YOU!"* the Orphanmaster screamed, and Leo flinched as she felt the sting of harsh breath on her cheek. *"YOU, BOY! You took my Agnes!"*

Through the panic, Leo's indignation cut white-hot.

"I'm NOT a boy!" she shouted back, summoning her courage.

*"You—"*

"No! NOT ME!"

All at once, the world was quiet again.

Then came a low hum: some tune that Leo didn't recognize, possibly an old lullaby. It hitched in what might have been a laugh, as though the voice was trying to stifle a smirk.

"You're mad!" Leo bit out impatiently, struggling underneath the hand again. "Why don't you GO AWAY and leave us alone?"

"Mad?" hissed the phantom voice, and Leo hesitated. It had taken on an oily quality that Leo had heard before—the sort of voice a venomous snake would have if it could speak. It might have been her imagination, but it sounded more . . . present than it had up to now. More awake.

The Orphanmaster was awake.

"Yes. Oh, I SEE you," he rumbled, his voice reverberating around Leo's head. "In the flesh. The VAMPIRE!"

There was a shrill whistle, like the squeal of the ghostly wind back in the gallery, and Leo winced. She couldn't move. There was no escape.

"H-how . . . ?" she croaked.

"It's a funny old thing, isn't it—becoming a ghost?" the Orphanmaster spat, the sound echoing through the armory. "Imagine for a moment that I cut off your leg. And your arms. And then your miserable head. And then I flung all the wretched parts away, into the furthest reaches of the forest, miles apart! Or buried them, deep underground! Or sunk them to the bottom of the sea!"

Leo gritted her teeth. "What are you *talking* about? You really are barmy!"

"Barmy, she says!" A shrill, crazed laugh made Leo wince, wishing she could cover her ears against the piercing sound. "Not quite yet! But tell me, vampire, wouldn't YOU go mad, caring for UNGRATEFUL CHILDREN every day? Suffering that terrible drudgery? The boredom? The annoyance?"

"You're a liar!" Leo gasped out. Her head was spinning. Fear gummed her throat, but she showed her fangs anyway. "That's not true and you know it—you never cared for them! Minna told me everything! I know what you were going to do!"

"Let me TELL you what I am going to do. I grow stronger by the hour. I will find that troublesome girl and I will crush her like a beetle beneath my boot. But, before I do, I'm going to crush YOU. With the two of you gone, nothing will stand in my way!" The Orphanmaster's voice shook with mirth. "I can finally do whatever I please! I never CHOSE that life, you know. I never WANTED to be saddled with miserable orphans, all on my own!"

Leo tried to kick. By some miracle, her wooden leg jerked upward, moving her body an inch farther up the ceiling.

*Yes!*

"Minna will find you first!" Leo cried, buying time. "She's coming for you; you can't stop her!"

"Oh, believe me, I'm counting on it." The Orphanmaster chuckled a greasy laugh. "Save me the trouble of coming to this horrible, drafty place again." He sighed. "It's what I'll do AFTERWARD that I still haven't decided. . . . But I'll have the CHILDREN, regardless. Walter and Karin and . . . whatever their names were. The money would have been nice, but they will work for ME now. Consider it payment for being their loving caretaker for these long, painful years."

"You leave them alone!" Wriggling harder, Leo's elbows lifted from the ceiling, her hands balling into furious fists. She could feel herself boiling over, her body starting to lengthen and change.

"And what will you do? Bite me? Drink my blood?"

Leo choked back an angry retort, hissing through her fangs.

"I wonder how best to get them," the Orphanmaster mused. "To turn them into ghosts too. The afterlife won't be so bad with some slaves to do my bidding. Not that you'll be around to see it, of course! No point keeping around a menace like you!"

*NO!*

Leo thrashed, pushing up with all her might, and finally managed to work a clawed hand free. She sliced blindly at the air, feeling a freezing bolt of some unseen force meet her bare skin and rocket up her arm. . . .

All at once, her head felt less full and the grip of the hand on her face loosened. The red mist was clearing. Pressure lifted from her chest, and her lungs filled out with a wheeze, her squashed organs settling back into their rightful places. There was a sighing breath, swept away on the air into nothingness.

Where had the Orphanmaster gone?

What had happened?

Leo's ears strained to hear, tuned to any little sound and—

WHH-THUMPH!

She fell hard and the floor rushed to meet her. She found herself in a crumpled heap, face down in a puddle of dirty water from the bucket. A multitude of different pains bloomed and muddled into each other until she couldn't quite detect what hurt the most.

Under her belly, there was a different feeling. Something was squirming.

"Ooomf . . . ARGH! What in the world?"

Leo flopped over, freeing Rodrigo where he had been squashed underneath her. He took a wobbly step sideways, looking very much like a disgruntled crab.

"Sorry, Rodri," Leo groaned. Her head was swimming as she wiped her face on her sleeve. "Did you . . . did you *hear* that?"

"Hear what?" Rodrigo groused, his fuzzy hair bristling one way and then the other. "You need to be more careful! You're not the only one who lives here, you know!"

Grunting out a vague apology, Leo checked her nose. Mercifully, it wasn't broken—though it was throbbing in time with each blink. As was her shoulder, her ribs, and her hip.

"Did you catch that beast, then?" Rodrigo asked nervously. "Before you decided to FLATTEN ME with your ridiculous gymnastics?"

Leo could imagine the hysterics if he knew the truth.

"I . . . I caught it, yes . . ."

"Humph. We should make a pact. We must never speak of this again. Ever."

Talking was too much effort; Leo couldn't get her lungs to slow down enough to get another word out. She was trembling so hard that her elbows were knocking against the floor.

She managed a nod. Even though Rodrigo couldn't see her, he seemed satisfied.

"I really thought I'd snarfed down all the other spiders in the castle. . . . I suppose I must have missed one—didn't it smell weird? Well—we sure showed *him*, didn't we? Hah!" Rodrigo crawled back up Leo's sleeve, pleased with himself.

Leo wasn't cruel enough to correct him.

Emmeline's threat was insignificant now; Leo had no intention of hanging around in the armory any longer. Getting unsteadily to her feet, she was bent nearly double as she limped across the chamber, leaving the mess behind her.

Somehow, Rodrigo had NO IDEA that the invader had been the Orphanmaster; it was almost as though she'd had some sort of hallucination.

*No,* Leo told herself, coming to the door. She cast a baleful glance back at the suits of armor, now innocently still. *Hallucinations aren't real. And that was DEFINITELY real.*

But some ghost trick, maybe? She licked her lips, worrying at the hem of her cape until a thread pulled loose. She would definitely have to ask Minna about it.

*Minna.* The seventh moon would be rising soon; there was only one more night to rid themselves of the Orphanmaster before he did something truly terrible. As soon as the sun was set and Leo could get away, she needed to warn her friend about his plans.

That was, if he wasn't already out there in Otto's End, after the other children. He was awake now, after all, and it was clear that his power was far more terrible than Leo had first thought. Maybe he was even a threat to rival Sieglinde. . . .

Leo's thoughts whirled the whole way up to the western tower, even as her healing powers activated and the hurt in her back dwindled to an ache. She was clammy all over, like she had spent all night running out in the forest. The sight of her room—and of her BED—made her feel suddenly more exhausted than she had initially realized.

She would snatch a couple of hours of precious sleep before going to help Minna. Leo's eyelids drooped as she let a yawning Rodrigo scuttle down her arm and into his drawer, nestling among the socks there.

Bright blood sloshed in the cup she kept at her bedside, at Marged's insistence. *(I won't have you going hungry, Miss Leo!)*

Leo held it with both hands, but they were equally shaky and didn't help much. She brought it to her mouth, letting the coppery tang soothe her whirling brain—

Her heart froze as something tough slid past her lips and bumped into the back of her throat.

Red droplets flew as she coughed, thumping her chest with one fist. She fumbled the cup back onto her nightstand. Her long tongue rolled out of her mouth. . . .

And two trembling clawtips plucked up a thick red-gray fingernail.

"BLERGH!" Leo flung the revolting thing away, her whole body seizing up in horror. The fingernail hit the wall in a vaporous puff and disintegrated, crumbling away into dust.

The faraway sound of sinister laughter was loud in her ears, even as Leo dived beneath her blanket and pulled her pillow over her head.

# 17
# Twice-Blessed Water

*Leo,*
*Seventh moon. Meet me at*
*the HH.*
*Minna*

The note was only paper, but it felt as heavy as a rock in Leo's cape pocket. It was a grim reminder of the seventh moon where it hung ominously above Castle Motteberg. The Orphanmaster was waiting for them; by the end of the night, they would have run out of time. . . .

Leo sweated and fidgeted and glanced over at the old grandfather clock, which stood in the corner of the dining room. Every ticking second that passed felt like a stake in her back—until the hands indicated it was *midnight* and—

*BONG!*

Leo catapulted her spoon off the side of her bowl, sending blood soup splattering across the otherwise pristine tablecloth.

*BONG!*

"Eleonore!" exclaimed Dad from the other end of the table, dabbing delicately at his mouth with a napkin. "What's gotten into you? You're as white as a sheet."

*BONG!*

If she was a little pale, it was probably her racing heart and her aching back. The Orphanmaster had really done his worst; despite Leo's healing abilities, she was still feeling the fall from a few hours previously. She hadn't had nearly enough sleep to properly recover. And *then* Marged had appeared at the crack of dusk, summoning Leo to family brunch with Mum. . . .

When the Great and Terrible Sieglinde von Motteberg called you to the dining room, to DISOBEY was out of the question.

"Sorry, sorry!" Leo gasped, dabbing at the soupy mess. She lowered her head as the clock continued to chime, counting out the twelfth hour.

"She's as white as a GHOST, Dad!" Emmeline cut in, slurping enthusiastically around her spoon. Her red-smeared chin only added to her menacing aura.

Leo gripped the edge of her chair. All around her, the faces of von Motteberg ancestors sneered from their portraits, judging her. At the head of the table Lady Sieglinde could have been one of the statues out on the bridge: carved from marble, severe and stony and cold.

Like a hawk spotting its prey, her flinty eyes flickered to Leo.

"What's wrong, child?" Sieglinde demanded. "You've barely touched your soup—aside from flinging it across the table like some COMMON girl."

Sieglinde's gown tonight was her favorite gray and had billowing sleeves that she had tucked back so as to avoid staining. The bones in her knobbly wrists reminded Leo of twining branches: graceful, elegant, strong . . .

The click of her claws against her spoon, however, made Leo's spine feel like jelly.

"Y-yes," Leo said, swallowing. Her mouth ran away with her before her brain could catch up: "I'm so sorry, Mum, it's just . . . I feel a bit poorly, actually."

She really did. She was sick with GUILT—her friend needed her and she was having lunch!

"Poorly?" Sieglinde's lip curled. She subtly leaned back in her seat, despite the considerable distance between Leo and Dad and Emmeline at one end of the table, and Sieglinde at the other in her grand, ornately carved chair.

While Dad's preoccupation with germs stemmed from his fear of rats and roaches and other vermin, Mum had an aversion to anything that might make her ill.

Sickness was weakness. The (future) Head of the Council needed to be in pristine health at all times in order to rule effectively. It was, in Lady Sieglinde's view, completely beneath a powerful vampire to get a sniffle or a fever or—perish the thought—to feel a bit POORLY.

That was it.

*I'm coming, Minna!* Leo thought, gritting her fangs.

"Mmm!" She put on her best "I don't feel so good" face. "I . . . I think maybe I've got TOAD TUMMY." Putting both hands below her ribs, she sucked in a breath to push her belly out as much as she could.

"You're FAKING it!" Emmeline accused, banging the end of her spoon on the table. "You're trying to sneak away, aren't you?"

"Now, now." Mum raised a hand—enough to cut Emmeline's tantrum short. "Leo, if you feel unwell, you should have stayed in your room!" she scolded, and then clicked her fingers twice when the sound of clattering announced the arrival of a suit of armor. "Marged, excellent. Escort this one back up to the western tower; she's full of . . ."

"Slime, probably," supplied Leo sadly.

Inwardly, she was shocked at herself; perhaps this lying business wasn't so difficult, after all. What was she becoming?

It was for a good cause, she reasoned. She HAD to get to Hollowhome and to Minna, to warn her friend about the Orphanmaster's awakening. They had to vanquish him—TONIGHT.

Even if Emmeline told Mum.

Even if Mum went mad.

After what Leo had seen, pinned to the armory ceiling last day . . . she had to be brave. It wasn't too late!

"Yes, yes, go! Off you go now!" Mum flapped a hand, her nostrils pinching in disgust.

From across the table Dad blinked owlishly at her, adjusting his glasses like he didn't quite know what to make of the scene.

"Miss Leo, you poor thing! You should have said that you felt off-color!" Marged fussed, balancing a platter of bloodloaf in one gauntlet in order to feel Leo's forehead with the other. "Come on. Let's get you off to bed. Don't I feel guilty now, for having you scrubbing swords yesternight. . . ."

Leo stood hastily, her chair scraping back across the flagstone floor.

"That's all right, Marged!" she blurted, before she could lose her resolve. She looked the knight in the eye—or in the visor—so she wouldn't be able to catch Emmeline's glower. "I'll be able to get myself up the stairs. You should stay; there's still the main course and dessert yet!"

"But, Miss Leo—"

"Enjoy your meal!" Leo called in the vague direction of the table, already shuffling to the door. "Don't worry about me. I'll be fine!" She kept an arm wrapped around her stomach until she was out in the hallway and safe from prying eyes.

She paused for a moment against the wall, unable to believe her own nerve. Slowly, she lifted her head.

Across from her, the parlor door was ajar. Standing innocently between two crystal glasses was a slim corked bottle, green in color and barely the length of her hand. From its position on the low table, it appeared to wink at her. It would be perfect for holding liquids: a potion or wine or *water* . . .

Leo steeled herself.

Then, finally, with Minna's note tucked around the little bottle and trepidation in her heart, she was away.

The seventh moon was high above her head as Leo ran through the stoic Dreadwald trees.

To be precise, she ran harder and faster and more desperately than she had ever done in living (or Undead) memory. She heard the snap of brittle leaves, felt the prickle of pine needles, and the night air was clean and dewy after yester-night's rain. She dipped and darted and dashed. Her bare foot found purchase on a knobbly tree trunk, and she used it to push herself higher, leaping from branch to branch.

*Hang on, Minna! I'm coming!*

She had messed up, she knew. Bowing to Emmeline and giving in to Marged—and to MUM—had cost her valuable time, time that they simply didn't have to waste. All around her, signs of the Orphanmaster's grip were starting to manifest in the forest: some rotten bark; a graying shrub collapsing in on itself; a dying tree, blackened and bent . . .

They could still do this, Leo told herself, blinking away tears. All wasn't lost. They could grab the twice-blessed water on their way through Otto's End and then go straight on to St. Frieda's. The Orphanmaster's Spirit Anchor was bound to be there, since it was the last place Leo had seen her lost leg. He didn't have the *Companion* to advise him, after all; Leo and Minna had the advantage of GHOSTLY KNOWLEDGE on their side.

When she reached the clearing in the forest, the ancient large-leaved lime tree rustled in greeting. She was as beautiful as ever, with not a streak of decay on her gargantuan trunk.

Leo dipped her head in respectful reply as she slipped through a gap in the silvery bark and inside Hollowhome.

Minna would understand her lateness, Leo thought with her last shred of optimism. She wiped her sweaty hands on her shorts. Minna *knew* that things were complicated, when you were part of a noble vampire family. She would totally get why it had taken Leo so long to slip away, if Leo apologized—

"LEO VON MOTTEBERG!" someone yelled in her ear, sending fireflies fleeing. "WHERE HAVE YOU BEEN?"

The heavy table upended on its side. The hammock turned inside out like a leaf in a storm, sending blankets flying. Leo flew too, caught in the ghostly whirlwind—she was pushed clear across the base and into the opposite wall, where a raging ball of furiously shimmering fog was on her in a heartbeat.

"Do you have ANY IDEA how long I've been camped out here? Waiting?" Minna shouted, appearing inches from Leo's nose. She bared her gappy teeth ferociously. "Is this a GAME to you? Did you just wander down when you fancied it?"

"Minna!" Leo gasped through a mouthful of Minna's ghostly hair. "I came as soon as I could! I was cleaning the armory and then, well, something happened! Something big! A-and then tonight, I couldn't get away until now . . . There was a-a-a family thing!" How on earth was she supposed to even *begin* to explain?

"A FAMILY THING! Oh!" Minna threw up her hands; she

was holding Leo up by sheer fury alone, but there was no time for Leo to be impressed. "I'm so sorry to have inconvenienced you! Did you forget what night it is?"

"No! I didn't! Not for one second—but you don't get what they're like! When you're a von Motteberg, you—"

"Oh, *please*, tell me again all about how you're rich and spoiled!"

"It's not like that. I—"

"Then what *is* it like, Leo?"

"Mum will KILL me if she finds out about you!" Leo roared, losing her temper. "I failed my Hunt! Okay—I FAILED it! I was never meant to make a ghost—let alone two!"

Minna was stunned into silence. Leo breathed deeply, coming back to herself.

Her belly flipped. *She had failed her Hunt.* The words were out there now; there was no taking them back. "I've made a huge mess of things," she admitted. "Mum might exile me—if I'm lucky—but PROBABLY she'll turn me to dust."

As Minna's hold loosened, Leo slipped down from the wall.

"I told you about my Waxing Moon," she said miserably. "My Hunt: the most important night for a young vampire. You heard what Emmeline said up in my bedroom . . ."

Minna didn't seem quite as moved as Leo had hoped she would be.

"If you're so worried about getting into trouble," Minna said, drifting down to fix Leo with a baleful look, "then WHY are you here? Why come back at all?"

"What?"

"Why bother? Why not stay up at the castle and play pretend, so your evil vampire mum never finds out?" Minna waved a hand wildly around her head, starting to float back and forth as if pacing in midair. "Why did I wait around all night and day for you? I'm such an *idiot.*"

The poker gleamed in the dim light, gripped hard in Minna's fist. Reflected in her vaporous body, the lights of the fireflies set Minna aglow.

"I'll go alone," Minna said. "I have what I need." The poker's sharp tip indicated one of the nooks in the wall in which the ghost-killing ingredients were safely nestled. The salt jar. The sulfur crystal. The box of matches to produce smoke. "I'll get the twice-blessed water myself. And then I'm going to end this. I stab the Spirit Anchor—your leg—and my mission is won. My friends are safe. My purpose is fulfilled and you never see me again."

Somehow, Minna's dismissal hurt far worse than anything Leo had endured up at Castle Motteberg.

She had let Minna down.

Dismayed, Leo shook her head. "You don't have to go

alone!" she cried. Quieter, she added, "I . . . I don't *want* you to go alone. I'm *sorry.* I shouldn't have taken so long. I was scared of my family. But I'm here now."

There was only one other thing she could think of that might convince Minna.

"The Orphanmaster spoke to me."

Her back turned, Minna froze. Though Hollowhome was already enormously cavernous by the standards of the average Dreadwald tree, the gulf between the two girls felt bigger than ever.

"What?"

"Please," Leo said, "something WEIRD happened in the day—something REALLY WEIRD. There was a hand in the castle armory. Er . . . unattached."

Slowly, suspiciously, Minna spun to look at her. "You don't usually keep an unattached hand in the armory?" she asked.

"Not a ghost hand, no." Leo swallowed. "It was angry. It chased . . . well . . . it ran up the wall and then I grabbed it and then IT grabbed ME . . ."

She had half expected Minna to scoff at her in disbelief. Instead, Minna just looked back at her—if a tad impatiently.

"And then what?"

"Well, it was the Orphanmaster's hand. It had his rings and his pajama sleeve and his horrible f-fingernails . . ." Leo blanched at the memory. She felt a bit sick again. "He was there. At the CASTLE, Minna."

"And it was *definitely* the Orphanmaster?"

Leo nodded so fervently she was surprised her head didn't fall off. "Yes! He was talking in his sleep, wailing about Agnes. Then he thought I was someone named Wilhelm—"

Leo stopped short, startled by the sudden flicker that rippled across Minna's pallid face.

"What? What is it?" Leo asked, feeling silly, as though she was missing a piece of the puzzle. "You said, back at St. Frieda's, that your name is Wilhelmina. Everyone calls you Minna, but the Orphanmaster was looking for Wilhelm."

"Wilhelm is a boy's name," Minna said sharply.

"I know! That's why I thought it was weird! He called me a boy, when he thought I was Wilhelm! He said that I had taken Agnes from him!"

For the first time since Leo had known her, Minna looked . . . small.

Not small from the top of her head to the tips of her toes, but small in the way she shrank further into herself, her shoulders hunching. Smaller even than when she was a Living girl, looking for clues in the room above the sleeping orphans, prepared to fight a monster.

"What's wrong?" Leo asked. "What aren't you telling me?"

Minna tried to protest. "We're wasting time." She closed her eyes and furrowed her brow. "You really think it will help? Knowing everything?"

"I think if you want me to help you, then I should know. It could help us in our fight."

"So you don't trust me."

"I do trust you, Minna," Leo said honestly. "What I don't trust is *him*. If there's any trick that the Orphanmaster might have up his sleeve, then we ought to both be fully prepared. Knowing the enemy is important."

"I see." Minna's thin shoulders slumped further. "I suppose you're right."

"Who is Wilhelm, Minna?"

Minna swallowed. She averted her eyes to the floor, watching as a stray firefly alighted on the fallen *Encyclopedia*.

"Agnes died," she said, "looking after an orphan as a volunteer at St. Frieda's. His name was Wilhelm. So that's probably why the Orphanmaster confused you for him at first—he was piecing his memories together, like I did before I came to find you."

Wilhelm was an orphan too, then. Leo nodded slowly, letting her brain catch up while Minna continued on.

"The boy, Wilhelm, he had . . . he had the kind of illness you don't get better from, not usually." This sounded like a story Minna knew well, one that had been told to her many times. "But he did—he got better, and he grew up and left. He was lucky. But Agnes, the wife of the Orphanmaster . . . she caught his sickness and she passed away. She was only young: *too* young to die. The Orphanmaster has hated children ever since. Orphans, especially. And ME especially."

"Why you?" Leo whispered. She didn't understand any of it; what was there to hate about Minna? Why would someone despise a child *so much*?

Minna's mouth downturned. She seemed to be fighting with herself.

Whichever part of her won out, it was the part that wanted to confess.

"The orphan—Wilhelm—he was *my dad*."

Leo couldn't believe it. Humans really were complicated; their fates were all intertwined like an elaborate tapestry. To think that Minna had ended up at St. Frieda's, just like her father . . . Just like her father who had passed on the sickness that took the Orphanmaster's wife . . .

"Minna . . ." The shock dissipated and Leo felt an emptiness inside: a numbness that made her heart hang heavy. "Why didn't you tell me? You know that you can tell me anything you want, don't you?"

"I thought . . ." Minna sucked in a deep breath—like Leo, she hadn't lost her habit of *breathing*. "I thought if you knew," she said, "that you wouldn't understand. You would feel sorry for the Orphanmaster and then you wouldn't want to help me."

Leo didn't know what to say. It was a tricky business, trying to comfort a friend. Especially when you couldn't even so much as touch them on the shoulder.

In the end, though, Minna spoke for her.

"I suppose the question is: Do you think it's okay for people who have been hurt . . . to hurt others in return? Because he will, you know. Once he is through with me and you, he won't stop there. People like him never stop." Though Minna didn't so much as blink, something fierce and barely contained had lit up inside her, like a hurricane on the horizon. Her narrow glare was blazing.

It was far better, Leo thought, than the sad, small Minna she had seen a moment before. She much preferred this version, vengefulness and all.

"I *don't* think it's okay," Leo said resolutely. "Not even the littlest bit. I'm right behind you, all the way to the end. And not only b-because of what Mum will do to me if she finds out I created two ghosts! I *want* to help you, Minna. I really do.

Feeling sorry for the Orphanmaster doesn't change that—not when he's become . . . become this . . ."

*This monster*, she thought privately, as though saying it aloud might summon him again.

"You were right about your friends being in danger," Leo continued instead. "The Orphanmaster means to find them, after we're out of the picture. He said that t-turning them into ghosts would be 'payment,' so they can work for him in the afterlife." She hung her head. "I'm sorry I'm so late. I made a mistake. Please take me with you to Otto's End."

Minna said nothing. At the mention of the other children and their peril she had balled her hands into trembling fists.

"Minna," Leo pressed. "Minna, please."

When Minna looked her way, Leo knew that they understood each other.

"Bring everything with you," Minna ordered tersely, shimmering with angry energy. "We won't be at the church for long. Every second we give him now makes him stronger. We can't let that seventh moon sink without him GONE."

As Minna swept out of Hollowhome, Leo paused at the base entrance, her attention caught.

There, nestled above the gap in the tree trunk, was a dark, oily smudge. It burbled as Leo peered up at it, bubbles rising on its slimy surface. A thick glob of the stuff fell, hanging on by a glutinous thread before splatting onto the dirt, inches from Leo's toes. The patch of earth sizzled, graying as though all life was being sucked out of it.

Hissing through her fangs, Leo charged out into the forest beyond.

If Minna was ready to fight the Orphanmaster, then so was she.

Leo crept silently alongside Minna as they slunk into town, passing by the huddled houses. The slant of the eaves made the buildings seem to frown forebodingly at them, as if their windows were eyes and their doors were mouths full of teeth. The darkness muted everything, made it softer and more comforting, but Leo could picture how scary Otto's End would be during the day.

As it was, the town was just as quiet and still as it had been on the night of the fire. The cobbled streets were empty. The market stalls had all been packed up and the stallholders gone home. None of the chimneys were smoking. It was as though the world had stopped, suspending the Living in time. Everywhere they looked, there was evidence of the Orphanmaster's presence; that strange, invasive rot had twisted its way through the town, pooling in dark nooks and growing in gaps in the stonework.

It sickened Leo to look at it for too long. She kept her head low as they passed by the deserted schoolhouse and finally arrived at St. Maja's church.

It was a friendlier place, at least outwardly, with its stained glass and foreboding gravestones. There wasn't an inky glob in sight here; perhaps, for some reason, the Orphanmaster didn't fancy hanging around the church.

Leo knew that this was no place for a VAMPIRE either. Her every nerve was on high alert. It didn't help that Minna hadn't said a single word to her since they had left Hollowhome—Leo was sure Minna was still angry with her.

Insects whirred and the open gate creaked in the wind. Mottled moths flapped clumsily around the lantern above the church entrance, drawn by its gleam. Outside the church, two figures, one dark and one pale, approached the door. A hollow had been worn into the step, created by the feet of generations of worshippers.

"This is it, then," Leo said awkwardly. She was a jumble of confused nerves, or nervous confusion; being this close to the church was making her itchy. "Do we . . . Should we knock?"

Minna tilted her head. Then she drifted right on through the door. There was a heavy *shh-clunk* as she opened it from the other side, sliding the iron bolts across.

"Problem solved!" she declared, all business as she appeared in the open doorway. "Would you like to come in?"

"Uh . . ." Leo floundered, inching her wooden foot closer to the threshold. She winced, feeling resistance. Something was pushing her away. "I'm not sure this will work, Minna. I think it might have to be Father Whatshisface."

*The first Vampiric Law. The Vampire will not enter uninvited.*

Minna puffed out her cheeks. "That's a bit silly, isn't it?"

"He's the one who lives here, so . . ." Leo cleared her throat, shifting from foot to foot. Above them, an owl hooted.

"I'll go in first, then," Minna huffed, like it was a huge amount of bother. "So you can do your vaaampire thing." She wiggled her fingers, disappearing off into the shadowy church.

Alone on the doorstep, Leo licked her lips.

She jiggled one leg and then the other.

She bounced her arms at her sides, swinging her clawed hands back and forth.

From deep within the building something smashed—perhaps a plate or a teacup. There was a pause, and then lamplight bloomed.

Eyes bulging, chin tucked low, Leo stayed very still. She willed her hand to move, to reach out for the brass door knocker. For a long moment, it refused to budge, and then—

*BANG! BANG-BANG!*

Leo knocked three times and snatched her arm back into

the safety of her cape. The air felt frostier now than when she left the castle.

A misshapen figure lumbered into view. It lurched unsteadily down the aisle between the pews, dragging its feet. Closer and closer the monster came, its crinkled eyes scrunching tighter in the moonlight and . . .

And . . . Leo realized, it wasn't a monster at all. It was the priest, blinking sleepily and swaddled in his floral blanket. His sparse gray hair was sticking up in the back. Locking eyes with the vampire at his door, Father Pavlov stopped in his tracks.

It had to be now. Drawing herself up to look bigger, Leo summoned her Vampiric Will. It rose within her like a swelling tide and then flowed from her mouth.

"*Human*," she intoned unblinkingly. "*You have something to ask.*"

*Invite me in.*

*Invite me in.*

Father Pavlov squinted at her. Then his bushy eyebrows curved upward in surprise.

"Eleonore?"

Leo wavered. "Pardon me?"

"Eleonore," the priest insisted. "Dietmar's daughter?"

*"I . . . er . . ."*

What was happening? Leo felt her Will stutter, puttering

out. Grown-ups, she decided, were all-around tricky. This wasn't the plan at all. She took a step backward, ready to run.

"Wait! Please wait. Any child of Dietmar's is welcome here," Father Pavlov said in a rush. "I'm sorry—you startled me, is all. My visitors are usually . . . well, *human*. I'd invite you in—b-but your father has never been one for the décor here. Vampires and churches, and all that."

Suddenly, Leo wasn't so sure about this. She battled with herself for a moment. The last time she had encountered a human—a fully grown human—she had almost lost her life for a second time. There was no such thing as a third do-over.

From the mossy wall next to her, Minna's quizzical face emerged.

"Go on, Leo!" she urged, glancing meaningfully at Father Pavlov. "Try your hypnotism thing again! We have a job to do!"

The priest didn't react; it seemed that, being human, he couldn't see or hear Minna at all. Oblivious, he nodded his gray head at Leo.

"I think I might know why you're here," he said. "It's about the . . . the wraith, isn't it? The spirit haunting the town?"

Minna leapt out of the wall. "AHA! He means the Orphan-master!" She darted back and forth, phasing harmlessly through the unwitting human.

Leo wanted to tell Minna to calm down, but the priest was waiting.

She had been standing at the open door for too long. A WRONG sort of feeling had come over her, like catching your funny bone or biting into something icy or missing a step in the dark . . . all at once. A full-body shiver racked Leo, making her hair sproing straight and her fangs grind together.

Behind Father Pavlov, past the stone font and the silent pews, the altar gleamed. It might have been her imagination, but it looked as though it was casting its own light—a pure white, whiter than Dad's lab or Minna's ghostly eyes, the kind of white that can stop a vampire's heart and end an unlife in a blink.

"Maybe," Father Pavlov interjected, "maybe we . . . we should sit outside? Meet me in the graveyard, my dear—I'll make some tea. No, no, I insist! You are my guest. You can tell your friend that they are most welcome to join us too." And before Leo could protest, the priest shuffled off back into the church, dragging his blanket with him.

Minna boggled at his retreating back, spooked. *He knows?* she mouthed in Leo's direction.

By way of a reply, Leo slumped against the wall.

"So," ventured Leo, a steaming cup of undrinkable tea in hand. They had business to get to, but this was such a strange turn. She just HAD to know something first . . . "How do you know Dad?"

The three of them had gathered in the graveyard and sat on a rickety bench among the gravestones. Nearby, the statue of an elegant lady kept her stony watch over them. Leo could feel her looking; the back of her neck prickled, though she kept her eyes warily on their human host.

Father Pavlov, halfway through sipping his tea, jumped as he scalded his mouth. "Oh! Mmm, of course! Your father often joins me for a chat and a friendly game of chess. We go way back—although, I suppose in vampire terms, the human life is but the flap of a butterfly's wing."

Leo lifted an eyebrow.

"We . . . have an unfortunate tendency to die," the priest explained, smiling ruefully. "But before me, Dietmar was also on good terms with Father Bartz. And with Father Bindrich before him. And Father Engelmann, and Father Egner. Father Rosenkranz, well, they hated each other—used to bicker terribly, let me tell you! But before *him* was Father Groth, and they were apparently terrific chums—"

"Right, I see," interrupted Leo, anticipating that they might be there a while. There was no time to waste chatting; the seventh moon was still on the move across the night sky. "It's just, Dad's never . . . he's never said anything. About having a friend that's . . ." She wafted a hand to indicate Father Pavlov; a HUMAN, she meant, or perhaps HUMAN PRIEST, which was even worse. Her belly turned another somersault.

"I can understand why he wasn't forthcoming," admitted Father Pavlov. "Humans can be dangerous creatures. That's partly why Dietmar began his tradition of visiting St. Maja's—to keep an eye on the Living neighbors, as it were. My dear, he wants to protect you! He would probably be horrified if he knew we had met! And . . . I take it he doesn't know about your friend here either?"

They both looked sideways. Leo saw Minna, sitting primly with her cup of tea. Father Pavlov, saw only the cup, floating eerily in midair.

"I knew I sensed something," he said uneasily. "There's been . . . ah . . . quite the ghostly activity in Otto's End lately. But this one really doesn't want to talk to me, does he?"

"You mean SHE," Leo corrected. She looked to Minna, who had turned her nose huffily up at that comment. "Really, Minna, come on. It will be quicker if you tell him yourself."

"Wait a moment . . ." Father Pavlov looked suddenly peaky. "Minna? *Wilhelmina?*"

Both Leo and Minna, still unseen, stared at him.

Then, with a startled cry, Father Pavlov promptly emptied his teacup into his own lap as Minna reappeared.

Leo was privately impressed; she hadn't been sure if Minna could manifest in front of a human. Father Pavlov, on the other claw, was less thrilled.

"As I live and breathe," the priest gasped, clutching at the bench beneath him. Leo worried for a moment that he might actually have a heart attack; he looked far too wrinkly for nasty shocks. "*Minna.* It's you."

"Father," Minna returned in her matter-of-fact sort of way. "It's you. As I do not live and do not breathe." There was a sour note to her voice. When she took a sip from her cup, the tea ran right through her to patter onto the bench. "Why are you so surprised to see me? Are my bones not buried here?"

"Well!" Leo squeaked, clapping her hands together briskly. "Now that we're all reacquainted, let's get down to it, shall we? Thing is, Father, we need the water from the font."

"The font?"

"Yes. But we'll need you to bless it once more, if it's not too much trouble. Just to be sure, you know. It has to be EXTRA HOLY."

"Right . . . well, that's . . ." Father Pavlov was having difficulty taking this in. He was as white as a sheet as he continued to stare at Minna.

Minna sighed. "We need the twice-blessed water to fight the Orphanmaster," she said plainly. "He has returned as a ghost. The *wraith* you were talking about earlier."

"He plans to go after the other children," Leo added. She caught Minna's eye. "We need to stop him before people get hurt."

"You mean Bill? *Bill* is the ghost causing all this trouble?" Father Pavlov looked off into Otto's End. "That's . . . We . . ." He scrubbed a hand down over his crinkly eyes. "My apologies, children. There have been some strange happenings in town lately. Unsettling occurrences. Unearthly events."

Leo nodded grimly. "My least favorite kind of events," she said.

Father Pavlov explained about the sightings of disembodied parts, and household items that had unexpectedly sprung to life. He told them of the foul, foggy stench and phantom laughter that rumbled from under beds and inside wardrobes. He described weird lights and swirling mists and a deep sense of disquiet that crept into dreams and turned them into nightmares. Then, of course, there was the black, oily slick that had appeared around town, which kept growing and growing no matter how often it was cleaned away.

"Father," Minna said, lighting up while Leo quietly cringed. They were on the Orphanmaster's trail for sure. "You were right. What you have here is most certainly a HAUNTING."

The priest pulled a handkerchief from his sleeve. "Quite," he croaked, mopping his brow. "Yes. A haunting."

"And I'm afraid it will only get worse. After the moon goes down tonight, the Orphanmaster will come into his true power. He's been bad, up until now—even in his sleep."

"He tried to crush me with a book," Leo pointed out.

"Yes—and THEN he turned into a gust of wind and tried to throw you down the mountain," added Minna.

"Yeah. And there was the ghost hand in the armory; THAT was terrifying."

"Can't believe I missed that one . . ."

"Mmm. I found his horrible fingernail in my cup of blood, did I tell you about *that*?"

"I might have an idea," Father Pavlov cut in over the girls, his voice thin and wheezing. "Have you heard before of PURGATORY? A state between Heaven and Hell?"

Minna nodded. "I know of it. A place between worlds."

"Perhaps your situation is similar. If you imagine . . . our world." Father Pavlov held out a veiny hand, his palm down. "And the next." He set his other hand on top of it. "Like pages of a book. And to get from one page to the next, you have to turn the first one over. Perhaps you and Bill are . . . between pages, as it were."

Leo and Minna looked at each other.

"What happens on the next page, then?" Leo wondered aloud.

*"Beneath the watch of the seventh sinking moon will a spirit's power be fully realized,"* quoted Minna. She turned to Father Pavlov. "It was a warning we found in an old book, *The Ghost-Hunter's Companion*. It will be bad news for us when day breaks this morning. For ALL of us."

Leo blinked. The way Father Pavlov described it, it sounded very much like a ghostly coming of age. A ghostly Waxing Moon. She wrapped her cape more firmly about herself, feeling suddenly cold.

Father Pavlov sighed. "I suppose the question now is, what the dickens to do about it."

Leo produced the little bottle she had pinched from Castle Motteberg, holding it delicately between two claws. Her smile was as wobbly as it was toothy.

"I think we already know the answer to that! But first you have to promise not to spill A SINGLE WORD to Dad. . . ."

# 18
# The Spirit Anchor

The wind nipped at Leo's heel as she darted through the cramped streets of Otto's End, wary of the seventh moon as it hung low over the ramshackle rooftops. Leo's failure to sneak away from the castle had cost them dearly, as had Father Pavlov's frightened rambling; soon they would be out of time. Her keen ears caught the faint mechanical whirr of the clock tower, its gears and pulleys counting out the seconds. The sound made Leo's heart quicken.

Minna sailed ahead, swooping in and out of the stone walls that crowded in on them. In just a few nights her piloting had improved tenfold—as had her mood.

"Almost there!" she called back, sounding a little too EAGER for Leo's liking. Minna couldn't wait to wrap her hands around the neck of her foe. Leo, on the other claw, was desperately hoping that they could find her lost leg and destroy it without encountering the Orphanmaster himself. . . .

Inside her cape pocket, Leo could feel the twice-blessed water. Even securely corked in its vial, it had a peculiar intensity that gave Leo the jitters. Its deadly power was at the forefront of her mind as she trailed after her guide, moving as though she was carrying a nest full of hornets.

Or perhaps the hornets' nest was actually their destination. Leo swallowed as they left the town behind and arrived at the iron gate.

At the top of the driveway, the ruin of St. Frieda's was somberly waiting. Leo's mouth dropped open as she took in the destruction—damage *she* had caused, however inadvertently. All that was left of the orphanage was a burnt-out husk, covered in a layer of soot that stirred on the breeze. The bitter smell of it reached Leo's nose as she crept closer to the gate. Only part of the outer wall was still standing; the whole building slumped sideways, its dreary brickwork blown out and scattered down the bank.

From this angle the remains of St. Frieda's looked like the gray, broken shell of a bird's egg, blackened with disease.

Anyone who hadn't seen the place before the fire, who didn't know that it was once an orphanage . . . would be forgiven for not knowing that St. Frieda's ever existed at all. Leo bit her lip and pushed down her guilty trepidation.

As they approached, clouds drifted over the pallid face of the moon. Minna stopped at the foot of the drive. Her confidence stalled. A solemn look came over her; this place still held so many memories that she would rather forget.

Leo peered at her. "You okay?"

Minna shook herself. "Yes! Of course I am—why wouldn't I be?" She schooled her face back into a carefully neutral mask. "Let's get up there."

Together, they flitted up the long drive to the wreck. Arriving at the double doors (or what remained of them, flame-eaten and hanging from melted hinges), Leo couldn't help but feel they were walking into the lair of something awful.

*We'll be quick about it,* she told herself, trying to be brave. Her hand left behind a long-fingered print in the ash as she took a deep breath and pushed one of the doors open.

They picked their way through St. Frieda's, creeping from room to ruined room. Leo left more prints—from her feet, this time, trailing behind her down the collapsed hallway. To their left, a landslide of rubble bulged through a misshapen door.

"This was the dormitory," Minna said numbly, eyeing the mess in disbelief. "It's where we all slept. The coldest room in the orphanage—except for the basement, of course."

"Probably even colder than the basement now. Looks like the roof caved in." Leo wasn't surprised. Dreadwald wood made sturdy, reliable supports for buildings. It was also, however, highly flammable. She drew her cape tightly around herself.

Minna hummed. "It got especially bad in winter. Last year, we had to chip ice from the window. It was frozen solid every morning. All the beds felt wet; it was so cold. . . ."

As they peered around, a sense of heavy melancholy came over Leo. She looked to Minna, who had plucked something out of the ashes.

"What's that?" Leo asked, but Minna didn't reply. She didn't have to.

It was a child's toy: a mechanical monkey made of tin. One of its arms had pinged loose, bobbling sadly on its spring.

"This . . . It was Wolfgang's." Minna's hands shook, making the monkey rattle. "I wonder if the others are okay. Do you think they've noticed the haunting? Do you think they're scared?"

"I'm sure they're being looked after," Leo said, even though she wasn't sure at all. She suspected Minna knew as much.

Minna placed the monkey down on a shard of upturned floorboard.

"It can't be any worse than here. Come on—we have a *you-know-what* to find," she said, as though the Orphanmaster himself might be spying on them. The thought made Leo shrink smaller—what if he WAS here? Laughing at them from the shadows? She looked furtively over her shoulder, seeing only the dark, soot-covered hallway down which they had come.

They continued on, past the scorched spine of the staircase. Above it, where the ceiling should have been, there was now open sky, dotted with faraway stars.

"We were hardly ever allowed upstairs," Minna said. "The Orphanmaster was suspicious of us, always calling us sly or light-fingered. We only went up there to dust or to sweep." She seemed to be talking to herself, remembering a life that, only nights ago, had been very much real.

The heavens grumbled, billowing black clouds starting to swirl together. Only hours before, it had been a clear night.

It could have been the ominous sky, the twice-blessed water, or Minna's closed-off expression, but Leo knew there was something BAD about this place. She couldn't see it or hear it, but she could feel it. Her gut told her to fly as far away as possible.

"My le—" Leo stopped and cleared her throat. "I mean, THE THING should be nearby, shouldn't it?"

*Let's grab it and go!* was what she didn't say, not wanting to be cowardly—but Minna seemed to get it.

"I feel like it's close," Minna whispered. "Don't ask me why. Come on, let's try this way."

She beckoned Leo to follow, flying through a crumbling heap of stone and singed wood that might have been another doorway. Leo climbed up and over, and then her feet thudded down in what was left of a vast drawing room. It was entirely exposed to the forest on one side and littered with burnt furniture. Somewhat ironically, considering the fate of St. Frieda's, the fireplace was the only thing still mostly standing, though its chimney had split right down the middle—

A shrieking, squeaking flock of bats suddenly took flight, flapping frantically from where they had been nestled inside the fireplace. They burst upward in a living cloud and flew away into the night.

Leo squeaked too—before an icy hand was clapped over her mouth.

"Shhh!" Minna hissed. Her blank eyes darted from side to side, searching for movement.

"What? What's wrong?" Leo whispered back, her voice burbling through Minna's misty hand. There was no sign of the Orphanmaster. The room was quiet and still, as frozen as the rest of Otto's End at this hour.

"I don't know," Minna said. "There's . . . there's a weird feeling here."

Leo felt her heart jolt as Minna released her. A zing of static ran all the way down to her toes and up to the top of her head. Around them, surrounded by broken floorboards and soot, the dark shapes of the ruined furniture were suddenly menacing.

"Is it him? Is he here?" she wheezed out.

"*Something's* here." Minna tapped the hilt of her poker—their weapon of intent. The weapon they would use to pierce their target. "Something we *need*, maybe."

*The Spirit Anchor,* Leo thought, gazing around at the chaos. All they had to do now was find it, and fast.

But where to start . . .

There was the four-poster bed, slumped on its side like a shipwreck. Half a writing desk. What might have once been an armchair, now reduced to four melted feet.

Looking up, Leo realized that the first and second floors . . . were not where she had left them the night she had fled St. Frieda's. In fact, they were entirely in the wrong place. There must have been a cave-in here too, because everything had come crashing downstairs into the drawing room, leaving the remnants of the Orphanmaster's bedroom strewn about. The light of the seventh moon, streaming in through the enormous hole eaten in the roof, made everything silvery and shadowy.

"Better get digging," Leo suggested, already wanting to be far away from this place. Minna's reminiscing was making her itchy—she *really* didn't want to stick around to meet the Orphanmaster himself.

She wasted no time in scrabbling through the debris. Pushing the soot aside revealed . . . more soot, which in turn uncovered even MORE soot. Before long, her gray hands and knee and face were thoroughly smudged, as though she had rolled around in a fireplace.

It *had* to be here. She dug in with her claws, fighting to ignore her irritated eyes and the gritty taste on her tongue.

"We might be too late—what if he's already snatched it? What if he knows?" Minna fretted. Leo tried not to stare as clumps of burnt wood and stone and ash began to float directly around Minna's dangling legs. If the Orphanmaster had figured out that Leo's lost leg was what kept him tethered to this world—if he had realized his one real WEAKNESS . . . they were in trouble. There was no backup plan. It was the *Companion*'s advice or nothing.

Together, the girls searched for the Spirit Anchor, until Minna began to droop tiredly and Leo's back ached from bending down. Leo was positively caked in ash, which clung to her hair and clothing in a dusty layer. Some of the horrid stuff had been drawn up into Minna's body, particles swirling through her before scattering like muddy snowflakes at her feet.

"This is hopeless," Minna bemoaned, looking despondently around them. "He definitely knows. He's taken it."

"He can't have! Don't give up!"

Minna didn't seem to hear her—she was too busy staring up at the circle of sky above them. The seventh moon continued to travel, steadily moving lower and lower along its inevitable path. It looked fainter now as the black night was tinged with a hint of red.

"We're losing the moon," Minna worried aloud. Then she turned to Leo. "At this rate the dawn will beat us to it."

Leo didn't need to be told. The morning sun would bring her certain demise, she knew—but they were SO CLOSE and there was still time. They had the ghost-killing ingredients. The missing leg was all they needed, and it was SOMEWHERE HERE. She was sure of it, in a way she couldn't explain.

All of this would be over. Minna would be free. The other children would be safe. Leo's beloved Dreadwald would be rid of the Orphanmaster's poisonous rot—and Mum would be none the wiser. All evidence of Leo's mistakes would be gone; she could go back to her old unlife as the vampire daughter she was always meant to be and get her first Hunt properly under her belt FOR REAL, and everything would be fine.

"Let's keep looking," she insisted. "It must— *Oof*!"

Soot billowed upward as Leo fell squarely onto her bottom, having tripped backward over something.

A something that jutted up from the burned mountain.

"Are you all right?" Minna was asking, but Leo was too busy *thinking* to properly listen. She scooted closer.

The something was made of wood, but treated with a coating that had melted and blackened and started to congeal like frogspawn jelly in the spring. It had escaped the devouring fire—at least, it was only half burnt. An idea sparking, Leo rolled forward onto her knees.

"Leo . . . ," Minna groaned, flinching as a handful of dirt flew her way. "Hey! Would you stop that? The Anchor isn't here; this is pointless! We'll try another room. I must have been wrong."

Leo wasn't so sure about that. She swept a great armful of ash from the top of the shape, which she recognized now as a huge box, longer than it was wide. The fallen wardrobe, she realized, cast aside and toppled onto its front. The wind had blown the soot about enough to obscure it from view, innocuous among the rest of the wreckage.

Hidden within, a mysterious power was calling out to them. Minna was too busy telling Leo off to hear it.

"Did you hear me? Are you listening? Leo, I said it's not—"

There was a tremendous CRUNCH as Leo punched her hand right through the fire-weakened wood, tearing a hole with her claws. Blue-white light erupted from inside, beaming out.

"Minna! My leg!"

Only, it wasn't hers any more. The actual physical leg was gone—presumably taken away when they'd recovered the Orphanmaster's body for burial. In the leg's place, a ghostly copy remained.

"The Spirit Anchor!" Minna gasped, suddenly right at Leo's side. Her eyes were huge. "H-how did you know?"

Leo shook her head. Inside the murky wound torn by her claws, the leg shone with otherworldly magic. She stared down at it from through Minna's shoulder. "Er . . . lucky guess? I sort of . . . sensed it."

Something had told her not to give up. Perhaps it was a vampire sixth sense, she reasoned. The leg looked almost as she'd remembered it, with Dad's handiwork in every lump and bump. The only real difference was its eerie shimmer.

"Well, I suppose it *was* yours!" Minna said. "It's still a part of you, in a way. Oh, I'm . . . I'm so . . ."

All at once, Leo was overcome with a chilly feeling—like being enveloped in marble. Her vision was obscured by a film of snowy hair.

Minna was hugging her.

Leo's brain came to a juddering halt. She was a frozen statue.

Minna was *hugging* her.

Minna was . . .

Minna . . .

"You are INCREDIBLE!" Minna roared into her ear. "We've got him! Leo, you weirdo genius!"

Leo felt strange inside; her chest was full of bubbles, like she could float away.

It had been a long time since she'd had a hug. A proper hug, from a proper friend. She cuddled Button the cat all the time, but this was different.

What was she supposed to do? It probably wasn't just to sit there stiffly, motionless. Should she put an arm around Minna—or was it both arms? Was she meant to squeeze back?

It didn't matter in the end, because Minna was quickly back on task. She broke away, reaching eagerly down into the wardrobe. . . .

Minna lifted the leg out, cradling it reverently. It hummed with power, its glassy gleam sending the shadows scurrying.

Leo's breath hitched.

They had really done it.

Now to destroy the Orphanmaster.

Above them, the cloudy sky was now a deep burgundy. Minna was right, Leo realized: it wouldn't be long before the seventh moon would disappear—and the sun would rise in its place, spilling its beautiful, radiant, lethal light over the awakening world. . . .

Vampires and sunlight did not mix.

*The second Vampiric Law. The Vampire will not stand in the light of day.*

Leo knew precisely what would happen to her if the sun touched her skin—the same thing that had happened to her great-aunt Claudia. Her flesh would sear like the hottest fire and she would be turned to crumbly stone. It was an excruciatingly painful fate. A ghastly way to go. A shelter could be her lifeline.

"M-maybe we should get this back to HH," she suggested. Yes—that was a good idea. The dense canopy of the forest would provide some protection from the light on their way. They could return to base and go from there.

Except . . .

In an instant Leo felt her face drain to a paler gray. Minna startled, almost dropping the leg.

The leg that was rapidly changing color, a red blot spreading through it like blood in water.

"Oh, *pox*."

Leo had seen this same shade of red before; it was the color of the mist in the armory, and it was the color of the Orphanmaster's memory when Minna had shared her story in Hollowhome.

RED, according to the *Encyclopedia*, was often a warning. Beetle-red. Toadstool-red. The red splotches on the abdomen of the black widow spider. I sting, I bite, I will make you sick. Do not touch, do not eat, leave well alone if you don't want boils on your bottom.

As Leo and Minna looked on, watching the Orphanmaster's Spirit Anchor turn the same crimson as the sky, Leo could only think that they were in VERY BIG TROUBLE indeed.

"Let's go!" she cried. She was already running, almost tripping over her own cape as she hurtled in the direction of the forest. . . .

They were too late. Leo had barely taken two strides before the ruined orphanage reared upward, junk and charred earth roiling. Ash began to move around their feet, flowing in swirling lines that whirled faster and faster, a cyclone in the center of the wrecked drawing room.

There a mound had formed, pushing higher, taller, broader, reaching up with alarming speed. Chunks of gray stone crumbled away, revealing a red light within that shone with the same ferocity as the lost leg.

"He's here!" Minna shouted over the deafening thunder. "THIS IS IT—it has to be now!" She was grinning, and madly at that—she practically *thrummed* as she drew her poker, zeroing in on her old enemy. Her hair whipped around as she summoned her own ghostly strength, lifting her farther from the ground. The leg fell from her grasp, forgotten in the dirt.

"Minna!" Leo shouted, battling to be heard. "Minna! The leg!"

From the rising mound more debris fell away to reveal a scarlet mouth full of putrid teeth leering at them.

Falling on all fours, Leo scrambled for the Spirit Anchor. Her claws went uselessly through it.

It couldn't be moved—not by a non-ghost. She would have to work right here. She uttered a dismayed groan; above her, Minna was totally fixated on her target, on the figure emerging from the ground like the most toxic of fungi. She was deaf to Leo's pleas.

A horrible laugh oozed into the air. It was quiet at first: a sinister chuckle that made Leo's skin prickle worse than being covered in ants. Then the laugh grew louder, rising to an ugly guffaw as the blood-red ghost shook away the last of his shell.

*"Oh,"* he purred in his oily voice, "I *knew* it would be you! Exactly like your repulsive father: always where he wasn't wanted!"

"Minna! We have to go! Minna! MINNA!"

Above them, the Orphanmaster seemed as tall as Mount Moth, his ghostly body a hulking mass of red light. He had the same large ears, scraggly sideburns, and crooked teeth. The wicked glare was familiar too, but this time his eyes flashed with a quite real, quite TERRIBLE power.

"So we meet again!" The Orphanmaster spread his arms wide. Each hand was as broad as a dinner plate. "Wilhelmina. I must say, you're looking . . . rather different. Did you cut your hair?"

"I could say the same to you!" Minna bit out. Her expression pinched with disgust. "Only, you've always been a loathsome beast, haven't you? At least now your outsides match your insides!"

*"Minna!"* Leo hissed, equally as forgotten as the leg. She was drowned out as the Orphanmaster bellowed another laugh, throwing his head back.

"It's over for you!" Minna continued, her chin lifted defiantly. "You've hurt us for the last time—there's NO WAY you're getting your hands on my friends!"

"My, my. Aren't we the warrior?" the Orphanmaster sneered. He pointed at the poker. "Do you actually know how to use that thing? I seem to recall that your last attempt on my life didn't go quite according to plan. . . ."

"Enough!"

"Would your friends really WANT saving? From a horror like you? Have you seen yourself?"

"ENOUGH!"

"THEY WILL RUN SCREAMING!" the Orphanmaster crowed, his whole body ablaze. "Oh, they'll make good little servants for me, I'm sure of it. What should I do to them, Minna? How should I make them into ghosts, JUST LIKE ME?"

*"Enough,"* cut in a new voice.

The ghosts looked around in surprise at the interruption, turning to the tall figure beside them. The creature bore its razor teeth, its stare like deep pits.

"We've heard *plenty* from you!" Leo rumbled. Her voice came out deeper, right from the bottom of her belly. She could feel her body starting to evolve, becoming more monstrous, more feral. Her ribs swelled with a deep breath, bones standing out beneath her skin.

Minna frowned at her. "Le—"

"Ah! The vampire again!" the Orphanmaster exclaimed gleefully. "This gets better and better, doesn't it? Not only am I trapped here with *you*"—he shot Minna a scathing glare—"but you bring along your demonic friend, too! I wonder what your little orphan pals would think of THAT."

Leo ignored him. Instead, she stepped closer to Minna.

*"You know what we have to do,"* she whispered into the shell of Minna's ear. She kept her gaze unflinchingly on the Orphanmaster, watching him through the back of Minna's translucent head. *"It has to be now. The moon, Minna."*

Minna looked around at her. Her jaw tensed. Her lips drew thin.

Over the pines, the seventh moon was sinking dangerously low.

*We'll fulfill your purpose,* Leo thought, willing Minna to somehow understand. *We'll banish the Orphanmaster forever, so you and your friends can be fr—*

*KK-WUMPH!*

Leo flew backward, bowled over by the stinging slap of gravel. She spluttered, rubbing her eyes. A great fistful of rubble had soared right through Minna, hitting Leo squarely in the face.

Minna whipped around, mouth agape. Jerking upright, Leo brushed dust and tiny stones from her front. The cuts on her cheeks were already healing, beaded with her inky blood.

The Orphanmaster smirked.

"If I *have* to be here, we might as well make the most of it!"

Snarling, Leo pulled at her cape. The tiniest movement was enough to allow a shred of the Holy light to peek out. Inside its glass prison, the twice-blessed water winked.

A signal.

Minna raised her poker, drawing her arm back until she could look down the weapon's length. There was a slight tremor in her pose, just for a beat, and then it stilled.

From within her frail body the yell of a fighter erupted.

"AaaaAAARGH!" Minna screamed, and charged.

# 19
# Hope and Hopelessness

Leo was beginning to see why ghosts weren't to be messed with.

Minna slashed with the poker, slicing at the air. Teeth gnashing, the Orphanmaster jerked back to avoid the blow. He swung heavily forward, riding the momentum so as to return the attack, but Minna was too fast; she spiraled up into the air, a stream of soot following her.

The Orphanmaster jumped to meet her as Minna plunged, and there was a horrible sound as they clashed, like the screech of pierced armor. They were nose to nose and grimacing.

Around them, the debris came alive, great slabs of earth floating upward.

St. Frieda's was an awakening giant, and they were on its back. Leo wobbled, trying to find her feet. What was left of the walls began to crumple, dust raining down and chunks of the stonework falling like hailstones.

Disturbed by the commotion, the Spirit Anchor began to roll.

*No, no, no!* Leo scrabbled after it, but her efforts to grab the leg were in vain. Still, she could follow it at least. Finally, it came to a stop, flopping stiffly next to a melted door handle. Leo fell to her knees beside it—but what now? She looked up to where Minna was battling on, throwing herself again and again at her foe.

Minna had truly lost her marbles. She was a mad thing, wild, screaming murder.

She was the perfect distraction.

Leo knew that they had to combine the ghost-killing ingredients, but she'd never imagined it would be under such pressure: crouched in the dirt while Minna and Orphanmaster fought, the orphanage collapsing around them. Leo's instinct was to build up a ring of burnt dirt around the leg—to scrape together a hasty barrier to keep everything contained. That done, she pulled out the vial of glowing water, her teeth chattering and her bones rattling—

And ducked in the nick of time as a broken pipe went sailing through the space where her head had been.

*Too close!* Leo flattened her body to the ground. The twice-blessed water sang urgently in her palm.

*Hurry!* it pressed. *Hurry!*

Bracing herself, Leo pulled the cork.

She poured out the twice-blessed water, which soaked into the ground around the leg. It gave a fizzling wheeze as it disappeared. Watching it, Leo's mind stuttered. What was next? She rummaged in her pockets, frantic.

Sulfur. Smoke. *Yes.* Leo took the matches in one hand and the crystal in the other. She fumbled, almost dropping them. Above her, Minna and the Orphanmaster spun in a deadly dance, reeling back and forth as they fought to best each other.

*Pffft.* The first match spluttered out, its faint plume vanishing in a pathetic puff. Leo growled under her breath, groping for another. In her haste she upended the fiddly box, spilling its contents into the makeshift pit.

*No!*

With a CRUNCH like breaking glass, the Orphanmaster finally grasped hold of Minna. He shook her like a doll, and then she went careening across the brightening sky, thin limbs flailing, turning a cartwheel as she went.

"Minna!" Leo cried, and the Orphanmaster's triumphant face turned her way.

Two pairs of eyes met, one set red and one pitch black.

"What do we have *here* . . . ?"

With a jolt of staticky panic that made her toes tingle, Leo froze.

"HEY!" a voice called out, and Leo snapped around to see Minna's furious face peeking out of a cracked ceramic pot. The rest of her body emerged, brandishing the poker. "Your fight is with ME!"

The Orphanmaster sneered. "Is it? Do you think me a fool?" His eyes zeroed in on Leo, flashing in suspicion. "You're UP TO SOMETHING!"

Leo barely had time to fling herself aside.

A gigantic fist smashed into her makeshift pit with the strength of a plummeting comet. Matches cracked and split. A shower of ash rained down, making Leo cough and cover her face.

When she looked up through streaming eyes, the Orphanmaster was clutching the yellow sulfur, holding it triumphantly aloft.

"My, my," he commented, turning the crystal curiously.

His face was tinged a sickly color as it reflected the pre-dawn light. "Isn't this an interesting find?"

And with that, he squeezed hard.

The sulfur crumbled to dust, blowing uselessly away between his fingers.

"No!" Minna gasped. Leo felt herself go cold all over.

"Oh, I'm so sorry! Was that yours?" the Orphanmaster asked, feigning dismay. He tutted down at his hand as though it had acted without him. "I'm guessing that was of some significance? And—this?"

Beneath his foot was the jar of salt. It had slipped free of Leo's cape when she'd rolled aside.

"Wouldn't it be devastating," continued the Orphanmaster, his voice rising, "if something were to happen to *this* too?"

The glass creaked, putting up a fight. But with a merciless stomp, the Orphanmaster crushed it, salt exploding out to mingle with the soot and broken glass, forming a stark starburst that shot out from where the Orphanmaster stood and reached all the way to Leo.

"Whoops!" the fiend crowed. The girls stared—Minna with pure, boiling hatred, and Leo with disbelief. She had been so foolish; they weren't ready at all. Their ghost-killing plan had been full of holes to begin with—neither of the girls knew exactly what was supposed to happen once they had all the components—but now it had been quite literally TRAMPLED on by the Orphanmaster.

Leo bent her head, screwing her eyes closed, her claws and fangs clenched tight. She felt hot lava rear up inside her.

"You . . . you remind me a lot of my big sister," she said with dangerous calm. In her mind she was sitting quietly in the eye of the storm that was swirling inside her.

The Orphanmaster stopped laughing.

Leo jabbed a clawed finger. "You're supposed to be an ADULT!" she shouted, letting her anger ignite. Her black eyes flashed and her fanged mouth snarled. "You became the Orphanmaster! It was your JOB to care—to finish Agnes's work—but you're nothing but a big, CRUEL BABY!"

The Orphanmaster's sunken face twisted. "Don't you speak her name. Don't you *dare*."

"What would Agnes think if she could see you now? Undoing everything she worked for! Hurting the children she wanted to help!"

At his sides the Orphanmaster's fists clenched. "You unbelievable, *ignorant* . . . Her *work* was hunting down MONSTERS like you!"

Leo blinked. What? Agnes . . . was a hunter?

"Hah!" bit out the Orphanmaster. "That's right!"

Hunters were so few and far between, these nights. Leo had

never in her unlife encountered a hunter in the Dreadwald; she had always assumed that Lady Sieglinde had eaten them all.

It couldn't be true. The kind, gentle Agnes from Minna's story—out slaying monsters? Slaying VAMPIRES?

The Orphanmaster lunged for Leo, taking advantage of her shocked stupor. Her claws went harmlessly through him, but the ghost's fist felt solid as he clipped her shoulder. The blow glanced off and Leo barely felt a thing—adrenaline had taken over, making her giddy. It was the feeling of bounding through the forest. It was the feeling of nosediving off the western tower. Leo snarled as she hit back, sailing uselessly through the Orphanmaster's body.

*So this is fighting a ghost*, Leo thought. It was terribly unfair; being untouchable was a fatal advantage. Leo swiped at her enemy's legs, trying to trip him with a low kick, but phased straight through him again. The Orphanmaster barked a laugh, twisting to follow her.

"Even I don't know how many vampires Agnes slayed! You presume to tell ME what she would have wanted—she would have staked you where you stood!"

A hard hand grasped her arm, fingernails digging in. The room did a somersault as the Orphanmaster flipped her.

Leo hit the ground and slammed into the dirt, and her brain sloshed in her skull.

The Orphanmaster was instantly in her ear. "I should be with her now! I'm dead, aren't I? I should be with Agnes! And what do I get? STUCK HERE, with YOU!"

Struggling, Leo tried to scratch, crying out in frustration as her claws went cleanly, harmlessly through him.

"DON'T YOU SEE?" the Orphanmaster gloated. "IT'S HOPELESS! Perhaps I will finish what Agnes started, after all! One more pathetic little vampire out the way, before I visit my orphan friends?"

Leo *couldn't* see; thick fingers covered her face. The Orphanmaster could very well crush her, like the sulfur and the salt jar. But though her heart fluttered with panic, Leo's mind was suddenly calm again.

Because the Orphanmaster was wrong, she realized.

They couldn't be hopeless. It was impossible to be hopeless.

Hope, in fact, was the only thing they had left. There had to be another way to win. A way to destroy him before all was lost . . .

Leo managed to wrench free enough to turn her head, before the Orphanmaster squashed her again.

Through her swimming vision, she thought she saw a familiar figure. A figure with long, pale hair and a tattered nightgown. A figure who bent over the pit with the red leg—the Spirit Anchor they had worked so hard to destroy.

*Leave it, Minna*, thought Leo floatily. *We need another way. No sulfur. No smoke.*

Leo had successfully added the twice-blessed water to the pit. Some of the salt had ended up in there too, after the jar had exploded beneath the Orphanmaster's foot. The matches had been strewn uselessly everywhere.

But it wasn't enough; the *Companion* had been clear about that. They needed all the components to kill a ghost.

Then, behind her curtain of hair, a smoky stream blew from Minna's mouth.

Leo blinked hard once, twice. It really looked like Minna was breathing smoke onto the Spirit Anchor.

It also seemed . . . like the leg was glowing, stronger and brighter than before. The red color bled away, shining instead with a white light, almost Holy light. Leo's black pupils turned to slits and she drew in a sharp breath.

The Orphanmaster's grasp faltered. Leo felt the pressure lift, felt herself drifting back.

"What are you doing?" someone demanded in a faraway voice. Leo winced as Minna's blazing form advanced toward her. She was a beacon, beaming out, a star fallen to earth. The poker glinted in her fist. She was more of an avenging angel than a ghost now.

*How?* Leo wondered numbly, in some dark and distant

part of her consciousness. She lay where she was, unmoving even as the Orphanmaster staggered over her. He was aflame too, drawing higher, broader, furiously ablaze.

"What have you done?" he rasped. "Minna . . . Wilhelmina, you . . ."

"This is it," Minna replied gravely. The ground made way for her as she moved, soot rippling away. She radiated a fierce power, in a way that reminded Leo unsettlingly of her mum. The look on Minna's face was the same one she had worn the night of the first moon, reading those life-ruining letters while the Orphanmaster slept. . . .

With a *thunk*, Minna tossed the white leg into what remained of the ashy nest. She raised the poker high above her head.

"This is for my friends. And for me. For all of us, for JUSTICE!"

"You know nothing of *justice*!" spat the Orphanmaster. His mouth twisted; he had realized the very real danger he was in. "Nothing in this world is *just*! It wasn't *just* to my Agnes! We ought to be together now, but here I am! Why should any of you be any different? What makes you so special that you should be spared?"

"Spared? I've never been spared, not by anything! But it's too late now. This is the end for both of us, for—"

But Minna didn't finish that thought.

In the distance, a glaring flood spilled from behind the peaks of Mount Moth.

It soared over the pine-topped Dreadwald forest.

It swept through Otto's End.

It filled every nook, every divot, every darkened doorway and gloomy alley.

Where there had been shadows, there was brilliant, gleaming, dreadful DAYLIGHT.

Minna jolted, looking back over her shoulder at the sunrise. In her hands the poker vanished into nothing. They had run out of time. The pale morning orb was emerging, tingeing the red sky with purples and blues as it went. Not even the thunderclouds could obscure it.

For a hundred years, Leo had only seen the dawn in paintings and in the illustrations in her books. She had forgotten how beautiful the real thing was. She was transfixed, even as her skin began to prickle.

"Leo!" someone called out to her, and then there Minna was, at her side. Leo felt a thin, icy grip shake her shoulder. "Leo—you have to go! The sun, it's coming up. Oh . . . oh no . . ."

Minna was fading away, her ghostly power depleted. She looked down at herself, at her hands as they began to turn into mist. Behind her, the Orphanmaster watched them. His mouth quirked upward and his thick arms were folded across his chest; he was the picture of smug satisfaction.

"No, no, no . . . I'm not finished here!" Minna cried. "I can't sleep now!"

"It's . . . it's okay, Minna—"

"It's not too late!" Minna looked frantically over at her, as though expecting Leo to burst into flames at any moment. "You can still run! You can make it to the forest!"

Leo wasn't so sure. Her mind was awhirl; the light was making it difficult to think. It felt like a bad dream.

"GO! I'll meet you at HH!" Minna choked, vanishing up to her shoulders. "You'd better be there! Don't you dare leave me!"

Looking out past the crumbling walls of the orphanage, Leo's gaze was drawn to where the dark tree line met the sky. Her breath caught in her chest. Her whole body hitched as though something was tugging at a wire pierced right through her heart. Minna was staring too, her dismayed face all that was left of her as she continued to vanish.

Leo hadn't known, up until that moment, that it was possible for something to be the most DREADFUL, DIRE thing you ever had the misfortune of witnessing—and, at the same time, for it to be an UTTER MIRACLE of impossible proportions.

Behind the Dreadwald pines, the white face of the seventh moon sunk down.

It fell lower.

And lower.

And was gone.

# 20
# The Seventh Sinking Moon

As abruptly as she had unraveled, Minna's body began to re-emerge.

Her arms knitted to her shoulders, joined by thin hands with bony fingers. Her nightgown flapped around her knobbly knees. Her delicate feet and toes, forever bare despite the cold, skimmed the ground. In her hand, the poker rematerialized as though unsheathed from the air.

"I'm still here? What . . . what is this?" Minna breathed, looking down at it. She was *glowing* now, brighter than any of the HH fireflies or the luminous mushrooms in the forest. She was like light trapped inside a crystal, reflected and amplified. Her poker glinted all the way to its pronged tip.

"The seventh moon!" Leo gasped out, feeling bizarrely as though she didn't have enough air in her body. Her useless heart was pounding. Her useless lungs were heaving. Looking at Minna stung her eyes.

"Then we're out of time," Minna choked out. She tried desperately to pull Leo upright, but Leo's legs wouldn't cooperate. "Please, Leo, I . . . I can't do this. He's won; the *Companion* WARNED us. We need to go!"

"You *can*. Look at yourself!" Leo wheezed out a frustrated groan. How could Minna not see? "It's your *fully realized power*, Minna. THAT'S what the *Companion* said. This is you! You're brilliant! And terrifying." The effort of speaking was too much. Leo crumpled, slumping into the ashes again. "Ugh . . . M-Minna, don't give up, it's not over y—"

She was cut off by a screeching crunch: the Orphanmaster's fist in Minna's back. The two flew over Leo's head, clear of the still glowing Spirit Anchor. Leo twisted in time to see Minna whip around and stick her foe with the poker, her gappy teeth bared furiously.

"What is THIS, then?" he crowed, seizing the poker in his chest as though to snap it in half, with Minna still doggedly attached to the other end. He flung them both aside. "Why, I feel as though I've been reborn, don't you?" The Orphanmaster too was burning brightly, easily three times the size of Minna. He swept a dramatic arm as if to gesture to the room around them, his face lighting up in malevolent glee. . . .

All around them, what was left of the orphanage sprang to life.

The ruined furniture rose up, taking on a malevolent red glow. The charred desk dragged itself forward on its two remaining legs, drawers clacking, oozing inky slime. The wardrobe flapped its blackened doors uselessly beneath itself. The armchair took a sagging step and its remaining feet crumbled under its weight.

"Oh!" the Orphanmaster breathed, looking down at his own hands. "Oh, I do LIKE this!" He thrummed with new strength, his fists crackling with energy when he clenched them tight. As he rose up into the air, tendrils of newfound power sunk down into St. Frieda's like evil roots.

Leo's eyes swiveled, frantically looking for Minna. Her body was heavy and uncooperative in the roiling ash. She wanted to cry out, but her throat stuck and her jaws wouldn't open. A smashed chandelier began to whirl like a spinning top, dancing madly toward her. She managed a clumsy roll before it smashed into the soot, inches from her face.

"WHAT ARE YOU DOING?" the chandelier bellowed, glass teeth gnashing like an angry dog. "YOU CALL THIS

FLOOR SCRUBBED? I'VE SEEN CLEANER TILES AT THE SLAUGHTERHOUSE!"

The poker whistled through the air, skewering the chandelier and sending crystal shards scattering.

"LAZY LITTLE BRATS!" The glass from the chandelier sputtered and pinged. "YOU'LL LICK THIS FLOOR BEFORE I'M DONE WITH YOU!"

"Oh, Leo!" Minna was there again, at her side, the poker flying faithfully back into her hand. She kicked the chandelier aside. "What IS this?"

Far away, from within the belly of the building, a thunderous racket heralded the awakening of more possessed furniture. The rubble bulged, disturbed by the movement.

"He's infected the whole orphanage!" Minna shouted over the din. "Hnngh!" She heaved Leo's useless body aside as the fireplace spat, a thick sludge of soot and wet dirt rolling out like a long tongue.

"LIGHTS OUT BY SIX O'CLOCK!" snapped the desk.

"I WANT ALL OF YOU UP BY FOUR IN THE MORNING, SHARP!" the fallen wardrobe added, strings of black rot sticking to its doors. "ANYONE NOT WORKING WILL HAVE TWENTY LASHES!"

A melted floor lamp took a swing at them both, forcing Minna to battle it away. All around them, the furniture was advancing like an Undead horde, phantom voices ringing out. In the midst of it all, the Orphanmaster floated serenely down to where Leo was lying. He was a rotten tyrant of a king, surveying his miserable kingdom. His beaming smile was mocking.

"What's the matter with you, then?" The Orphanmaster turned his face to the sun. "Looks like it will be a beautiful day! Aaah . . ." He planted his huge hands on his hips. "You know, Agnes used to love these sorts of days. Crisp and clear. Perfect for going for a walk, perhaps painting by the river—but, of course, this was after a long night hunting the likes of YOU."

"Leave her alone!" Minna shouted, wringing the lamp by its skinny neck. A black-splattered picture frame swooped down like an enraged hawk.

"WHAT'S THAT?" it mocked. "YOU WANT YOUR *MUM*? ARE YOU STUPID, CHILD?"

The WRONG sort of feeling was back, spreading all over as Leo flinched away from the Orphanmaster. Her Undead nerves were sparking in a way they never had before. Shakily, stiffly, she managed to pull her feet beneath herself. The motion opened a sizzling wound on her exposed knee, bubbling and splitting. Another on her cheek sent agony lancing up into her temple and down her neck.

Leo was glad that Minna hadn't seen it. She didn't want

to be remembered like this, turning gruesomely inside out in the sun. Behind her, her friend was still desperately fighting back the advancing furniture. Minna grasped the squawking picture frame like a shield, deflecting an inky glob of rot before it could reach her. The desk rattled its drawers and growled.

The Orphanmaster squatted down to scrutinize Leo. "My Agnes always had a stake hidden on her belt, even after she quit," he said cheerily. "Truly her mother's daughter. Came from a long line of noble vampire hunters, cut unfairly short. You should have seen her—she really was BRUTAL. She knew all the most painful ways to kill a beast like you."

Leo's skull was too tight. When she dipped her head, a horrible pressure mounted behind her eyes, threatening to explode them in their sockets. Still, she managed a warning snarl, pitching higher as the Orphanmaster lifted her chin to look into her face.

"You know," he murmured, "I've always been so very CURIOUS about what happens to a vampire in sunlight."

He would soon have his answer. Her gray skin was turning patchy in places, flaking away on the breeze like ancient paint. Beneath, the flesh was pale and veiny, struck through with marbling lines. Leo was burning up and freezing to her core.

There was a yell from somewhere far away: a war cry.

Minna came blasting in on a wave of smoke, slicing with the poker, trailing the remains of a smashed table behind her. She was so fast, she was almost a blur as she barreled into the Orphanmaster. The ghosts clashed over Leo's head, swinging each other around. Leo's skin burned as they swept over and through her.

Minna dragged the Orphanmaster by his hair, then by his ear, clawing madly at whatever part of him she could reach. The Spirit Anchor was lying beneath the Orphanmaster's feet, kicked about in the ash. A sooty cloud rose about them, half concealing them from view. Where Leo lay, the menacing army of furniture was drawing alarmingly close. . . .

There was a rush of air, the ripple of a sonic explosion, and then Minna was flying backward, the force propelling her through the rubble. The Orphanmaster smoothed down his pajamas and stretched out a crick in his neck. With an amused huff, he bent to scoop up the Spirit Anchor where it was still pulsating with its brilliant radiance and gave the leg a few experimental swings.

Minna came back at him, undeterred and snarling—only to be sent careening away by the Spirit Anchor when it swung to meet her.

"I should have been a sportsman!" The Orphanmaster laughed, pleased with himself. He turned to Leo, puffing with the effort of fending off Minna's attack. "Don't you agree?"

Leo wasn't listening. The ghosts were evenly matched; for all Minna's ferocious agility, the Orphanmaster had the advantage of size. But Minna had something that the Orphanmaster didn't. She had a hidden trick up the sleeve of her nightgown—even if she didn't believe it herself.

Minna had a VAMPIRE.

"C'mon, Leo," Leo slurred to herself, struggling to speak with her swollen tongue and locked jaw. Her blood, dormant for a century, was now fizzing in her veins. "Grub-for-brains. Cockroach. Mealyworm."

"What? What was that?"

The ache was like pressing on a bruise, dull and throbbing. There was no way Leo could stand, not like this, but her mind screamed at her body to move. The Spirit Anchor hummed in the Orphanmaster's meaty hands, beckoning her.

"Rude to the very end. Can't say I'm surprised." A ghostly hand punched her in the chest, flipping her onto her back. "Looks like our time is up!" He smirked, noticing Minna now struggling with the possessed wardrobe, its flapping doors dangerously close to where Leo lay.

Leo panted, seizing up all over. Her limbs felt stony-stiff. Her scorched flesh pulled her tight in a withering cocoon, trapping Leo in her own skin.

She was dying. Again.

"Ugh. Now, isn't this a grisly sight?" The Orphanmaster grimaced down at her. "So *this* is what happens to a vampire in the sun. No less than you deserve."

He held up a hand to halt the possessed furniture; he wanted his kill for himself. Minna looked up through her pale hair, withdrawing the poker from the wardrobe's back with a snarl.

Leo twitched. She couldn't speak; only a guttural sound came forth, her throat sticking shut.

*Mum*, she thought desperately, black tears pattering to the ground. *Mum. Dad.*

They weren't coming, of course. How could they? They had no idea where she was or what she'd been doing. They thought she was safe in her bed, just like every other day.

"This," the Orphanmaster continued, his whiskered face looming closer to hers, "is what you get for helping a *trespassing criminal.* Not to mention a MAD criminal! Wrong in the head—exactly like her miserable father, probably, and whatever woman was stupid enough to marry him. What did you think was going to happen?" He straightened up again, spreading his arms wide. "Come, now. You wanted to be the hero, didn't you? You wanted to swoop in and save POOR MINNA and the other orphans—boohoo! So sad!

"I *would* feel sorry for you, but I've wasted so much of my pity on undeserving children. I'm afraid there is none left for you, vampire." He perked up, making eye contact with Minna where she had been silently seething, stunned by his horrible speech. "Ah! And by the way, please don't worry about your precious friend there. I'll be sure to take very good care of her—and the other orphans, of course."

Leo's eyes swiveled to stare at him.

"Perhaps they should burn alive," the Orphanmaster said slowly. "As I did."

Leo wanted to scream. She wanted to lash out. Though she couldn't see Minna, she could feel her rage like an echo of her own.

Slowly, her gaze was pulled to a pointed shape, lying innocently in the soot. It was slightly curved and bound in a pouch of worn leather. Carved into the handle was an ancient inscription, written in a mysterious language.

There was no mistaking it: it was Minna's dagger. Leo had carried it with her this whole time; it must have tumbled from her cape when she fell. A sliver of an idea crawled across her mind and rooted there.

*Salt, sulfur, smoke.*

"I told you, YOU LEAVE HER ALONE!" someone yelled—Minna, erupting from directly beneath them, a livid firework of white light. In a fit of desperation Minna flung the poker with all her might, aiming for the Spirit Anchor.

The rod screamed through the air like a javelin and hit the Orphanmaster in the shoulder instead, puncturing all the way through to the other side. The fiend roared, spit flying.

It was so bright now, Leo could hardly see. Her whole arm shuddered, her claws fluttering as if to try to close into a fist.

*Salt-sulfur-smoke, twice-blessed water, the glow of a sunrise . . .*

With a tortured groan, Leo heaved her body sideways, curling in on herself, reaching . . .

And fell uselessly back again. The ghosts grappled above her, Minna darting forward, battling the Orphanmaster away from where Leo lay.

*The glow of a sunrise! And . . . and . . .*

It was torment. Leo was fading in and out of herself; her mind was blanking, snapping back and forth between consciousness and oblivion. The narrow world flashed in and out, punctuated by an agony worse than anything she'd ever felt.

A final, desperate push rolled Leo onto her front, tipping forward. Her shaking arm folded beneath her, claws closing around the dagger.

*A weapon of intent!*

The dagger thrummed to life, an impossible force awakening in her hand. In the distance a clanging sound registered on the edge of her consciousness, over the song of the Otto's End clock tower as the bells began their morning greeting.

*I'm not done!*

*I'm not THROUGH WITH YOU, ORPHANMASTER!*

But Leo was on the brink of death: a shadowy precipice over which there was no returning. Her wretched body was all but done for, ready to give up.

Except.

Clutching the dagger so hard it was an extension of her own arm, Leo let out a tormented hiss. She couldn't let Minna be hurt; she couldn't lose her only friend—not after she had been so lonely for so long.

There was one thing she had left to give. Even if it didn't work, she had to try.

Leo's mind's eye turned inward, tuning into something deeply, darkly powerful. Something instinctive for the vampire. Something she had sworn that she would never, EVER do again. If she could have howled, she would have.

*I can do it, I can do it, I can, I CAN!*

In a flurrying frenzy of frantic wings, Leo's shriveled body burst into a swarm of black bats.

Leo swept toward the Orphanmaster, zeroing in on her target, despite being left dizzied by her GRIMWALK. Her two eyes had become numerous, multiple little bodies moving as one. The rush of air beneath her many wings was exhilarating. She felt victorious, unstoppable . . .

She was going to die, she knew. But she would go out fighting. She wouldn't lie there and crumble away.

*I'm not afraid of YOU!*

The bat swarm sped through the Orphanmaster's scarlet body, through the white Spirit Anchor that had once been Leo's leg. Angry squeaks were her war cry. The flapping of wings was oncoming thunder.

Leo's true form—by now hairless and horrifying, the skin almost entirely peeled away—materialized in front of her enemy, falling forward into the Orphanmaster as she dispelled the GRIMWALK. She pulled the dagger free of its sheath, her stony fingers cracking painfully. Whether it was enough, she couldn't know, but the look of shock on the Orphanmaster's face was an image she would take with her into the after-afterlife.

Letting gravity carry her, Leo plunged Minna's dagger through the Spirit Anchor.

And stuck there.

The air frosted over. There was a peculiar smell—like wet earth, seconds before a lightning strike. If Leo had any hair left, she was sure it would be standing on end. She sagged backward, looking down in shock at where the dagger was sticking out of the Spirit Anchor, still clutched in the Orphanmaster's arms.

The Orphanmaster's eyes bulged. His mouth cracked open in disbelief.

"YOU—" he managed, before a beaming light rose up in his throat, choking him. It poured from his mouth and his ears and his eye sockets, consuming him from the inside out. His body began to splinter into motes of floating ghostly energy. The Spirit Anchor disappeared, melting away through the Orphanmaster's grasping fingers.

*Not me,* Leo thought, boggling at the dagger. *Minna.*

It was meant to be Minna's POKER, wasn't it? The weapon of intent. She looked up, letting her head tilt back. Minna stared down at her, wide-eyed.

Leo wanted to laugh. She wanted to cry. Instead, only a thin wheeze erupted from her as the girls tumbled into the ash. Reality appeared to tear apart before their astonished eyes.

With a sucking WHOOSH, a curious rupture opened in the air to the Orphanmaster's left; a seam in the VERY FABRIC OF EXISTENCE had split wide open. Leo had never seen anything like it—not in the Dreadwald, not in Dad's lab, not even in the library. Behind the rupture, a frothing, spitting, churning vortex of time and space began to draw the Orphanmaster through, pulling him away in ribbons.

The dagger and the poker clattered to the ground. All around them, the watching furniture collapsed, slumping lifelessly back into its own ooze.

Minna was saying something in Leo's ear—something frantic, something important—but it was lost in the shrill whistling of the vortex.

*You were wrong to do what you did,* Leo thought, strangely peaceful as she watched the Orphanmaster go, his contorted face silently screaming. *I'm sorry about your Agnes. But you were wrong. She wouldn't have wanted you to become THIS.*

There was an airy rush and a faint *pop*, and the hungry rupture closed, coiled in on itself, and vanished—taking the Orphanmaster with it.

A final, rattling breath emerged from Leo's collapsed throat.

The world was calming. The Orphanmaster's corrupting rot was dying away, each inky, oily fingerprint beginning to dry up.

The bustle of the awakening town sounded far, far away; perhaps soon Father Pavlov would come by and find her. Rather, he would find Leo's dry, crumbling body, blowing away on the wind. The pain had morphed into a kind of numbness, sliding over the line between wakefulness and sleep. She didn't feel Minna clasp her ruined hand; she was too busy drifting.

It was done. Minna's purpose was fulfilled. Her mission was complete; she had defeated the Orphanmaster and, unknown to her friends, saved all of their lives.

*We did it. We did it.*

*It's over.*

*Mum . . . It wasn't a human . . . but it was a hunt. . . .*

In that moment, the battle won, Leo the vampire slipped quietly away.

Or she would have, but for the HORRENDOUS RACKET that assaulted her ears, like a stack of pots being upended. Then the cutlery drawer. Then the entire kitchen.

"MISS LEO!"

# 21
# A Knight of the Land

"OH, MISS LEO! Oh—OH, little one . . ."

A bulky shadow fell over Leo. There was merciful darkness and merciless light. Leo—if indeed Leo even existed any more—was no longer in control.

Then there were hands on her shoulder and her hip. Or perhaps not hands at all: *gauntlets*, turning her gently. Even the slightest movement caused a new wave of nauseous pain to come creeping back in. Leo's eyes rolled in their lidless sockets and a high, thin sound escaped her.

"Hang on, Miss Leo! Hold on! Don't you go anywhere!"

*Mar . . . ged?* she thought, considering that maybe she truly HAD gone mad.

Her whole body lurched, handled clumsily upright. She could feel herself sliding down, her arms and legs slotting into place.

It was cooler inside the armor, and blessedly black. Marged's visor came down with a fang-rattling KH-CHUNK, sealing what was left of Leo inside. Through the slats, Leo saw the red plume bobbing forward into her field of vision.

"Don't you worry!" Marged's voice echoed around her. "Don't you fret! I'm here. Let's get you home."

*Wait!* Leo wanted to say. She gnashed her teeth. Her dry eyes had no tears left to shed; instead, she wriggled sharply, feeling like an insect in its chrysalis. Or rather, an insect that had been repeatedly set on fire, thrown off a cliff, and run over by a herd of cattle.

"Hgggh . . . ," she gritted out, her ruined voice box stuttering to life in the dark. Talking felt like swallowing sand, scraping and scratching her throat. "'Ar-ged . . ."

Leo couldn't feel her face. Her lips didn't move, if indeed she had any lips left. She could only imagine the state she was in.

"Hush now; you must save your strength!"

Her first step was a cacophony of metal, impossibly loud from inside. The next step was even more deafening still, making Leo's ears ring as Marged clomped her way up and over the heap of rubble.

Rattling, crashing, clanking. A tinny sound, echoing within the confined space.

They left Otto's End behind, each of Marged's long strides covering more and more ground. Every flying step jarred Leo's battered body, jostled inside the armor. Her joints cried for mercy. Her skull pulsated with a tired ache.

From through the sliver of the visor, the forest floor flashed by at a startling pace. Gauntlets pistoned back and forth. Every now and again, the feathery plume flopped forward into view and then bobbed back again.

It was too much for sore eyes.

"Hold on, Miss Leo! Miss . . . Miss Leo?"

Then, to the immediate relief of what was left of her, there ceased to be anything of Leo von Motteberg at all.

For a long time afterward, a select few in Otto's End would swear they had seen a knight dressed in armor, with a bright red plume in their helmet, emerging from the St. Frieda's ruin and running toward the forest. No one believed them;

they were only children, after all, with the wild imaginations of youth.

The *sensible* people knew that it was impossible. The Royal Guard never ventured this far from the city limits. Nothing of importance ever happened in a town like Otto's End.

The rumors persisted, however, and would do so for years to come. Years after St. Frieda's Home was rebuilt into something warm and welcoming, years after the children had themselves grown up and grown old with their families, the stories remained, of wraiths and hauntings and of a mysterious knight.

*Something* had happened in Otto's End, Minna's friends were sure of it.

Back in the present and wrapped in his blanket, the boy called Walter leaned out of the attic window above the baker's. He swore he could hear the clanging clatter of armor, echoing through the distant pines. Growing fainter and fainter, it sounded as though it was heading toward the mountain.

# 22
# Freedom

Resurfacing from beneath a slumberous sea, the girl called Leo opened her eyes.

She was in her room and tucked so tightly into bed she had to fight her arms free. Sitting weakly upright, she saw that the shutters were safely closed and the drapes were safely drawn, and at the foot of her bed was Button, also safe and sound. His thin back rose and fell as he slept, and his toilet-brush fur stuck up in its usual tufts.

Looking blearily around, it took a while for her exhausted eyes to make sense of what she was seeing. Her bedroom was mostly as Leo had left it—if less dusty than before. Marged had probably fussed in here; a suspiciously tidy room was her calling card. Pulling herself out from her blanket, Leo scooted on her bottom until her toes could touch the floorboards.

She stretched, all the way from her left foot to the tips of her fingers, her long spine bending back with a satisfying pop. Her right leg was waiting for her, resting against the bedside table. As always, it buckled easily into place.

Crossing the floor, Leo hobbled stiffly to the bathroom. The water was icier than usual against her skin as she stood at the sink and washed her face clean, lingering over her healed nose and mouth. She traced the new skin with her clawtips, marveling at the familiar shapes of her face. Everything seemed to be present and mostly correct. Her fingertips felt tender when she swiped them over her scalp, and she was briefly grateful that she didn't have a reflection to see what she actually looked like.

Her hair was growing back, short and particularly bristly in places, but starting to curl in others. Her eyebrows were reappearing too. Only her eyelashes were still lagging—but then, she *had* regrown her actual eyelids, which had probably taken a while. Leo swallowed queasily, trying not to linger on the thought.

But.

She was alive.

Well, as alive as a vampire could be. *Undead* would be more accurate; that was to say, she hadn't completely turned to stone and crumbled away at St. Frieda's.

But it had been close. Leo held on to the sink for support, her knee trembling. What had happened? It had been like a cyclone that had swept her up and spun her about. She remembered the Orphanmaster, spit flying as he laughed. She remembered Minna at her side, fiercely battling the fiend back, protecting Leo from the possessed furniture. . . .

*Minna.* What had happened to Minna? Trying to remember was like trying to hold on to water in her cupped hands; the details flowed away from her before she could grasp them. . . .

"Miss Leo?" someone said, and Leo jerked her head up. Marged was in the doorway, having moved more quietly than she had ever managed before. Either that, or Leo really had been distracted. "You're awake! Oh, thank goodness!"

"It looks that way," Leo said, her voice coming out in an ugly croak. "Marged . . . I . . . How long?"

"H-how long, Miss Leo?"

"How long was I asleep? I feel . . . I feel . . ." She looked at her hands, inspecting her claws. They felt weird beneath even the slightest pressure.

She couldn't quite put the sensation into words. Perhaps *raw* would be closest. It was like being brand-new.

Marged nodded. "I know, little one. It's been some time. The healing process—it takes a lot." She shuffled the pointed sabbatons where her feet would have been, seemingly reluctant to explain. "That is . . . You see, it was weeks before I could even move you from the crypt. . . ."

"I was in the crypt?" Leo's stomach flip-flopped. The crypt was the murky warren where their ancestors slept: some as ashes in urns, some as bones in coffins, others as stony statues that had been burned to death in sunlight, their agonized faces contorted. All were suspended in their deathly eternity.

Every von Motteberg (or what was left of them) ended up there, sooner or later. If a stake or the sun didn't get you, there was a kind of vampiric madness that took over the mind after a few thousand years. Immortality was nice and all, but it came at a cost. Leo had only visited the crypt on special occasions, and only ever with Dad to supervise.

"I'm afraid so," Marged confirmed. "Lady Sieglinde thought it best to take you down there—you really were in the most terrible state. On the very brink. I wasn't sure if . . . if I was too late, after all. After you went to sleep, we feared you might be lost to us."

With a clanking clatter, Marged marched over. Her gauntlets were gentle when she took Leo's face between them. "I am very glad, Miss Leo, that you are still here," she said seriously.

"If not for your friend, if you had been exposed to the sun for even a moment longer . . . I'm afraid you would have perished."

*My friend?* Leo looked to the doorway, where the fuzzy bottom of a brown, eight-legged creature was scuttling out of view. *Ah. Rodrigo. I should have guessed.*

"I must say, the shock of encountering a talking spider was somewhat eclipsed by his news," Marged said drily, turning Leo's face back toward her. "It is not every night that you are told that the young lady of the house is off *battling ghosts*, hmmm?"

Leo's mouth cracked open. CAUGHT. She groped for an excuse, any excuse, but Marged just shook her helmet in exasperation. Her red plume puffed up and she finally let it out. . . .

"Oh, Miss Leo, WHAT WERE YOU THINKING? You have been raised better than this! You *know* how dangerous they are!" Marged scolded, smushing Leo's cheeks. "There is a reason why vampires and ghosts have fought each other for so long. *That there* is a truly ancient and bloody feud, the sort of thing a young girl should never get herself entangled in!"

"I . . . I . . ."

Behind her visor, the empty space in Marged's head managed to look especially disappointed.

Leo knew what came next.

"I was *so worried* about you," Marged told her, and Leo's heart weighed as heavy as a rock. Carefully, she took hold of Marged's gauntlets, coaxing them to rest on her shoulders instead. Her mouth wobbled and her eyebrows pinched together.

What could she say? That it was her fault? That she needed to help Minna, no matter the cost?

That she'd finally found a real friend . . . ?

"I'm sorry, Marged. I know you must have been scared." Leo gnawed on her lower lip, which felt softer and not as chapped as it used to be. "I was scared too—really, *really* scared."

"You have to promise me. Promise you'll never, EVER do anything like that again."

"I promise, Marged, I promise. . . ."

Letting her go, Marged rattled where she stood; Leo had never known her to get this worked up. "Honestly, when I took the job, I never knew being a nanny would be so difficult—"

"Butler," Leo interjected, but was ignored.

"That moment, when the spider told me where you were . . . I felt I might burst. The thought that we might never see you again—it was too much, little one. It was the most . . . unspeakably awful feeling in the world. I hope you NEVER know it for yourself."

Realization overcame Leo, listening to the knight. A

disjointed memory trickled across her mind: the agonizing throb of her battered body, banged around inside a suit of armor.

*It was you*, she thought, staring. *You knew I was in trouble and you came to help.*

*You came to save me.*

Her eyes stung. Her face felt hot.

Leo leapt at Marged, wrapping her arms around her cool body and burying her face into her metal breastplate.

*I'm sorry,* she thought over and over. The enormity of what she'd done came barreling in. Tears overflowed as she finally, finally allowed herself to cry, so hard that her back heaved and her shoulders hitched. *I'm sorry*, she thought, *I'm sorry*, but what came out of her mouth was, "Thank you, thank you . . ."

"There now, Miss Leo—don't you cry. You have to save your strength."

"I'm really sorry, M-Marged, I had no idea. . . ."

"I know."

"It was so horrible." More tears bubbled; Marged's armor was smeared with black. Leo drew in a wet breath, swiping her pajama sleeve beneath her runny nose. "It was the *worst thing*. I thought I was done. I was ready to die."

"But you didn't." Marged's gauntlet was comforting on

top of Leo's head, stroking her stubbly hair. "You did what you had to do to help your friend."

The Orphanmaster. He truly was gone.

And, therefore, so was Minna. Her mission was won. She could go into the afterlife in peace, no longer trapped as a ghost.

They would never see each other again.

*This is what you wanted*, Leo reminded herself, letting Marged rock her. She felt so small, like a helpless baby. Her heart was painfully hollow, like part of her was missing now. *This was the plan. To help Minna fulfill her purpose, and set her free.*

"In spite of everything . . . even though you SHOULD HAVE TOLD ME what you were doing"—Marged sighed grudgingly—"I am so very *proud* of you. But do not under any circumstances tell Lady Sieglinde."

"Mum doesn't know?"

"She believes there was an accident, while you were playing in the Dreadwald. That you had been trapped by a falling tree. I had to think fast, Miss Leo; it was the best I could do at the time. A lie—however necessary—is not an easy thing, and especially not when you are lying to *your* mother."

Leo sucked in a breath. She knew very well what Marged was referring to—the problem of the Waxing Moon was still one that she would need to tackle, when her strength had returned. There was no time to reflect, however, as Marged spoke up again above her head:

"Lady Sieglinde didn't leave your side for nights down in the crypt. None of us could coax her away, not even to eat. We really did think . . . you might not come back. She will be so relieved to hear you are awake."

Mum had . . . looked over her? While she was asleep?

Mum had WORRIED for her. Leo couldn't believe it. This had never happened before.

"A-and Dad?" she asked. "Does he know what really happened?"

Marged shrugged, ushering Leo back to bed. "Lord Dietmar knows better than to argue with Lady Sieglinde. He worries for you girls, but I do not think he will uncover the truth; he's not exactly an expert detective. He's been spending even more time in his lab—I think perhaps he rather needed the distraction of a fiddly experiment or two. We've all been worried sick about you, Miss Leo. And I do mean all of us."

The visor turned meaningfully toward the nightstand, where, to Leo's astonished eyes, there was a GET WELL SOON card written in wobbly, childish handwriting. Whoever had penned it would have had to use their whole fist to hold the quill steady. The ink had still smudged. On the front was a crude drawing of Leo, complete with cape and wild hair and Button sitting at her feet. The inside read:

*Don't actually die, stinkworm.*
*From Emmeline*

Next to it was a boxy parcel wrapped in brown paper, neatly bound with string. It looked like the corners had been pressed to make it extra neat.

"What's this?" Leo asked, placing a weak hand on top of it.

Marged inclined her head. "Why don't we open it and find out?"

Sitting up in bed, propped up by a ridiculous amount of pillows, Leo looked over the attached note. Her cheeks felt suddenly wet again.

*For my youngest daughter on her birthnight.*
*Happy birthnight, Eleonore! Your mother and I are so proud of you.*
*Love, Dad*

"He remembered," she murmured to herself, wiping her nose on her shoulder. Marged flinched at her bad manners but didn't say anything—instead, she helped Leo's stiff fingers deal with the tightly knotted string. Leo already knew she would love the gift; she could feel the hard cover and pages through the wrapping.

"A book!" she exclaimed, as though it was a surprise, and Marged's laugh echoed within her metal body.

It was indeed a book, beautifully bound and heavy enough to make Leo's knee ache as she cradled it on her lap.

*The Encyclopedia Silva*, the gilded cover read. *Volume II.*

Leo gasped. She hadn't known there was more—she had never found another L. Hinterblatt book in the library. It seemed Dad was full of surprises, and not just who he chose to play chess with. Leo's hands shook as she reverently traced the lettering, curving around the image of what could have been a large-leaved lime tree.

*It's incredible*, she wanted to say, or maybe even, *Please tell Dad THANK YOU from me, even though he is very late!* but then Marged couldn't hold back her urge to fuss any longer.

"Oh my nights, what am I going to do?" Marged lamented, tucking Leo's sheets around her extra snugly, new book and all. "One hundred and eleven years old, and already off hunting her first ghost! You know, vampires typically start with a human. They're much tastier."

The Dreadwald was elegant in its winter clothing, a thick layer of fluffy snow. It clung to every branch, every stone, and every fallen tree, and the river was icy and slow and clear as crystal. Still more was falling; fat white snowflakes drifted earthward, erasing the fresh tracks that lead toward the ancient large-leaved lime.

With a flurrying leap, Leo hurtled through the trees. Powdery snow flew in her wake, whipped up by her nimble feet. The air was cool in her shriveled lungs, making her feel as though she could run and run forever.

The forest never failed to make her feel alive again.

"YAHOOOOO!" Leo whooped, sending a robin fluttering for cover as she vaulted over a log. She stumbled on touchdown—almost toppling over—but her wooden leg caught her weight and she was zooming off again.

Finally, winding down to a jog, she came to the clearing.

There, glittering with icicles, was the silvery tree she had come to know as her second home.

Hollowhome. HH.

She had made more memories here in a few nights than in her entire unlife. She'd even brought a friend—and then it had been Minna's base too. Leo touched a hand to the frigid bark, finding it smooth and mercifully clear of any black rot; the forest had really bounced back after its ordeal now that the Orphanmaster was vanquished. She dipped her head respectfully.

"Hello, old girl," she said aloud, though she wasn't sure why. Perhaps she just didn't want to feel so alone.

Fireflies winked as she slipped inside, brushing the snow from her boots. The frost was too much for her toes in the wintertime; her usually bare foot needed the protection. Leo left the boots at the entrance, shaking her cape and her head while she was at it.

More than a month had passed since she had awoken in her bed, in the aftermath of the battle with the Orphanmaster. Her hair had grown back completely, and was now messier than it had ever been, sticking up like a startled shrub. For some reason, Marged had stopped nagging her about a trim. Maybe it was a welcome reminder that Leo had survived.

And Leo felt physically better than ever, in fact, now that her body had been given the chance to properly heal. She'd been desperate to get out of the tower ever since her awakening, but this was the first time she had been allowed. Bed rest had made her impatiently itchy, or itchily impatient. No amount of whining or wheedling had been enough to make Mum and Dad and Marged budge—until now.

Freedom tasted sweet . . . even if she had a strict curfew to stick to. She had to be back at the castle an hour before sunrise, at the latest. The closer eye her parents were keeping on her was a worry; Leo hoped it wouldn't stop her from TRULY completing her Hunt and biting her first human. . . .

When she was ready, of course. Somehow, fighting an evil ghost had put Leo off hunting for a while, Waxing Moon or otherwise. As long as Emmeline didn't blab and Marged was still on her side, Leo had the breathing room. It was funny how almost burning to death in the sun could put things into perspective.

Leo hopped up into her hammock, letting her head tilt back to lean against the frosty wall. She watched the fireflies bumble back and forth, floating down to touch on the low table, on the books where they had waited patiently all this time.

At least she still had the *Encyclopedia* (and its younger cousin, courtesy of Dad). The book had always been a loyal friend to her, if a quiet one. And it was so quiet here too, gripped in wintry slumber. Much of the Dreadwald lay dormant beneath the snow, plants falling back to seed, animals in hiding, insects returning to the hard, cold earth.

A firefly landed on the tip of Leo's nose, its wings twitching. Leo blew it off with a gentle puff of breath and it fluttered away. For a long time, she had suspected that there was something weird about her beloved HH—about an actual, living tree of such gargantuan size, with its hollow base that could easily rival Leo's bedroom back in Castle Motteberg. And somehow, its insect guardians lived here year-round instead of going into the drawn-out sleep of other species.

It was a mystery that even the *Encyclopedia* didn't have the answer to. With a sigh, Leo approached the table, running her hand down the book's spine. It sat there, unmoving and unhelpful next to the heftier *Companion*, the book that had started Leo and Minna on their journey. . . .

Leo paused, her fingertips still hovering over the *Encyclopedia.* She tilted her head, frowning to herself.

Because lying between the two books, oh so innocuously, was something she had missed.

Something that made her breath catch.

*It's you?* Leo thought, picking up Minna's dagger with trembling hands. She turned the blade this way and that; there was no mistaking it. The inscription and leather pouch were the same. As was the way it fit into her palm, easy and powerful.

It was their weapon of intent, the final piece to defeating the Orphanmaster.

How had it ended up back here? She had left it at the orphanage.

Leo couldn't stop herself shaking, overcome with an empty sort of feeling as she unsheathed the dagger. In the polished blade the bark of the tree was reflected back at her, the hammock hanging behind where Leo's reflection would have once been, were she still human.

It made sense, she thought numbly, that this would be the thing to end it. Minna was about to use the dagger the night they had first met, after all. She'd been readying herself for murder when Leo had appeared at the Orphanmaster's window and ruined everything. In a way, the dagger felt like part of Minna herself.

*Oh, Minna. I miss you. . . .*

Leo clutched the dagger to her chest. She tried to collect herself; she'd cried so much lately, it was a wonder there was even a drop of blood left in her. Running her fingers over the carving in the handle, Leo bit the inside of her cheek. Perhaps she could learn to read whatever the inscription said. A new project—a diversion from eternity on her own.

But.

There, right at the hilt, were two letters that Leo could already make out. They looked as though they'd been carved by a different hand, scratched into the wood.

A.H.

*A.H.?*

Leo wracked her brain but came up with nothing. She turned the dagger over, trying to see if it looked any different from another angle.

That was how, reflected in the shiny blade, she saw her.

"Hello, Leo," Minna's reflection greeted, and Leo dropped the dagger into her wooden foot.

"Minna?"

"Hi."

"MINNA?"

"You should close your mouth before the fireflies get in," Minna grumped. "Yes—it's me. In the flesh. Or not in the flesh . . . you get what I mean. Stop looking at me like that!"

Leo obediently snapped her fangs shut, hopping on one leg to hold up her foot. She looked her friend up and down within the dagger. The ghost called Minna was as wispy as ever, floaty and translucent. She had her frayed nightgown and hairband, the poker through her shoulder, and an irritated twitch in her eyelid that was definitely the same too.

There was one problem: Leo simply couldn't believe what she was seeing.

"I . . . I . . . Y-you're . . ."

"If you're not going to start making sense, then I'll go, shall I?"

"You're here! I can't believe it!" Leo blurted. "But . . . Oh no." Her mouth downturned. "Are you . . . are you trapped in the dagger now? How did this happen?"

Minna laughed at her. "Trapped? No—no, I'm not trapped. I'm . . . wherever we go next." She waved a hand. "Wherever ghosts go, I mean. There's too much to explain, Leo—it's just GHOST STUFF. You'll have to take my word for it."

"I still can't believe it's you! I thought I'd never see you again!"

"And *I* thought I'd never see YOU again." Minna rolled her eyes. "I've been looking in on HH every night. It was too risky to float around the castle—I didn't know you had an *actual* knight in shining armor."

"Oh, Marged? She's my butler. She fusses after me too much, but"—Leo sighed—"she's been my guardian since I was first turned."

"Hmmm. Well, I'm glad you managed to get away. Your butler-knight looked STRAIGHT AT ME on that first night, when I came to your bedroom and you weren't there. I'm sure I was invisible, but it was almost like . . ." Minna shook her head as if to dispel a ridiculous thought. "Never mind. You're here now."

Leo felt her heart do a tiny leap. Minna had come looking for her?

"Listen, Leo . . ." Minna balled her fists, getting that strange stubborn look she used to get before saying something difficult. "What you did back there—I'm really glad. I'm glad you're still here too. I know that you finished what I started and . . . and I'm grateful that you didn't give up. If it wasn't for you, that monster might still be out there. I wouldn't have made it on my own. It had to be both of us."

"But . . . how did you *do that* with the Spirit Anchor?" Leo asked. "I don't understand. The sulfur, it was gone! And the smoke—well, okay, I get that part. Of course you could breathe smoke; I'd forgotten all about it—"

"The matches. There's sulfur in the matches."

Leo's mouth opened on a silent *oh*. Minna nodded in a *yes, there you go* sort of way, and then she frowned.

"I guess there's a lot that I had forgotten too. I used to sell matches out on the streets, for a while. After my parents passed away, I mean," Minna clarified, and Leo could only nod uselessly. "They have sulfur in the match heads to make them spark when struck."

"How did you know it would work?" Leo asked. "How did you know it would be enough?"

"I didn't. I guess I just hoped."

She'd *hoped*, and that was it. Just like Leo and the dagger, their replacement weapon of intent. Leo didn't know whether to laugh or to cry again; her body was trying to do both at once, making her quake where she stood.

"What's . . . what's wrong with you?" Minna asked, eyeing Leo warily as the movement made the dagger shake too. "Are you sick? Did you catch some sort of weird vampire disease while you were asleep?"

"No, no! I'm . . . I'm so glad too. That you're here," Leo said earnestly. She knew she was being embarrassing—maybe even embarrassing enough to rival one of Marged's lectures—but she couldn't help it. "It's selfish of me, but I . . . I'm so happy to see you again. Even though it's not what you want, is it? Being stuck as a ghost?"

"Mmm. It wasn't what I hoped." Minna raised an eyebrow. "I don't know if I have a *different* purpose, or if you stole my mission from me. You know. By being the one to kill the Orphanmaster."

Leo squeaked.

"Oh—don't overreact. You've been getting in my way from the beginning, why should this be any different?" Minna rolled her eyes, but she didn't look cross. Instead, she wore what might have been the beginnings of a smile. "Maybe it was for the best. Do you think it counts for your Wax Moon?"

"Wax*ing* Moon," Leo corrected gently. She was pleased that Minna had remembered. "I . . . I don't think so. I didn't bite him, after all. The victim has to be Living—and the Orphanmaster was already dead."

"Well. You hunted him down. I think it should count."

Minna was right. And more than that . . .

Leo had GRIMWALKed. She couldn't believe it. It had been barely a few feet, but she had definitely pulled it off, after all this time.

A sick, cold feeling bubbled up inside her. It burst almost as quickly as it had taken hold, simmering down again. She was grateful she still had her three limbs. She wouldn't be trying it again in a hurry.

"Leo," Minna interrupted her thoughts, "if we're done here—there's someone you need to see. A couple of someones, actually. Take me out of your foot?"

Leo did as she was asked, yanking the dagger free. She squinted down at its shiny surface, watching as Minna pointed to something that seemed far away in the foggy background.

It almost looked like . . . Dreadwald trees in the snow. Beyond Minna's finger, two equally ghostly figures stood huddled beneath the falling flakes. They became clearer and clearer beneath Leo's stunned gaze.

One was tall, with round spectacles balanced on his crooked nose. He wore the apron and long gloves of some sort of smith. His lips were thin and his teeth were large, with a noticeable gap between the two front ones.

The other was shorter, plumper, clad in the kind of gear one might wear to ride a horse. Her hair was braided into buns on either side of her head. Beneath her spattering of pale freckles, she had a kind face—in fact, both of them did. Spotting Minna—or could they see Leo too?—the woman leaned up to murmur something to the man. They clasped their hands tightly between them.

"Mum and Dad," Minna said, so quietly that Leo wasn't sure she'd properly heard.

"Minna?"

Turning to her, Minna shot her a watery grin. "Can you believe it? They waited for me to find them. Those seven nights, I was . . . between the pages, like Father Pavlov said. Between worlds. I didn't think I would ever see them again, and here they are. . . ."

*Minna's mum and dad.*

Leo stared. She felt a lump in her throat. "That's what parents do, Minna. You deserve it."

She felt an icy shock touch her arm, as though some of Minna's ghost energy had shot through the dagger.

"Thank you, Leo the vampire. For everything you've done for me. You're a good friend."

It took a moment of stunned realization, but Leo coaxed

herself to squeeze the handle of the dagger back, as tightly as though it was Minna's own hand.

"Will I . . . will I see you again?" Leo asked. Her voice came out scratchy; her tongue felt as though it was made out of sandpaper.

Minna pulled a face. "Yes you will, you idiot," she huffed tearily. She scrubbed her forearm across her eyes. "Tomorrow night! I'll be back here, for real. Don't leave me waiting this time!"

Leo watched Minna go, flying to her parents. She watched as Minna's mum clapped her daughter heartily on the back, and Minna's dad kissed the top of her head. Leo's toes curled and she gripped the dagger tightly. The three ghosts walked away, arms around each other and holding close.

*Tomorrow night?* Leo suspected that she might be dreaming. She clamped her eyes closed and gave her arm a painful pinch, but when she looked again, there she still was: standing in the silent HH, watching as Minna and her parents melted away.

"See you tomorrow," Leo said softly, setting the dagger down. She stood for a long moment, jiggling her wooden leg. She was a *good friend.* To a GHOST. It was unheard of: a phenomenon not seen in the entire written history of vampirekind.

Whistling to herself while wrapping her books safely in her cape, Leo didn't see the new figure appear in the dagger.

Nor did she hear the warning buzz of the fireflies.

From within the blade a mysterious woman stared out at the young vampire who had changed everything. Around her ghostly silhouette, the wintry trees bowed and shriveled. She turned abruptly, unseen, her skirts rustling behind her, and left no footprints as she disappeared.

Leo turned too late to look back at the dagger, at where Minna and her parents had been, the view now completely obscured by falling snow. Little by little, the toothiest smile broke out on her face.

*Marged is really going to hate this!*